TURN BACK,
IT'S A TRICK!

Turn Back, It's A Trick!

Bill Blackarm

authorHOUSE®

AuthorHouse™
1663 Liberty Drive
Bloomington, IN 47403
www.authorhouse.com
Phone: 1-800-839-8640

First published by AuthorHouse   10/05/2011

ISBN: 978-1-4670-4083-9 (sc)
ISBN: 978-1-4670-4082-2 (hc)
ISBN: 978-1-4670-4081-5 (ebk)

Library of Congress Control Number: 2011917244

Printed in the United States of America

Any people depicted in stock imagery provided by Thinkstock are models, and such images are being used for illustrative purposes only.
Certain stock imagery © Thinkstock.

This book is printed on acid-free paper.

Turn back, it's a trick.

By Bill Blackarm
(Not my real name and you'll play hell getting it)

You didn't think I would give you my real name did you? They are watching right now. They want my name. They want this manuscript. They will stop at nothing to find it. They don't want you to know what I am about to tell you. If I were you, I would keep the information contained here in, to yourself. If I should not survive, I have made provisions to publish this manuscript after my death. But then, taking me down won't be easy.

"I believe that imagination is stronger than knowledge, myth is more potent than history, dreams are more powerful than facts, hope always triumphs over experience, laughter is a cure for grief and love is stronger than death."

Robert Fulgham

"Don't be afraid your life will end, be afraid that it will never begin."

Grace Hansen

2. Computer laws: Any given program when running is obsolete.
3. Commerce Law: To err is human, to forgive is not Company policy.
4. War law: Friendly fire—isn't.
5. Cop's Law: Bullet proof law: Bullet Proof vests—aren't.
6. Photography Law: Auto focus-won't.
7. Sewing Law: The scissors cut easiest past the button hole.
8. Nurse's Law: Doctors only ask your name if the patient is not doing well.
9. Bus Law: If you are running late the Bus will too.
10. Toddler Law: When you forget the stroller, they will want to ride.
11. Political Law: No matter who gets in, "Government" always gets in.
12. Office Law: When you don't have much work, all your colleagues will be busy.
13. Horse Laws: Horses you hate cannot be sold and will out live you.
14. Love Laws: Goon like guys always bag the best gals in town.
15. Parking Law: The furthest parking place is the closest.

Corollaries to Murphy's law are:

1. Nothing is as easy as it looks.
2. Everything takes longer than you think it will.
3. If there is a possibility of something going wrong, the one that can cause the most damage will be the one that goes wrong.
4. Left to themselves, things tend to go from bad to worse.

5. It is impossible to make anything foolproof because fools are so ingenious.
6. Mother nature is a bitch.

But you say there are a lot more laws than Murphy's law "Garlic Breath". And I would say: "I know. I have done my research". Here is a partial list:

Finagle's Law: "Anything that can go wrong will go wrong at the worst possible time."

Hanlon's Razor: "Never attribute to malice to what is adequately explained by stupidity."

Clark's Law: "Sufficiently advanced cluelessness is indistinguishable from malice."

Occam's Razor: "The simplest explanation is more likely the correct one."

Sturgeon's Law: "Nothing is always absolutely so" and the second and more famous law: "Ninety percent of everything is Crap."

Segal's Law: "A man with a watch knows what time it is. A man with two watches is never sure."

Shermer's Law: "Any sufficiently advanced alien intelligence is indistinguishable from God."

Skitt's Law: "Any posting correcting an error in another post will contain at least one error itself."

Goodhart's Law: "When a measure becomes a target, it ceases to be a good measure."

Herblock's Law: "If it is good, they will stop making it"

Hutber's Law: "Improvement means deterioration."

Kranzbery's Law of Technology: "Technology is neither good nor bad, nor neutral."

Leinbniz's Law: "If two objects have their properties in common, then they are one in the same."

Meadow's Law: "One is a tragedy, two is suspicious and three is murder until proven otherwise."

Parkinson's Law: "Work expands to fill the time available for it's completion."

Peter Principle: "In a Hierarchy every employee tends to rise to his level of incompetence."

Petronius Paradox: "Practice modernization on all things including moderation."

Dr. Who's law: First things first, but not necessarily in that order.

Otoole's Law in commentary on Murphy's Law: "Murphy was an optimist."

Unknown: "I was wrong once, but then I found I was mistaken."

And of course the famous Conundrum, The Crocodile Dilemma: "If a Crocodile steals a child and promises to return it if the father can correctly guess what the Crocodile will do, how should the Crocodile respond in the case where the father guesses that the child will not be returned."

Zen Teachings:

1. Do not walk behind me for I may not lead. Do not walk in front of me, for I may not follow. Do not walk beside me for the path is too narrow. In fact, just leave me the Hell alone.
2. Always remember you're unique. Just like everyone else.
3. Before you criticize someone, you should walk a mile in their shoes. That way when you criticize them, you are a mile away and you have their shoes.
4. Some days you are the dog, and some days you are the tree.
5. A closed mouth gathers no foot.
6. Experience is something you don't get until just after you need it.
7. You are born naked wet and hungry and get slapped on your ass. Then things just keep getting worse.

Unknown

1. Remember when you throw dirt you will always loose ground.

Oxymoron's

1. Why is the third hand on a watch called the second hand?
2. Why do we say something is out of "whack"? What is a whack?
3. Why do we call it after dark when it's really after light?
4. Doesn't "expecting the unexpected" make the unexpected expected?
5. If work is so terrific, why do we have to pay you to do it?
6. How come abbreviation is such a long word?

Finally, but not necessarily of lesser consequence, Renn's Law: "Bad begets social interaction, therefore bad is good."

Example #1001: A man breaks his leg. That's bad. The accident causes financial and social stress to the family. That's bad. But, friends and family pull together to help the man overcome his adversity. That's good. The friends and family meet hospital staff and interact. That's good. The hospital staff feel valued. That's good. The man is back to work and feels that he has overcome adversity. That's good. Thus the bad of the broken leg brought many goods.—You buy that? Think about it. You have been buying it all this time.

Social Support, Residual Adversity and Depressive Outcome*
P. G. Surtees
MRC Unit for Epidemiological Studies in Psychiatry, University Department of Psychiatry, Royal Edinburgh Hospital, Edinburgh, UK

SUMMARY

"Investigators of the relationship between life stress and illness onset have been criticized for paying too little attention to factors which may protect individuals from the adverse consequences of stress. A major factor neglected in this regard has been social support. The present study investigates the relationship between social support, residual adversity and symptom severity in patients seven months after onset of a depressive illness. The results, whilst possibly lacking causal significance, suggested that the presence of social support conferred partial immunity against the recurrence of symptoms in individuals suffering a high level of residual adversity. Confiding relationships with reciprocity between confidant and patient concerning their personal affairs had the greatest protective qualities."

PROLOGUE

Over the years since the first "coining" of some of these famous phrases, man seemed content to put a tangible depiction to many things that caused physical or emotional pain many of which were unexplained. In other words, if the unexplained could have a name then maybe this made it acceptable.

But was this also a way of hiding from the unknown? The author's contention is that man was made to fight back. The human spirit is not automatically set to accept anything "dished out" to it. There is no predestined arrangement set for man. Could we be in a big "pin ball" game with most things happening by accident? Maybe. But then you forgot about the "flippers". Who is catching the ball just before the ball goes down the "end of round" hole. If the ball goes down the hole, the game might be over. However, another "run" of unplanned circumstances, could be easily introduced by sending the ball back in play. "It makes for more challenges, maybe more than challenges. Maybe it makes for grief."

Figuring out what is happening in a pin ball machine game seems overwhelming. There are an infinite number of possibilities. Recording the possibilities could be some mindless exercise. But maybe some are "blind alleys", maybe made to make the exercise daunting. But, we were given brains and the ability to question. More than that, we were given the ability to "act". Most people don't question turns in life. Maybe it's time that someone did. No one will believe what I have written in this book. Man has been programmed to accept almost anything. Everyone . . . except me.

Renn's Chart. The following chart is given to the reader to score how many unusual events that happen in his life. I realize that the reader will be skeptical and I have provided for that. The chart allows the reader to be as bold or as conservative or as non-believing as he wants. The result after reading this book to someone who truly can be honest with himself will be startling. Be as honest as you can in scoring this chart.

RENN'S CHART

A number of these events may have happened to the reader. A Chart has been supplied for your use. Keep a running tally, but don't let anyone know you are doing it. It could be fatal. A number of events will be numbered in this book. They may be a little different than the events that have happened to you. Then again, maybe they have not happened to you. Just don't judge the premise until you're through with the book. Then you will know why I cannot give you my name.

1 to 3 .... Hardly worth scoring. My life is a ship on smooth seas.

3 to 6 .... Well . . . maybe some of these events may have happened, but I can explain them all. Even if I can't, maybe some of these are divine intervention. I shouldn't even be questioning any of them.

6 to 9 .... Well, I think this book is still full of crap. But on the other hand I guess I have had some of these unexplained events happen to me. But don't get any ideas. I still think you still are off base.

9 to 12........ I still think you're way out in left field. But I have actually experienced these events and they did give me some torment. I never had anyone stand up and point them out until now.

12 to 15...... Wow! Renn, you are on the right track.

15 to 20...... Renn! I'm joining you! We've got to fight back.

Renn's moto to the believer's . . . "Keep it going" Which means "fight the fight". Or: "Never give in."

Keep score so you can refer back to how many torments have affected your life. Please take notes as you read. It may be more important than you think. Time is running out.

Don't be too quick to discount some of the ideas in this book. They may have just happened to you. By the way, that cup of Coke you put on the desk . . . it's about to fall. But it won't fall on the floor. That would be too easy to fix. It will fall onto the key board of your laptop. You laugh. I can see it now. You may not see it yet. But maybe it's because you already "toast".

CHAPTER 1

Just The Start

It all started a long time ago. I was a kid in Oklahoma. Well, maybe it didn't start then at all. But you won't believe anything I am about to tell you unless you know a little about me, the author. Part of this book aims at studying social interaction or maybe it doesn't do that at all. But still, you might expect that I want to get closer to the reader, so he will identify with my story a little more. We can become buddies. Maybe we can go out for drinks. I actually think your mother and my mother went to different schools together.

But wait, you misunderstand me. I question why man needs to be social at all. I suppose it is necessary to give you a little glimpse of my back ground. However, I have placed a "mind scrubber" somewhere hidden in this book. When you turn the correct page, it will emit an odor that will cause you to forget everything you will learn about me in the following pages. It's just a well.

Anyone associated with me might pay the ultimate price. You think that is death. But the dead sleep well. No, as you will find out later, it is the tormented who slosh through the slurry of life every day. Sorry. Don't be angry with me. I am just the messenger.

CHAPTER 2

Childhood

My childhood was not too unusual. I was average, I guess. I was not a great athlete or a scholar or a ladies man. But, I wanted to be an athlete. One day I decided to take the basketball from the best basketball player on our high school team.

He was really "cocky". The day came when the scrubs (that's my group) were running scrimmage against the "A" team. The moment flashed before my eyes as I saw "him" dribbling toward me. There was some movement on my left and it caught his attention for just a millisecond. It was the time.

With a startling flash, I was in action. It was all my legs could do to propel my body as quickly as my mind commanded. I jumped forward and hit the ball from his hands. It was amazing. Everyone stopped to see the miracle. I had done the impossible. I had stolen his ball. I would be heralded as a "star of stars". Except, . . . that I was . . . (wait for it) . . . running toward the wrong goal. Yes, maybe that was a premonition and sort of mini "sketch" of what the rest of my life would be; "flying a mock speed toward the wrong goal."

That was when I first thought that I was different. But, for just a second I was someone special. I savored the idea for a long time, even if it was "the man who went the wrong way."

Stardom was intoxicating. But then, I started to wonder why we were brought up to seek stardom. A star is easily identified. He glows in the sky. He is on everyone's mind. People expected good from a star. A cousin to "stardom" is "popularity". Why do we seek this mind expanding concept called "popularity?

We all go though life with the idea that we are special. And . . . the idea was, being special can only be achieved if people know us. I'm asking you. I really don't know. Treat me as if I just landed from another planet. It appears that we crave the "lime light". But why do we need this? We walk down the street and they say . . . "I know him". Or they really say: "I can identify him". Does it appear that somewhere along the line, popularity and invasion of privacy got mixed. Funny, how that happens. Now in order to be popular we have to lay the complete story of our lives out for public view. We relish it or we are told that we should.

The police check our ID on a traffic stop. We check into a Hotel room. They want your ID. What? If you were not who you said you were you might want to set up a terrorist camp right there in the Hotel room. Too far fetched? Maybe, but just to set the record straight, you could set one up in your room under your actual name too. So why do they need any particular name?

Your automobile tag addresses who you are. Anyone with the interest can go to the Department of Motor Vehicles and find out your address for a dollar. We have electronic boxes that allow us to drive on a turnpike without stopping to pay tolls. They know when we enter the Turnpike, they tag us at the ½ way point and know when we exit. They also know our average speed while on the Turnpike. We have numbers on our license plate identifying us. We have unique ID numbers that tie us to the tax collector and Social Security. We have phone numbers. Our cell phones have "chips" that ties us to an account. But more threatening, they can tie us to a GPS location within 12 inches.

We check in at the airport and they ask for our Government issued ID. If we don't want to give it out, we are refused a boarding pass or worse. We might be branded a "terrorist". "What do you have to hide" they say. You must have done something wrong. Does wanting to keep your life private, mean that you are a criminal?

Now, they have something on the internet call "Socially Verified". What does that mean? Of course, the first thought is that they want to know if we are criminals. I looked up some statistics on internet usage and social crimes. Of the events reported, 1/10 of 1% is connected to someone trying to commit a crime. Even fewer are related to affairs of the heart. In fact what is a crime related to the heart? What do they want? Now, I am sure there are a lot of people out there who have shady pasts. But of those people, how many are using the internet for a crime. Again, after some research of at least what was available, I found next to none were on the Internet. So, we are back to the same question. Why do these people running the "Socially Verified" service want to know your background? Whatever it was, I wasn't buying it.

Life is all about relationships isn't it? We hang degrees on the wall. We join clubs. We can be found on the Internet. We join Facebook and other social networks and ask people to visit our private social sites. We build a "background". We are proud of our lives both on the internet and off. But why? Do we really need social support? Will this help us overcome life's adversities? Do we think that we get some sort of protection from what life brings us? When "circumstances" start circling around us, will there be someone there to help? Catastrophic events happen. The "man" comes after you. Will your social network be able to help you? If you say yes then you have watched too many "Little House On The Prairie" episodes.

I had a dream several years ago. In the dream I was lying on an operating table. In each arm I had a large number of needles connected to tubes. They were all sucking the life out of me. They were all labeled. (Nice of them.) Each tube was something different. In the right arm starting at the top was the electric bill, then the gas bill, then the cable bill, then the food bill, then the cell phone bill, then taxes and insurance. On the left arm were odd bills like "Napster" that charges me every month even though I have never "down loaded" a single song.

Then there is: Gasoline for the car, expenses for business lunches, costs of broken equipment. Then there are the sneaky bills that you never ordered like luggage insurance, and "trip insurance",etc. The list seems to double about every three years. In the dream I was in "Intensive Care".

I remember seeing them wheel my body down the hall as though I would expire soon.
There's very little you can do about life's "bills". But then what about life's "relationships"? I once tried to get into the movie business.

I really didn't know what I was doing. Getting into the right circles was almost impossible. It was an exclusive club that didn't allow anyone in who had not paid their dues. It seemed that if I had written a book called: "Gone With The Wind" or the "Bible". They would have said: "Sorry, it doesn't resolve". But what they really meant was, "we don't know who you are". Or "You haven't been working in the business long enough". Then, you find yourself asking if all challenges and all successes are really about how you relate to others? If you take that line of reasoning you could turn out a stack of pancakes and if you had the right connections and people liked you, then the savory masterpiece would be an "object art" and placed on a pedestal.

But everyone is thinking the same way. There is a certain order to life. Should I fall in "lock step" with everyone else and carry heavy stones on my back. After all that's what you do if adversity hits. I considered hefting the weights of life and showing everyone that I could carry the heavy stones too. I thought and thought and then things changed. My mind stopped processing this "crap". I had another idea . . . I was gonna run.

CHAPTER **3**

Running

This whole idea of leaving a set of circumstances and starting over somewhere else had become intoxicating for me. Why not wake up some morning with a completely different life? But that was not all I wanted. To merely change positions in life wasn't enough. After all, changing the color of your car doesn't protect you from getting a parking ticket.

No, I wanted a protected existence. Maybe this was not possible, but I had decided to make a complete investigation. There are books about disappearing and then reappearing.

I would study them.

The Authors argument was that you could start a new life by getting married again, getting a job and paying taxes. Then if someone from your past found you later, you could say that you simply had changed your life and that you had become a model citizen. That still didn't sit right with me. I didn't want to just start the whole process again. My argument was: Could someone disappear and not reappear and still enjoy everything that is out there?

I started a notebook keeping track of the information I gained in my research. It would become invaluable later. I became obsessed with this information. I first started by reading articles about disappearing. The point most of the Authors of the books I read was made, was to make you understand what you were hiding from. Another question was: "Are you running from the law or just your life?" For example, if it was the police, you would most likely get caught.

Hiding from them would produce one set of requirements. If you were running from an abusive spouse, then that was a different set of problems. If you were running from the IRS, then that was a third set of requirements depending on how much you owed the Government, and so on. So, I found myself asking what I was running from. For most people that would be a very easy question. "I robbed a Bank and I want to run away with the loot." "My spouse is abusive and I don't want him or her to find me." But for me, it was not so "cut and dried". I started out imagining a life with out "requirements".

You might say: "But Renn, everyone needs to accept responsibility. And, I would say: "But, I have carried as many stones as anyone. I have pulled on the ropes of life. I was always there when the situation required it. I was an example of a model citizen. But I struggled and struggled and after many "trips and falls", I began to think that that line of thinking was a "hook" with a big piece of meat on it. Up to now I had swallowed the whole bait. The hook gouged into my throat wall every day, but I over looked it. The pain might have been imagined, but then again maybe not. I was caught, gutted, filleted, packaged and set aside ready to eat. Most people lay there all boxed up ready to be consumed. But when they captured me, I always figured a way to leave at least one hand outside the box. It was a funny box going down the processing plants assembly line. You might have heard a sleepy attendant who had the job of counting products coming down the line. He might have said: "Paper box, paper box, paper box, paper box with hand sticking out, paper box." Of course, this was just my day dream. You thought I really got boxed up. You are more screwed up than me. Maybe you are not. But the system was hard to break. Most people didn't try. However, I still thought there might be another way.

I have read about Americans moving to Costa Rica. Lodging is very cheap. A retirement lifestyle is easy to set up. "One can live like a king for $800.00 per month. He can look at the ocean across the lawn of his sea side house as the gardener tends his garden and the cook prepares his meal." That was yesterday. You read about it all the time. But today in the electronic world "the man" can find you anywhere, well . . . unless, you took extreme precautions.

So, I set about to do research. If I was to disappear whether here or in another Country, I would need to follow some guidelines.

CHAPTER 4

Renn's Conglomerate of Guide lines for disappearing based on research information.

Disappearing is a very unusual way to solve life's problems. First of all, at this time in my research there seems to be no way to completely disappear. The idea was, as I discovered, to create the illusion that you have disappeared. Notes on this point and part of my research are as follows:

The actual act:

1. Disappearing requires advanced planning.
2. If you decide the pick a location outside the US, know that you will have left a record if you use your original passport. I lost a passport a number of years ago.

I applied for a new one and quickly noticed that the passport had different ID numbers on it. Had I found the first one and used it, the authorities would have wanted some explanation immediately. Moving inside the US is of course easier since there are no State border checks. However the USA is a giant web of electronic mechanisms that allow almost instantaneous responses sending authorities to your exact location should you use any form of ID media such as credit cards, driver's licenses, hunting and fishing licenses, etc. Many other Countries are not nearly as sophisticated.

3. The author of this information was suggesting that you acquire two separate identities. He says at a bare minimum, that you should have a valid driver's license, social security card, birth certificate and health card. The forgeries should be done with the latest technology and be of excellent quality. Note: Prepare for expensive fees.

4. The slow process of becoming less known:
    a. Decrease the contact with people you normally have contact with.
    b. Don't return phone calls.
    c. Don't attend meetings.
    d. Increase your absence so that people don't become suspicious.
    e. Remove all financial assets from the bank. Close all accounts several weeks before your departure. Too much time before you leave could cause questions. Two weeks seems about right.
    f. Sell all your physical assets. Turn them all into cash.
    g. Discard all things you can't sell. The author of this information suggested keeping your car and then selling it to your new identity in the new city of your choice. Take out a PO Box there, register the car and buy insurance.
    h. Cut the items you will take with you primarily clothes to two suitcases. Destroy everything else.
    i. Burn all documentation that links you to your old identity.

j. The author's final comment was "No mental Health Professional would recommend this technique as a means of solving life's problems." He also notes that this information was presented as a "means of entertainment". (I laughed a little. The original author had no idea how Government pressures would change in the future.)

CHAPTER **5**

Other ideas gleaned from my research:

1. The Authors all agreed that you should burn your old clothes. You should change your life style. Wear styles you would never have worn before. Cut your hair but not too short.

2. Burn all your family pictures. If the authorities were to put pressure on your relatives, the pictures would come out. Make them have to use a police artist's sketch. Facial recognition becomes much harder.

3. There is also the old adage: Three can keep a secret, . . . if . . . two are dead. Make new friends. Don't keep the old ones.

4. Destroy all of your credit cards. And no, this didn't mean to save one for an emergency. Most of the government agencies FBI, CIA, Police, etc. can track electronic use of a credit card within two minutes. They can pinpoint a location within 10 feet. They can be sitting on your doorstep in 20 minutes.

5. Get rid of your cell phone. Of course the bill can give away your location, but so can the cell phone signal. Each cell phone has a unique signal. Use of cell phones in war time has enabled the Government to use drones to track and fire missiles at a given location.

6. Don't talk near glass. Satellites can read vibrations off of glass.

7. Keep from depositing traces of yourself. Every where you go you leave pieces of yourself. Every article of clothing, every door knob, every telephone, every toilet seat will contain traces of you. You will need to decide if investigators will be tracking you through your DNA. A single human hair gives out enough information to establish a DNA. Skin is a perfect source of DNA. It is left every where. Human skin comprises 15 to 20% of an average adults body weight. A skin cell is born in the lower layer of skin called the "dermis". It slowly migrates to the top layer called the "epidermis" over two weeks.

Then, the skin cell spends another two weeks at this top layer gradually flattening out and continuing to move toward the surface. After that, it dies and is shed. Two billion to three billion skin cells are shed daily. The body goes through this process every 30 days because the skin constitutes the first line of defense against dehydration, infection, injuries and temperature extremes.

If you have decided that this method of tracking maybe be used, there are a number of ways to reduce your risk.

1. Wear a hat indoors. This reduces the amount of hair falling from your head.
2. Cutting your hair short will also reduce this risk.
3. Always use a toilet seat protector. Skin, sweat and body fluids can be used to track you.
4. Blood is hard to cover up. Don't even try. If you spill your blood you have left a clue. Some people use gasoline and soaps to try to scrub away the blood. They now have methods of reading DNA off of blood that

appeared to be completely cleaned up. Even burning the building down won't help.

5. Never lick an envelope. If you do so, you may as well take out an advertisement in the paper stating where you are.

6. Wipe everything down. Use soap and water. Keep in mind that that simply using a rag will just smudge the finger prints. They now have computers that can piece the finger prints back together. Throw your wiping material in the toilet.

7. Wear gloves when no one is watching. Never wear gloves when someone is around.

8. Don't eat in restaurants. Eating utensils will contain traces of you.

9. Most fast food restaurants and Mini marts have cameras that run continuously.

Like it or not, we live in a world that accepts strip searches at airports, surveillance cameras, discount cards that record our buying habits, "cookies" and spyware on our computers, on line access to technology that can image our back yards from a satellite, a microchip that allows tracking of the family dog and overseas contract labor that transcribes my medical history with no regard for privacy.

I also studied what to do while on the run. Some interesting items were:

1. Satellites can read heat signatures through roofing of cabins. If for example you are in a cabin at night and there is no corresponding heat signature for your automobile different than yours but still readable, then they might assume that you are there in hiding.

2. If you are being tracked by dogs always double back. Make circles around large objects. Walk down stream in water.
3. No Human is capable of outrunning a healthy dog.
4. Dogs will go for your feet and hands when running and your hands when you are down.
5. Dogs are trained not to go for the throat.
6. Even if you don't suspect that you are being trailed, it's a good idea to break your trail occasionally.

But, after much thought and of course fear of dogs and guns, I decided that I would try not to get in that situation. I decided that I would disappear in "plain site".

CHAPTER 6

Misinformation: (Another Author)

Lay a false trail. The best bet is for you to make it look like you went to the place you had most talked about visiting. Instead, you go to the one place that is as far away from the first place as can be; the one that you never told a soul about. Tell everyone that you are moving somewhere, or going overseas to teach English as a second language, joining the Peace Corps, or going tree planting with some volunteer non-profit group.

If you don't have a Facebook profile, create one and load it with all kinds of fake information. Set the privacy settings way down to zero so that you are 100% visible. Again, do the opposite, if you already have one with legit information.

My research was the start of this manuscript. I am not selling fiction. I am recording the rules of withdrawing from a controlled life. You may not see what is coming but then, "they" don't expect you to. I warn you, there is impending doom. It will not come as an explosion or a car wreck. There will be no bridge collapse. It will be and has been, a lot more subtle than that? What if it comes so slowly that it engulfs you and before you know it. Then you cannot escape. Face it, you're done for.

Let me get something straight right now. I had no plan to continue anymore thoughts that addressed the possible collapse of mankind. There probably wasn't any money in telling people of impending doom. I could yell about it until I was blue in the face, but no one would listen, especially from "Mr. Wrong Way Basketball Man". I will tell my tale anyway and at the end, I will rest my case. But for now, I am getting ahead of myself.

CHAPTER 7

Nothing special

Several years ago before my thought of running, I had rented a small apartment and dedicated part of my time to investigating man's need for relationships. It seemed simple enough. I wrote several essays. I joined a writing club. I even got two articles published in a magazine. I would get up every morning and after fixing some coffee and I would either research man's need for acceptance into society or even better I would sit and read other's commentaries on the subject. The Authors were trying to warn us. Reading their thoughts helped me find my true self. I sat and let the light of the warnings of adversity filter into my soul. After receiving this mind expanding information from my research, I would sit and contemplate the future of man. It was self fulfilling. It was delicious. It was necessary.

I joined several writing groups. I enjoyed them immensely. During my stint in one of the writing groups I met a girl. Her name was Anna. At first we just looked across the room at each other during breaks. But then, just the discourse of the class brought two very reserved individuals closer together. She was very special. I was young and shy. She seemed amused at my hapless tries to get her attention. One time I was paying more attention to her than the class and with one clumsy move, I spilled my papers all over the floor. Everyone in the class turned and looked at me. I shrank back in my seat. It would have been interminable, but the class bell rang and I escaped any social interaction.

A week later I finally got her to go to dinner with me. It was enchanting. We enjoyed the time immensely. Weeks went by and we met more and more. Most all the meetings produced great joy. I thought I had found my life mate.

Anna would say: "Renn, you are such a sweet man. Why do you write such alarming articles?" Then, she would think for a minute and try to "water down" her comments: "Yes, they don't seem to come from the same person." And I would think a minute and then say: "Dr. Jeckle and Mr. Hyde" . . . and, laugh it off.

Then reflecting, I might say: "I'm calling them as I see them. Do you know the story of the Emperor's new clothes?" But I don't think she ever understood. In general it was comment about people seeing a change or injustice in life, but being afraid to comment on it. That said, I never really defended the continuation of my pointed articles. They didn't change and of course, I always questioned social interaction.

Social interaction also came with the job I did from 6:00am to 3:00pm week days and in that context, I actually thrived. Come on, you thought I was independently wealthy? Well, let me be the first to burst your bubble. The day job helped me pay for my night work with the idea that someday I might not need the day job. But, let's get back to my thoughts. I worked at a nursing home as an orderly.

And as I said, I actually enjoyed it. I had a knack for helping people even though there was a hidden yearning to pull away from them. (Now I am starting to sound really screwed up.) They would say: "Oh, here comes Brad." Or "Brad can you help me with my puzzle?" Or "Brad, you're such an interesting man, tell me again about your childhood".

I actually was given an award for best employee of the year at South East Regional Nursing Home. During that stent of my life, I got to know a number of old people. The relationships I had with them were priceless even though I found myself pulling away at the same time I was taking their love in. One time I had ten people I was taking care of all at the same time. Some still come to mind.

There was Mrs. Jenkins. She loved to work with plants. I would wheel her into the back of the building where there was small garden. She would tell me what each plant was. I listened with all sincerity. It was amazing the knowledge she had.

Mr. Smith was a real character. He wanted to tell me about his experiences during World War II. He was a very resourceful man. He was a mechanic during the War. He told me that they were always running out of Jeep parts. So he made the parts out of found objects. One time he cut several timing gears out of a steel wheel. He was so proud. I learned to live his life with him. I found his strength could become my strength and the experience became very meaningful in the dark days that were to follow.

Bill Mathews was fairly quiet. He acted like he didn't want my company, but I knew better. Maybe he was the most like me; always placing obstacles in front of relationships.

But different from me, after he warmed up to you, he would not let you leave. We would have long talks by the fireside. He was the CEO of a large Company. The day he retired he came to the Home run by the Hospital. His wife had died several years earlier. Now as I look back. If it weren't for our talks each day, he might have slipped away sooner.

Betty Mitchell was a planner. She had been President of several "service" clubs. She wanted to help people even more than I did. I took dictation from her since she had had a stroke and could not use her right arm.

But all the old people I worked with, seemed to become frozen in place as they progressed to the end of their lives and of course, as I watched. They died of natural causes mostly. Some had arthritis which was not a killer by itself but tended to open the back door to something more. Some had bad hearts. Some died of Pneumonia. All of them were missed by me in many secret ways. Most of the people never questioned why they were taken. My heart was shattered every time one of them "stepped to the other side".

It was a natural event. I should have accepted it. But while I seemed to project a strong silent image of someone in mourning, I also had a small nagging feeling that the end of life and the journey to the next life was not as easy as it seemed. That maybe, we the living, could not see the real truth. But then, I would find myself feeling ashamed of my thoughts, and resolved to banish them from my mind.

One night after I had seen at least six old people leave this life, in as many hours, I found myself standing by a stream several hundred yards from the nursing home. It was dark and I should have gone home long ago. But, somehow, I had wandered away from the building in a delirium. I kept feeling that life was more than just an end to a struggle. I stood shaking in the blackness. The mold growing everywhere filled my olfactory senses. The rush of the water battered my hearing and chilled my feet.

Bill Mathews had passed this afternoon of no apparent cause. I was in shock. Someone said it was just old age. I had finished my shift and heard the details from someone who had come from the Hospital. He was gone.

They all had accepted it. But I found myself not wanting to be told the familiar line. "I am sorry my son, he has passed." I dropped to my knees in the stream and questioned my sanity. I closed my eyes and tried to picture a happier time; hoping my insecurity would vanish like a fading wind. I shook my head and tried to drive out the errant thoughts of disbelief.

But in the end, I raised up and lifted my arms to the heavens and screamed: "Why! . . ." Then, remembering the long list of friends who had died, I yelled: "I don't believe it!" I fell silent. Shortly thereafter, a mighty flash of lightening interrupted the solemn distant horizon.

There was a storm coming. It might be a bad one. There was a second flash of lightening as I turned to go and I swear, the tree next to me had grown and giant month with glistening teeth. It opened wider as I passed by. Seconds later, I looked back at it and upon the third flash of light and it was simply a somewhat twisted tree again. The rolls of thunder that followed caused my stomach to churn. Rain would shortly follow. People would say it brought a cleansing sense to the land. I thought differently.

The next night I had dream. I dreamed that I was wandering through some sort of portal and through a dark mist. As I sifted through long wet vines hanging from grotesque trees I saw a long line of old people coming over the horizon in the distance all holding candles. The line wove back into the hills and disappeared. It slowly curled like a snake as it moved toward me.

They did not speak to me, but I felt their presence. Somewhere deep in their very essence, they were trying to communicate with me. They were asking me for two things: To pay them respect for their lives and to find out why they died. I was aghast. I stepped back and slipped on a rock. I fell to the ground, but never lost sight of them. I had no answers. If they didn't know why they were in this limbo situation, who would?

The long line of souls seemed to drift past me in silence. I was close enough to see the sadness in their eyes, though they never looked at me. The line continued to pass me and finally faded away. I awoke in a full sweat. I tried to bring back the images, but try as I might, I could not remember exactly what I had seen.

After two years I quit my job as an Orderly. Relationships with people had brought me to the brink of sanity. I had experienced a boat load of "heart break". I pulled away and tried to control my feelings. But, as much as I tried resist, I still gave in to sorrow and fell victim to wanting social acceptance. My belief in relationships would catch me again in future months off guard and I would reap the consequences.

CHAPTER **8**

Anna

Anna and I had really become a pair. We were seen every where. We were inseparable except when we worked. She had a part time job with a printer. I think her family had some money and the small amount she received from them allowed her to pursue her interest in writing all the more. She would get lost in her work and lose track of time. Many evenings I had to go find her at the Library doing research. But, most things come to an end. And, lots of relationships break apart.

One day I used the key to her apartment she had given me. I was going to surprise her with an early Birthday present. Actually, I thought it would be another joyous day.

We had so much going for us. Time with her seemed to rush by. She was the joy in my life. But it changed quickly. On her breakfast table was a simple note. "Brad, (that was my name at the time) I have to go away. I may not return. I am sorry. Please do not try to find me. I will love you forever.
Anna."

I read the note and then reread the note a hundred times. I really could not believe what I was reading. The shock came slowly as I realized that part of my soul had been stolen. I was numb. I tried to argue to myself that I didn't know her well enough to question why she was gone. Maybe, I would file the whole segment of my life in my "mental file cabinet" under "my bad luck". That file was already pretty full. In fact I think I had pushed so much in there, that the back of that mental file cabinet was coming off. I would need one of those file extenders. Just joking but at the time there was no humor.

She truly was gone. I could not find any solace. Days turned into nights and nights turned into pits of sorrow. I found myself swimming in a cave filled with "muck" and worms. Not really. Well, maybe it had been real. Of course, you and I can rationalize that my feelings were just imagined because of a "traumatic event". My nerves were a like chewed Romex electrical cable. The aberrations seemed real and blocking the whole segment out of my life seemed the most rational solution. It all seemed logical except for the mud on my shirts in the morning. But let's not go there now.

Time passed, I left it alone for a while, but I was really hooked on her. So I called a couple of her friends. I called the school. No one knew any more than I did, except the school did receive a form officially "with-drawing" her from her school courses. It was a set of life events destroyed. All I had were some snap shots we had taken.

Gloom visited me every night. There were nights when I woke up with my stomach tied in knots. Throwing up became a normal thing. I tried to live on. I bought stomach medicine by the case. After a while I found I could only "dry heave". In my "non sick" moments, I buried myself in my writing. The air around me had turned sour. I tried to loose myself, but things were not the same with out her. I became very depressed.

My life was a "trash can" with a lost lid. That meant I would never stop more sadness from being stuffed in. But, after several months of lying on the floor of my apartment in a scrap pile of pizza boxes, I snapped out of it. Maybe I changed. I could finally start to get up every morning and found myself looking forward to a new day. Things seemed to be heading in some positive direction. I was back to writing. I buried myself in research. My articles were even more to the point, but not too threatening. Maybe they had had their "stinger" blunted.

My research allowed me to compile articles that studied many concepts depicting the socialization of man. They were up to date and factual. They probed all of our social mores. I felt I had one article that went even deeper than most. It might cause man to re-access his understanding to the meaning of life. It was not story book. It was not popular. It had a lot of truth to it. Unwittingly however, I stumbled on something far more onerous.

CHAPTER 9

Social networks as a means to . . .

At first, no one took much notice of a poor "hack" writer working out of a garage apartment. However, after several very pointed articles about social interaction came out with my name on them, I started to feel observation from places unknown.

And then, the final straw the broke the camel's back happened when I started a web site called "Back of Head Book". It was a spoof on FaceBook. Where FaceBook tried to bring you closer to your fellow man, "Back of head book" turned your head away so that no one could see your face. More to follow. Story at 10:00. That's how this whole set of events that you are about to read started.

The concept was that instead of embracing technology that could bring man closer together socially for no reason that I could understand, I took the opposite position and started a web site that would allow users to slowly disappear. After all, did we really want to be in the public eye?

No. Did we want people to paw through our personal chest of drawers and pull out our dirty underwear and show it to the world? No. Did we want people that we did not know to be our friends? No. Am I a criminal? No. Could this book and its ideas bring special unwanted interest to me? Yes.

I remember when a magazine came out in the early 2000's and said that security cameras would be used in many cities. They said maybe every city would have cameras in 4 or 5 locations. But before the writing of this book, there were lots of cameras. There were four cameras at every major street intersection and every public building in every City in the Country.

Cameras were located at public events. There were cameras facing all four directions at almost all street intersections. They said it was to catch terrorists or not as important, but as they said," almost as important" they were to catch people breaking traffic laws. After all people who were running red lights in sleepy subdivisions were running rampant. Points worth thinking about, but I believe their intentions were much deeper.

An organization was started called GREMIS. GREMIS was an acronym for Government Run Educational Media Intervention System. Catchy huh? Yes, leave it to the Government. The personality and strength of the organization was very slowly brought into society. One moment they were only an organization dedicated to protecting the general population from Terrorist control of the social media. The next moment, actually a year later, they were dictating what could be talked about and what could not. They became ruthless all in the name of protecting us from ourselves. Man, would, if left to his own devices, they contended, unknowingly destroy himself. I am so thankful that there are people out there whose only concern is protecting me from myself.

At one point, at the height of GREMIS's control, the Government introduced an electric blanket that they gave away to everyone. People picked the blankets up a convenient GREMIS pick up points all over the central part of the State. The blankets were actually soft and very nice. Word spread that the GREMIS electric blanket was a very high quality blanket and it was something special to own. But the citizens didn't realize that this blanket had completed the triangle. Now the Government had visual records via security cameras mounted everywhere. And from Face Book and MySpace and Twitter and others, the Government had digital social records. And now, with the blanket, they had a method of securing that "special candidate"; the one they had decided was that special "person of interest".

When decision came down from the Director, a radio signal was sent over the internet and picked up by a small receiver on the specially coded Electric Blanket. Seconds later the soft blanket became completely rigid and attached itself to the bed. The hapless occupant, the one GREMIS wanted to talk to, was held fast to the bed until Government representatives could arrive. They of course, had a key to the front door, again courtesy of the digital age. Nothing was sacred. Nothing.

But you say: "Renn, I have nothing to hide, do you? What wrong with the Government control and management of our lives?" I look at you and shake my head. I remember coming home one day and some one had gone through my dirty clothes. I don't mean this as a figure of speech. I mean, they had my underwear out and had analyzed the excrement on the inside of the seat of the underwear. I was surprised the next day to have a call from the Pharmacy. Someone had turned in a prescription for antibiotics. It seems that I had a urinary tract infection. How thoughtful of them to look after me. They even charged it to one of my credit cards.

The Government at the time my "Back of Head Book" web site came out had just figured out how to profile the entire human population. Well, not that much, but at least all the population of the in several adjoining States. This organization had gotten behind the social web sites and created a myth that theses sites and all people who used them were "very special". They were high tech, cutting edge, maybe the people were even "extra smart". You say "Smart" and everyone falls for it.

But, with the help of several of the Social Media web sites they could instantly have access to personal information on anyone listed on the sites. Of course GREMIS was the brains behind this maneuver. With some covert planning, it had become the electronic arm of the Government. And as you read earlier, "they were from the Government and they were here to help".

GREMIS was touted as the "new age" media control, "bringing us a better way". All our needs would be anticipated. It would be revolutionary. It was a sort of friendly "Big Electronic Brother" on steroids. It would find you, place your activities in a file, and tax you and place the tax on your credit cards. It could reach into your very soul, literally. If you didn't have room on your credit card it didn't matter. Your credit card would be over drawn and you would not be able to use it until you paid off the balance.

All the Credit Card companies were ordered to pay the tax and then collect it from you by one means or another. Some Card Companies had gotten very aggressive. I saw several men with their arms in slings. I think it was too much to ask of the general public to believe that one third on the male population had fallen and broken their arms.

So when my "Back of Head Book" came out, it sounded an immediate alarm. You see GREMIS had linked a nation wide camera network to the various social media. And with both written and visual information on everyone, you would find you were under the "public Microscope", but not until they let you know. By then, of course, it was too late.
My idea was different. In fact it threatened to destroy them. It worked silently. The more your "Face" on my "Back of head" page was uploaded to the site, the farther away your information got.

The harder and harder it became to find you. One link I had designed actually changes the features on the web site owner's face. One change to your face was made with every hit on your site. At the same time, the web site changed your information to believable but untrue information with each hit.

It was when I put in the last feature on my site, that finally set the government "dogs" loose. The new feature actually changed information about the site user. For example John Doe could log on to my web site to find out information about me. He would not only, "not" find out anything, he would actually log out as John Dole. The next time he logged in, he would leave the site as living in Denver Colorado instead of his home, Oklahoma City.

I knew this was a little much, but I thought it was "just punishment" for the "social tracking freaks". I had nothing to hide. I was not trying to promote any crime. I just wanted a life without personal ID. That's when they came after me.

CHAPTER **10**

Rain, Rain and more Rain

I had just finished my research on disappearing. That's when it happened. Call it intuition. Maybe it was just an odd set of circumstances. Maybe they had read my last social article. Maybe it was my web site. It was something. But thankfully, I was ready. There was a knock at my door. The first knock was a give away since I do not answer knocks at doors. By the way, I don't use overhead lights either; just small reading lights. And, I don't answer phones. Nor do I play music that can be heard. The blinds are always drawn. Any meetings I had with Anna or my few friends were set in advance.

Then there was a more threatening sound: "Mister Gains?" (not my real name . . . well, not any more) . . . long silence. "Mr. Gains? Are you there?" another knock: "Rap Rap Rap". I remained silent until the person or persons went away. I heard them say as they walked down the stairs: "Call Security. I think we've got a runner." With that, I knew I had very little time.

I had to pull together two years' worth of odd possessions and head out. I had not pulled money out of my bank account, but I would do it within 30 minutes. If I was lucky, GREMIS would not have activated a "search and retain" order yet. Plan

#79, the long study that you read above and were so aghast at, had actually gone into effect.

Within an hour all bank accounts linked to me or anyone with accounts with a similar name were frozen. Phone records were appropriated. Utility bills were conscripted. No fly and no ride orders were issued to all transportation carriers. My apartment was raided. The contents were boxed up and taken to some computer "cultural" assessment site. I suppose a nice name for an organization whose sole purpose was to collect information on "runners". This was serious business. Anna's records were even pulled as I found out later, but to their bad luck and mine too, there was no trail.

The word was out. The Men in Black Coats, as I called them later, were out on the streets. No man would be left uninvestigated. The pressure was stifling. Food and water were cut off to certain areas. Neighbors were investigated. Even my class mates were drug in to be examined. This was very serious. It was the movements of an organization that did not take failure as a possibility.

CHAPTER 11

The Trunk

I sat in my secret place in the trunk of my car and watched the waves of water come down over the front windshield. I still thought about Anna. She had been a breath of fresh air in my otherwise "stale" life.

However, I had hardened a little. My new creed was: "Maybe my life sucked, but it was better than no life". Catchy huh? One protected his way of existence, however so mundane, anyway he could. That's why I liked it where I was. I felt a certain security in the separation that the wall of water outside afforded me. No one would be out in weather like this. I could rest for the moment.

I already had a schedule. I would stay in the trunk until dawn. Actually the bigger cars had fairly comfortable trunks. I had a sleeping bag and a sack lunch. I even had rigged up a "trucker's helper". I called it a "trunker's helper". It was a small funnel and plastic tube led through a hole in the floor of the car and set to empty close to one of the back tires. The wetness by the tire actually looked like a dog had come by and relieved itself. Well, that was pretty close to true anyway if you count me as a two legged dog. My additions to a "General Motors" vehicle allowed all the comforts of home.

The car had a back seat center console that folded down. If anyone walked too close, I could pull up the console and the back seat would look completely unused. It was my "rolling fortress", at least until I found out a few things. Then, I would move on. You see living in the normal man's world had become very hard for me. My apartment had been sealed off. There was no going back. Many of the precautions I had written down had been forfeited with such short notice. They could not find them, but neither could I get to them. They had acted very quickly. Most people would have been caught. But then life in this part of the Country, had become very challenging anyway. You had Government checks everywhere. You had a Government that wanted more and more personal information.

But then, I was beyond that now. I had broken the grip so far. I had chosen another path. Everything was right here. But "right" the way I chose, not the way someone else wanted it. You could make your own rules. And if the rules didn't work, you could change them.

I called myself "Renn", but now I can't remember why. It didn't matter, I changed it every two months. I only know that "names" brought GREMIS closer to me. Maybe GREMIS was the "man"; maybe, the one who always seems to have things work better for himself. It could have been "Mr. basketball" man from my high school days. Maybe you have guessed by now that the role of Mr. Right had not worked for me.

Lighting flashed and brought me back to the present life for a short instant. What was I doing? Why had I done it? My mind raced. It tried to place my thoughts in order, but all efforts found nothing very substantial. Thunder shook the car. I never knew that a simple lighten strike could bring such a shutter.

I remember earlier, the rain had started. It pelted the car with freezing drops as I flew out of the door beside the garage. I kept the car in by my garage apartment. I knew they were after me. I jumped into the car and drove to this spot. That was the last memory of the GREMIS world. I dropped everything. And now I was here in my safe haven. It was all now just a flash in a race for escape.

Life after my escape seemed to have the taste of a stale cracker. It would start to taste ok, but after half the cracker was in your mouth and chewed into a wet cud, you would realize that you were eating something tasteless and debase (sort of like this book.) It was the thought of stale crackers that drove me out of the trunk. I guess I was speaking only metaphorically but then again I had a cracker crumb still on my lip. You figure it out, it's beyond me.

Anyway, you can buy my story this far or not, I'm moving on. It all comes together in the end (hopefully). So, I would leave the trunk occasionally and find a safe place to breathe the fresh air. I sat behind several trash dumpsters trying to find a direction in my new life. Thinking back, I had considered what would be involved in a quick escape from my apartment, but I admit, I had not really believed it would happen.

Now, it was more than an idea, it was staring me in the face like a hungry wolverine.

So, thinking back, I had been more interested in eating cookies and laying on the bed than thinking about what I would do if

I were to find myself on the run. Now, considering my current situation, I could have eaten a few less cookies. After the initial shock of changing lives, I found myself sitting in the rain. I guess there were two sides to every coin except for the trick coin I had once. But, that's another story. Reflecting back I guess the coin had two sides. I would remember the Hobo I watched eating a sandwich leaning up against the locked door of a "defunct" grocery store. He seemed to like his dinner. He ate the food as it were the greatest delicacy. I found myself feeling sorry for him. After all he had nothing. He had lots of nothing. I caught my self picturing his existence. He had "no bills, no mortgage, no car payment, no family responsibilities. Yes, he had nothing and I started to envy him. But then after some more thought, maybe he had everything and I had nothing.

I heard a dog bark and pulled my arm rest back into the back seat with silent speed. You would think by now that I would be used to living off the land. But then, I also liked the thrill of danger. Danger gave you an "edge". Man all the way back to prehistoric times learned to live on the "edge". The people that are not with us today took a different tact; the ones that didn't see danger all around. You know . . . the dead ones.

You think I dreaded adversity? Well, yes I guess at first, I did. Now, after many nights of reckoning with my soul, I had found comfort in the anonymous life. It made being President of the "out world" all worthwhile. I had taken a vote several months ago. There had been no opposition. I had won by a landside. I had voted myself "President" of the "here and now." My kingdom was a felt lined trunk. I commanded all you could see (in the trunk). And to celebrate my victory, I had eaten sardines out of a can and treated myself to a whole sleeve of biscuits. My current "palatial" habitat, would not win any awards, but then, I was avoiding the people who gave out awards. I could have made a case. That is, stood before them in a great echoing dark hall. I could just imagine myself erect in position in my best suit, acting like a New York Lawyer. The board of executives would sit in front of me with jaundice expressions. But, I would show them life's real truths. I would tell them of the true relaxations I found in a private of life.

I found myself enjoying every turn in the felt lined card board liner of the trunk that surrounded me. I would spend hours exploring every connection and every redirection of the trunk walls. It was truly an adventure inside metal walls. The dog bark now was fading. Still the rain hammered the top of the trunk.

I had wired the trunk light to a little switch. It came on at my command and allowed me use of my "reading room". I laughed. I truly was the "sultan" of confined spaces. I found the book I had been reading and opened it to my last dog ear. The book seemed to crawl into my mind and transport me away. It was truly freedom in a cramped dim world.

I was careful not to drift too far away. Or, at least, that was my plan. But it didn't work. I drifted off. There was a noise outside. I jumped back awake. Maybe I was off fighting dragons . . . I can't remember now, but I think I was about to win.

The same time the noise awoke me a drip hit me right in the eye. What kind of luck is that? Why couldn't it hit me in the chest or on the top of my head. Was it a notification of something? Notices came all the time. Maybe some of you don't notice. But then, there are some notices you do. It reminded me of older men's need to urinate. At some point in their life, most men had a very adamant need to pee. (Excuse my language)

With this need to pee came a terrible pain. It said "Renn . . . You need to pee right now!" I usually abided. But, I kept asking myself why the pain. When you think about it, there are many methods of "notification". There could be a "buzz" or maybe a "vibration". Your pulse might go up. You might start to sweat. Your eyes could flash light and dark. But no, the notification of choice was extreme pain. I always wondered why. Was there more to the task than just notifying someone of a needed duty? Pain to one individual could mean joy to the inflictor. #1000.

Oh yes, back to the drop of water in my eye. It was not pee. Good thing. But, that does bring to mind some great imagery. Don't let me drift off on another tale. After deciding that I was not drowning, thanks to the dream I was having, I rubbed my eye and found myself back in my felt covered domain. The rain had almost stopped. I leaned the arm rest forward but it was still dark out.

I always loved that. Darkness told me I had another hour to float in the "safe world". My feet where completely outstretched. The car was "factory" finished, well, except for one thing. I had cut a slot in the right side of the back seat. The hole was just big enough to stick my feet through. The hole was below the seat surface. I did remove some seat springs. And as a final thought I had glued some card board inside and to the bottom side of the seat. You would probably notice if you sat on that side of the back seat. But looking in from the windows, it appeared to be completely un-touched. It was my rolling bedroom. Also it was my living room, dining room and reading room. It was my "pee" room too with the use of the "trunker's helper". But then, when my bowels moved I had to find a way to get out of the trunk long enough to make things right.

CHAPTER **12**

More than the Trunk

I was not born in a trunk figuratively. It took time to find my correct place in life. Ha ha . . . , just joking, but then again, maybe not. It took time to get hit with everything that life had to throw. I was just starting to think about how all this happened, when I saw him though the fake trunk light.

Yes, I spent some time mounting several mirrors into the middle break light behind the rear window. It was impossible to tell that this was my private periscope. You could very easily miss him. He moved quickly with his long black leather flowing coat. But I had seen him several times before. "Mr. Black Leather Coat" was one of many government informers. I saw them come before the "great restructuring" when GREMIS had taken over. They were there after the crash of society as we know it. They were the eyes and ears when security cameras weren't present. They were the foot soldiers of a government gone aerie. They looked for people like me. Most all of the rest of the world had missed me. Of course, that's what I had counted on.

The rain had slowed down, but now had just become an irritant. My neck started to tense up. My mind raced back to memories of death and destruction, of ruined lives. People's personal computers had been turned into becoming an accomplice of the State. Anyone questioning the new State run "web" was conscripted to virtual cells in their own homes.

All this jarred my senses. The memories ran back to me like sawdust shooting up into my eyes from a circular saw. Rage took hold, and before I could formulate a plan, my hand was on the trunk release. The was a "pop" and the trunk lid flew open. He was standing near the car and the noise caught him completely by surprise.

My body simply spewed out of the trunk. An eerie wail came from my mouth as he faced me full on. "EEEEEEEEEEHHHHHHHHHHHHHHH" The cigarette dropped from his mouth as he felt my boots both driving into his kidneys. The kick was good, but we both knew that he was not quite human. The leather cape absorbed part of my kick.

His eyes bulged, but most of the force had been deflected. He seemed to whirl into a mass of smoke and loose skin. He fell back, but at the same time throwing something into my eyes. I shrieked and rolled at him again. I could not see. But, I would not give up that easily. Something deep inside me took over. Something that said: "I will not give in!" I was a full fledge maniac. My body turned and flipped and again kicked at him. This time I really hit something, He stumbled and fell back. As he fell he seemed to recompose. His eyes bulged again. Yellow liquid spewed from his eyes. The whole scene appeared like something spilling out of a blender with the top off.

I was just about to grab his head when the darkness took me over.

I screamed and screamed and then the scream turned into some sort of gargle. I started to loose control of my legs. He had gotten to me again with some sort of gas or powder. I was falling and he was laughing as he ran off.

Scene over? No! . . . You think that I was just a man who would try and then accept failure from this new society . . . No. No! You are wrong! I would reach inside my failing body and pull out every last ounce of strength. I would burn organs for fuel. I would bite my tongue and drink the blood for energy. I would scratch the day lights out of anything in front of me. Taking me down won't be that easy! Not without a last fight! You see I was a "new man", someone that they had not prepared for.

I whirled off the pavement completely blind and tore after his sound. I caught him as he was turning a corner and grabbed his neck. He fell against a low brick wall and I continued to beat his head into it. I would not give up. He screamed and screamed. But the scream shortly turned into a laugh. The more I grabbed him the more he seemed to turn to dust.

I stumbled and fell but with a "concrete" lock on his neck. He dissolved. I lay there in shock. He slowly he raised himself up and reformed into a man. He stood there a minute, long enough to look down at me in disgust. He brushed himself off and moved away, but he did have a noticeable limp.

You see? The system is not invincible. I had inflicted some damage. It had not been a complete loss. Maybe they could be beaten; just not here and just not now. But I would find a way to beat them and then pass it on. And . . . speaking of passing, I passed out.

Time raced by. Later, somehow, I really can't tell you how, I pulled myself back in the trunk and pulled the lid shut. The blackness was complete. The secrecy would sooth my wounds. The silence would flush my mind. The softness of the trunk lining would help me find my peace again. I slept away from "the man". I would have to move my rolling palace soon. I was sure that Mr. "dust man" would turn my location in.

Later that morning when I was still sleeping it off, a cop approached my car and was preparing to give my car a ticket for an unpaid parking meter. I would place it with the three hundred or so others in the glove compartment, that is if I could get the glove compartment lid closed again. I had turned my break light periscope to look forwards. Someone looking in the car might have thought it a little funny to see the break light facing to the front of the car, but so far it had not happened. I did have a little "get back" device planned for just such event. I was still seething from my fight with Mr. "Dust man". But now I would take it out on this unsuspecting COP. I had wired the battery to the frame of the car with a switch inline.

When the police man lifted the metal windshield wipers to place the ticket under the wiper, I flipped my switch. There was a sharp snap of electricity. The man jumped back in a cry of pain. It threw him back so hard he almost lost his balance. He walked away holding his burnt finger tips and maybe showing just a small dampness down in the middle of his crotch.

I chuckled in silence. But, I hadn't done much. I still had the ticket and he would probably take the rest of the day off. It was not that I had a dislike of police. It was my disgust for ideas that made no sense. The Cities were dying, yet the city officials made it very difficult to park and buy anything or do any business in the City. It would start the same way any other bureaucratic organization started. The office would be small at first. But then, over the years they would add personnel. Maybe a friend would hire another friend. Maybe a grant would allow them to hire several more workers for a short time. But, at the end of the year, they would need to raise the budget for the department. That's when the idea of raising more funds through parking meters would come in to play. Of course it happened in every department. And now the City was broke and looking for any revenue stream.

CHAPTER **13**

Boyhood dreams

When I was a boy I dreamed of building an Armoire that would set in ones living room. It would look like any normal Armoire, except that I could get inside it and take control from another world in a nice cozy seat complete with arm rests.

I tried to build one once. I took an old cabinet and lined the insides with foam. My idea was that I could sit in my hidden room inside the Armoire and be left completely alone. It was my kingdom inside the "outer world" It was a world I controlled. It was my only real peace.

After I got the cabinet in place, I decided to cut a little pinhole in the side.

Then I mounted a piece of white cardboard on the opposite wall next to me. The hole acted like a small lens. I could watch people walk by without the knowledge that they were being watched. There was one problem. Their images were all up side down. But who cares about details?

Later, I would dream of mounting a curved monitor inside the same Armoire from which I could watch TV, flip to a closed circuit camera and look around the house. Even later, I got interested in a computer program that would let me build my own world digitally. I built many fantasy worlds. One odd thing, there was never any people in the landscapes.

It usually showed a vast sea or land mass with all sorts of lonely conditions. You could build sand storms or great clouds of fog. I was in my element and without my knowledge, I was preparing for the future.

The cop had just left. I watched him go through my rear break light periscope. He turned and looked back at the car one last time. I could swear he looked right at the periscope. He looked so hard at me I felt a rash coming on. But then, he turned and walked away. It was then that I thought I noticed some similarity in his walk and the walk of the "dust" man last night. Then again . . . maybe not. Although, it was something that held my imagination for a minute more than it should have, if it was nothing

That's when it hit me. I was late. I had to get to train station. It was almost 8:00 am. He was always there at 8:00; "the man with the brief case". Well, actually the brief case that seemed to be fading out. It's hard to describe. You'll just have to bear with me while I try to explain. I had seen him twice before at the same time and place. I, of course, was wearing one of my disguises.

No one would recognize me, because I was someone different everyday. I was doing some research in the area and happened to be standing behind this man in a long black coat carrying a briefcase. It's not what you think. I mean he really wasn't completely there. The brief case actually was minus several thousand pixels in the lower corner causing it to look like a computer generated his image and at the last second had a "hick up". That's technical talk. I don't expect you to follow everything.

I could see glancing at my watch that it would be a miracle if I got back to the same place at the train station. After first scanning the area with my periscope and determining that the drunk laying on the sidewalk next to my car would not be a threat, I popped the trunk lid and allowed the "out world" to flow into my private space.

The rain had stopped now, but the rain must have made a pack with the wind. The wind probably said "Ok, I'll take over for now. I'll make it as unbearable as possible. But, get back to me tonight. Maybe we can flood a couple of areas down by the river." And with that, the rain stopped and the wind took over.

I jumped out of the trunk, not wanting to call attention to myself. Little seeds from an adjoining tree slashed at my face with their little propellers. The ozone from the morning rain wanted to fill my senses with wonderment, but I was not interested. I knew it was a trick. Instead, I was quickly whisked away by the evil wind. I pulled on my hooded sweat shirt as I stumbled down the sidewalk all the time receiving physical blows from the "bandit" wind. Pulling the hood over my head was sanctifying. It always afforded me some privacy when I didn't have time to get into "Character".

Wardrobe and facial changes were now not only a good idea, they were required. That is, unless you wanted to spend some time in a jail cell or worse. I would have to run. It was just now 8:00am. The grey buildings hanging over me were still dripping from the overnight drenching. They reared over me on either side of the narrow street. They seemed to lean forward as if they wanted to crush me. I let my imagination run loose. It would be a embracing "wet" crush, this feeling from the grey buildings. The crush would be sort of like kissing you as the life was sucked out of your poor defenseless body. The falling and hitting the pavement would not even be felt. Did I say that? "Ouuuu" . . . I need to get some more sleep. But for now, I started to run. With the hood over my head, I felt I could take on the world.

The train station was just around the corner. I was starting to slow. I expected to see the large building that housed the trains. I touched the side of the last structure on my way so as to fling myself into the short straight path required to get to the large grey building when: "Smash!!!" I ran into someone coming around the building the other way. It would have been a much bigger hit except the person started to decompose into dust. Then as quickly as it happened, it recomposed behind me. I turned and looked. It was a woman.

She was as surprised as I was. She stared at me in disbelief, then, she turned and ran. I staggered and fell to my knees; completely out of breath. My mind was blurred trying to put some order to what just happened. Was it just my mind working overtime? I convinced myself that it had not happened. I sat on the sidewalk leaning against an old wrought iron fence. Two battles in one morning could break a guy up.

After sitting there for a few minutes, my head started to clear. I got up and walked over to the Train ramp and walked down the stairs to the tracks where I had seen the man with the partially formed briefcase. There were still lots of people waiting for numerous trains going almost anywhere, but the man with the disappearing briefcase was not there. I had missed him.

I was tired anyway. I would need to slip back into the darkness of the trunk for a while. This exposure to daylight, people and what I had started to call the "out world", had drawn the energy from me. I would try it again tomorrow, to find the man with the briefcase. I wondered how he must be related to something much deeper.

As I walked out of the train shelter, I walked past a dark area with some signs that were burned out and humming. The result was more dark than light. There was lots of trash blowing around. The whole scene reminded me of a movie set. There was an image of a running man on the wall beside the sign. Then there was some writing scrawled in chalk. It caught my eye. I usually don't read graffiti, but the writing style got my attention. It had big flowing arcs that made up the letters. It seemed to be the writing of a very literate person. The person to want say something important. I stopped and read the writing. It said: "In the end, everything will be ok . . . But if it's not ok, then . . . it's not the end." I let the words filter into my mind. At first it didn't mean much, just a catchy saying. But then the meaning of the words started to hit me like a giant punch. Who wrote this and what did they mean? What did "the end" mean? Did it mean that life would end as we know it? And what did it mean when it said that things might not be ok? Did it mean that if "things were not ok" then, because things were not ok, that situation would prolong the end of life? And if things "not ok" went along in this limbo of a life, then would that mean that the plan was to prolong life with everyone being "not ok" or . . . in other words . . . In torment? I didn't know. I stood there for longer than I should have. But, I thought the statement was very profound. I decided to double my security and intensify my observations.

I wrote the phrase down in my black book for future study. I quickly headed back to the car.

I still had a ways to go to get back to the car. It was starting to rain. I might get soaked before I got to my black felt jungle. I was stepping up my pace when I saw another saying written this time on the back side of an real estate sign still hanging on to a wrought iron fence. It said: "Today is the tomorrow you worried about yesterday . . . and you were right to worry."

I quickly pulled out my black book and wrote that down. Now this saying was more to the point. It actually had a "ring" about it. Today was the day I had worried about. But, so was tomorrow. I put the black book back in my back pack just as huge drops of rain started to come down. I raised my arm to protect myself, but thought: "Yes, I could identify with this last one. Today did seem a little like my fears of yesterday". Ha (I thought) . . . I'm a poet too. Then the saying from my youth kept coming back: "He's a poet and don't know it but his big feet show it, because they are "long fellows." I know that makes some of you cringe . . . but hey, when you're living the life with a soon to be "super hero", you gott'a take it all in. You can tell your kids.

CHAPTER **14**

Suspicions

You know how you sometimes start to have a feeling that everything is not quite right. It's like it's almost right, but not quite. I was thinking of that very issue as I shook the gas pump spout. A few weeks earlier, I had filled my car up at a run down gas station using savings that I really shouldn't have spent. But this was "research" and I was committed. I shook the spout while it was in the car gas filler pipe. I shook it and shook it. I pulled it up but not completely out. I shook it some more. I waited. Then I pulled it out and what happened? A number of drops of gas still fell out on the concrete pavement of the gas station.

You are going to say: "OK Renn, so what? How does that relate to the price of eggs in Russia?" But then I would say to you: "There's more here than meets the eye. There should have been no drops of gas." I paused: Then: "The spout had plenty of time to drain out." I paused: "Where did the drops of gas come from?" You might say: Well Renn . . . You've got me." But I would say: "They have taken you over . . . I don't know who . . . but I am going to find out." Ok . . . Go try it. You think that I am not right? The gas will always spill a few drops no matter how many times you shake the spout. But, why?

Why? Was there a global effort to pollute the world eight drops at a time? That could take a long time. Maybe there is no idea of complete devastation of anything. This concept is underlined later in the book. Complete devastation would mean ending or stopping. And that would mean that there would be no soils to torture. And with no "tormenting" , what else would there be to do? So taking out a small black book , I started my research numbering this observation as #1001.

I was not always mistrusting. I suppose it was the incident on the airplane that really stands out as the first real introduction to tormenting. If nothing else before had been apparent, this incident caught my attention. Maybe it started my quest to find out what was really happening.

I wasn't getting off. I was flying through. In other words, we had stopped at a City on route, but I was not required to get off since my destination city was the next stop. A friendly man got into the seat next to me. He was placing his belonging in their proper places when he looked down at the floor. He quickly asked: "Are those your car keys?" I looked and sure enough they were. They had fallen out of my briefcase.

Now you say: "Renn, what's so strange about that?" At first nothing seemed wrong. After all, sometimes items fall out of your briefcase. I thought about this for a few minutes. But then my keys weren't any item. They went to two different cars. Both had electronic chips embedded in the key.

There would be no duplicating of these keys at the local Home Depot. The duplicate process would involve significant money and a long wait for the factory to duplicate them. I remember thinking that I had another key for one car but none for the other. And the car I had driven to the airport was not the car I had a duplicate to. So as all this information started to flow into my mind I realized that a number of items could have fallen out of my briefcase and not caused any problems.

I might have lost my reading book. Maybe my reading glasses could have slipped out. I could replace them for $10. I might have lost several pens. I might have lost a notebook with information really not that useful. I keep my black book zipped up in the brief case. Other items flashed through my mind. All could have been lost except the keys. Losing the keys would cause me the greatest torment. You say "But Renn, you probably would have seen them just sitting there waiting to take off.". I would scratch my head and think about this. I would whisper to you this: "When the plane took off, the keys would have slid backwards as silently as the night. They would end up under a seat at the back of the plane." It was brilliant. It was incredible. It was heinous. I was incensed. From that moment I vowed to continue recording all similar events. #1002

Oh, as a side note, I recorded that this incident had been "interrupted". The man had pointed out that my keys were on the floor. I picked them up and stopped the whole miserable chain of events that would have surely followed. But, this revelation meant that this process could be overridden. It was very interesting. Whoever could control a torment, could be beaten. I had just stumbled on the surface of the iceberg. I was to find out later that the ice ran much deeper below the surface.

During the flight after the key event I started making a mental list of several items I would investigate. The black book I had started earlier would see a lot of use in the future. The next item on my list and one that had been "dogging" me for a long time: "Yellow lights". You know that in the red, yellow, green cycle of a stop light there is only a small segment of time in the yellow light cycle that will cause you to have to slam on the breaks or run through the light. I had calculated that the total cycle is about 67 seconds.

There's 30 seconds of green, then 7 seconds of yellow and then 30 seconds of red. It varies a little from location to location but the proportion remains the same. In fact you will say: "Renn, different intersections have different lengths of time. But I would say that the yellow portion remains the same. Accepting the argument that the red and the green take longer only emphasizes my point. The yellow is actually a smaller portion. But to continue my point, it is the "approach time" that is really in question here. During the last few seconds of yellow is a time that you might get caught approaching and intersection. Obviously you would not go on red.

And like wise, you would go on green. So explain to me how it is that I am caught 75% of the time in this "limbo time", the last 1 second of yellow prior to entering and intersection. If you figure the math, it's 1 second out of 67 seconds or .05% of the time that I hit 75% of the time. I started to keep track. The amount of time this small segment appeared was staggering. And thus I added to my research book #1003.

I was back to the present. I was in the Trunk. It was close to weird time. I should head home. Oh? . . . you thought I lived in the car . . . Well . . . that's only partly true. I will get in the car and show you. It's a little place I have lived in for the past 2 years. And you say what is "weird time"? Well, I have pointed out some unusual events that have been plaguing the earth for several years. It could have been much longer. At "weird time", events seemed to happen closer together. It was a kind of "rush hour" for dirty tricks. It happens about once a week, usually on Thursdays and many Holidays. And today was Thursday.

I reflected back: "I saw the worst car wreck in my life on Christmas Eve as a boy. It was a holiday and people were rushing to get to relatives houses. It was evening; that time when it's not light, but not completely dark. It was that time that seemed define itself as different than any other time of the day. The occupants of the car were speeding with thoughts only of the evening celebration. I was riding with my parents when we approached the intersection at the north end of my Grandmother's block. We were late too. But we weren't speeding. I was looking the other way when I heard a screeching sound and turned to see two cars collide at maybe 50 mph. Both cars flew into the air on impact.

There was a terrible screeching and smashing and the breaking of glass. My parents rushed me to my grandmothers one half block down the street and called the police.

I never knew what happened to the poor souls in the cars. But the idea struck me that the mind can be manipulated to be more or less alert. Why? Maybe it was under the premise of "teaching a lesson about being more careful?"

Is that it? Are we always being taught lessons? Thanks very much, but I have had all the learning I want. Or is the idea may be to "torment?" I didn't understand then and I don't really understand now, but I was to meet someone much later who would give me some good arguments. But for now, I called this one. #1004.

"Weird time' was here again. I just had enough time to get into the driver's seat of my car and head to the house. It would be close. Fifteen minutes later I am pulling into my driveway. My driveway was in a junk yard. My house is a shipping container. I stopped the car and got out. I quickly opened the door of the container. After listening for a few moments and searching for movement, I pull the car in. It was just big enough for the car; leaving only a space at the front of the container.

There, my friend, I have cut a hatch that opens to an old basement. You could not see the foundation walls from the outside because of a large pile of scrap metal to the right and then of course, the container itself was hiding the rest.

Just as I closed the door to the container I heard the first of the screams that would dot the night. It sounded like the sounds of victims who had had their insides ripped out. What puzzled me is that most of these tormented souls didn't know that they were being stocked. That was my theory anyway. More to come on the 5:00 news.

A giant rat ran across the floor of my basement as I dropped down the metal ladder. I didn't care. Actually I identified with rats. Think about it. Here is a creature that exist's under it's own rules while the world around it goes through prolonged stages of horror.

The domestic brown rat is called the "fancy" rat or Rattus Norvegicus. Rats raised as pets are decedents of the brown rat. Brown rats are bigger and bolder and have pretty much taken over the position of the black rat or Rattus Rattus. Legend says that the black rat was the carrier of fleas that in turn carried the black plague all over Europe. Brown rats were first bread for blood sport, but more recently many after thousands of generations are now more docile and friendly to humans.

The rat lives by his wits. His vision is poor but every other sense is far superior to man. There are some not so obvious differences. The rat lives for today. Man lives for the future. The rat does not make any plans for the future. It lives only for today. The rat sees no problems, just opportunities. Man lives through the mighty trial of problems. And what's just as interesting, is that most of the time man does not know that he is being put though theses tribulations. Man takes life as a bit in his mouth and he pulls until he dies. And, all this flagellation, in the guise of making life better. By now, most of us must be perfect, because we have been "made better" so many times.

But we're not . . . and yet we go on with very few complaints. Yet the rat lives amongst the men, not affected by his inadequacies; living only for today. In fact the rat lives on in spite of man's triumphs and failures. So, I began to covet the company of the rats. I dropped to the floor and felt for the candle I kept by the ladder. Mr. Fitz as I called the rat was now no where to be seen. He was, "hiding in plain sight"; another Rat trait that I would study thoroughly.

The rain had started again outside, but my space was for the most part dry. It was a study in low energy consumption. In fact, it was a study in no energy consumption except for the battery operated radio that I used to plot the locations of the weird ones. I located the stick matches and lit the candle. The room glowed in soft light. I had found an old army bed in the junk yard and after slipping several blankets under my coat at the day shelter, I was in business. I opened the refrigerator that of course, didn't work. It did keep out the bugs and mice. Inside I had several packages of dried beef jerky. I found the jerky kept for months.

I also had some soda pop that I obtained by changing the "expires Oct 31" (Not the real date. You might use that date to try to locate me) coupon that the store gives out knowing that you only have 3 days to get there. The magnetic strip was simple to alter. I figured that I had every right in using the altered coupon because they were making a public effort to show that they were rewarding people for shopping with them. But in reality they only expected to get back about 10% of the coupons. So to recap that, the store advertised that they refunded 5%, but as it turned out only 10% of the coupons came in so in fact they were only refunding ½ of 1%. I numbered this one #1005.

My food supply was getting low. I would have to make another run. There was no bathroom. It was just a detail. You always have to bring up "details". I guess it was something about no sewer lines. But I did have a "chamber pot". Nothing but the best for me. I actually had found an old toilet in the junk yard. I had placed it near a block out in the basement floor. Some day I would dig a trench to the city sewer line, but it would have to be done at night. Instead, I would carry water down from a fountain in the park.
I would prime the toilet before each use. But there was just a bucket in a hole under the toilet so the whole exercise was a little protracted.

This junk yard actually did function during the day. There was an old grizzly guy that looked at dirty magazines and sat behind the counter of a small shack where some old rusty scales were placed. He did a big business when the weird ones were not out prowling and of course when he was sober.

CHAPTER 15

The trail starts

The small manuscript was on the table by my bed. I had read it and read it. It made no sense except that I knew it was important. It had come to me by accident. It had been so simple. I had turned the corner just like before. I guess I was running again though I can't remember why. It was almost like the race to the train station yesterday. I had run into another "dust man". I hit him hard as we collided. He was taken by complete surprise.

The blow had caused his right side to completely de-copy. It was like watching a 3d copier only in reverse. The whole right side of his body started to slowly turn to dust and fall to the ground. I think he was as scared as I was. His mouth dropped open as he saw his right side turn to small particles and then reform. He looked down at his arm and leg in a state of dust and then looked at me.

As soon as he was whole again, he broke and ran. I was still reeling from the impact. I staggered and caught myself against a building edge, just as I was going to fall. My eyes glazed the then re-focused. That's when I saw it. It was a manuscript in a leather pouch. I stared at it a moment and then realizing that the dust man had dropped it and might be back to get it, I grabbed the packet and tore off in the opposite direction.

Now, I sat there and stared at it. First of all it had a seal on it. That meant they wanted to know if anyone had opened it. Ha ha . . . that would be me . . . ha ha. I had opened it and stared at the text expecting to see right into the maze. Yes, I would straighten everything out. But alas . . . it was in code.

There were also charts and graphs; again described in code. The code was good. It would take me months to break it. But the graphs were graphs. There were graphic descriptions of some sort of projection. The code kept me from reading what they were showing but the graphic nature of the graph did not shelter the code. Something was projected to get larger. Just what that might be, caused me to loose sleep every night thereafter. But then the howling outside didn't help either.

I had opened the book for the first time three days ago. I was staring at it not knowing where to go with it when I heard the sharp crack outside. It was of course, one of my traps. Something was in big trouble. Maybe it was me.

I had worked on the traps after one of the howling things had gotten into my basement. I was taken completely by surprise. He had me very literally dead in my bed. I was only half awake. He had stepped forward to end my feeble life. I had seen him and I soiled my underwear. I started to think of what I might like to be in a new life. My existence was about to be history in this life and would have, except for one thing; my sewer connection.

I forgot to tell you that I started digging it last week in a fit of sleeplessness. I had dug most of it in the last few days. In my earlier life I had been the "king of procrastination." This life was no different. The hole was still there. I had made the connections but was too tired to fill it in. I had placed a piece if card board over the hole instead. I had been meaning fill it in. But every time I thought about it something else took precedence.

Or maybe I just didn't want to shovel the dirt back in the hole. Anyway, I just had to remember to not walk in that area. It was only ten feet deep. Actually, I would have expected the creature to come screaming out of the hole and slice my worthless body into millions of pieces. I huddled in the corner waiting to see my life end. But there was complete silence. I finally grabbed the one flash light I had hidden for an emergency. I peered down the hole and there was the most gruesome creature I had ever seen staring directly back at me. I shrank back expecting it to lunge right out of the hole, but it didn't. I looked again and that's when I saw that it's neck was at a odd angle from it's body. Son of a bitch! It had broken it's neck. Now maybe I would get the hole filled in a little sooner, like maybe before sun up! . . . ha ha Yes, at least that soon.

CHAPTER 16

More thoughts

I was washing my car several years ago. I put in some quarters in the selector box and the digital numbers showed 150. I, of course, assumed I had 2 minutes and 30 seconds. I started washing the car spraying soap all over it. It would be a good washing. Forty Five seconds had gone by. I was just turning the selector switch to rinse, when the machine shut off. The digital read out read "0". But forty five seconds had actually gone by. I would have to put in the same amount of coins to get the rest of my minute and a half that I thought I had left.

It was a rip off! And, of course even back then, I would not bow to "the man", so I got in the car pissed off and drove off with the suds all over the car. People walking along the sidewalks must have laughed at me. But, I would not pay more to be fooled again. The day went by with no further events. I went on with my day to day activities. But, after a while the whole concept started to come back to me.

Are we on this earth with an expectation of a certain length of time, but in fact some one or group of beings have changed the time increments. We go through life planning all sorts of valiant projects not knowing that a group or individual has a little surprise for us. I don't mind the idea that if someone wants to charge for 150 units. When the units run out, your time is up. No one can argue with that. That's pretty straight forward. It's the idea that you are being fooled into thinking one thing; that is of having two minutes and thirty seconds and really it's something completely different; that of having half that length of time. That's where I saw the evilness. How many people did this concept affect? I made up my mind right then to try find out more, and I eventually found much more. I might even do something about it someday. #1005.

As a side note, the next day I was back at the car wash. I had several items in my pocket. One item was a large magnet. Another was a coin with a string run through a hole in the coin. I had decided that I was not one to be taken advantage of. I would see if some other outcome could be introduced. I was in the process of trying to affect the digital readout with the magnet when a large bear of a man came around the corner. He wiped his hands with a rag and then yelled at me. "Hey! What are you doin?" I stammered a little; something about the price of sanitary napkins or something equally as foolish. He started to move towards me but I quickly threw all my devices into my pocket, jumped into the car and peeled out of the car wash. As I pulled out, I noticed the digital read out was at 170. It was strange. As I drove on I started to realize that maybe everything was not so "under control."

Or, at the very least, I decided that I might find a way to foul up the guy setting the "timing". I was just putting my ideas in order in my mind when it hit me. "They might be able to read my thoughts." The whole concept really staggered me. Should I really have my plans in my mind at all? How would I shield them? I resolved to find an answer.

Last year in June, I began starting my plan for a "Comprehensive guide to protecting your ass". I called it: Partial Ass Protection or : PAP for short. I had several ideas. The incident of yellow light had intrigued me. And of course, the gas pump begged for attention.

Now, I was noticing that drops of gas that flew out when you took the pump spout off the side of the pump. Remember the spout was facing up and there was at least three feet of hose going to the concrete surface where my car was parked. Any liquid would have long sense fallen to the bottom of the hose. So when the gas drops came out, what did that mean? Was this a maneuver to cause pollution? Was there a plan to so make man's plight just a little harder? At 7 drops per pump, that would take a long time, but then maybe that was the idea. Was the idea: "A world of small misfortunes". Had every mechanical device had been manipulated as well? Did your electric meter spin just a little faster than it should? Did your washing machine that was just out of warranty, break? And it would cost more to fix it than to buy a new one? Where did it stop?

Was the world meant to slowly "go down"? My theory was that it was meant to find a "level" of torment. I conjectured that there were several levels of degradation.
"You gonna use that pump or you just gonna "milk it" there?" The voice brought me back to reality. I turned around to see an old withered woman looking at me. I quickly finished my business with the hose and put it back in place but still noticing that a small puddle of spilled gas lay at my feet as I got in the car and drove down the block. I stopped and made note and then continued to drive off.

Months passed. The world remained the same and the world changed at the same time. Someone else said that, misfortune was the "candy" of life. I am sure they were joking or making social discourse. But the time at the pump there were no jokes. There was nothing pleasant related to social discourse. People went along with their lives, unsuspectingly. But, maybe there was more to it. Maybe their lives were being manipulated. And I started to think that only I knew what might be really happening. I resolved to continue my journal. I was reminded of the saying: "If ignorance is bliss, then why are most people not happy?"

CHAPTER 17

More deeds

The five dollar bill stared up at me as if it had been caught doing something wrong. It was mine of course. It was lying on the ground beside me. I had a bad habit of taking bills and just shoving them in my pocket. I had pulled something out of my pocket and the five dollar bills had come too. Not that strange you say. That has happened to me too. Well . . . Hello . . . I have been keeping track. It turns out that the five dollar bill will come out of my pocket 90% of the time.

I had a theory. I put a Foreign Currency one dollar bill in the same pocket and proceeded to pull different items out of the pocket at different times during the day. The Foreign Currency one dollar bill never came out. But the five dollar bill came out 90% of the time. What could this mean? Was someone controlling this situation as well? Was it an attempt to give some less fortunate soul my money? Maybe it was. Was the foreign one dollar bill not enough to make it worth while? Was the proposed loss of the five dollar bill among a list of small torments that would make up the day? I marked the event for the 67th time in my book #1006 and placed the book back in my backpack.

The sun was just coming through the crack in the slab above me. The small streak of light would start across on the opposite wall and slowly track across the walls of the room. It was my natural alarm clock. The light meant several things. The most reassuring thing was that I was still alive. I liked that one. It had a kind of a "ring" to it.

Second, it meant that the mindless souls that searched for me or anything else for that matter; the one's that walked in the night, would have contracted back into the stinking hole they slept in during the day. I liked that one too, the contracting part that is.

Also, it meant that I had to get moving. Most days I would go looking for some food. Nothing except can goods could be found, but I actually had developed a taste for canned meat. There were of course, diners serving aromatic meals and they were hard to avoid. You could smell bacon and eggs cooking on a grill. Most people sat there at a diner mindlessly staring out the window.

I thought I could join the group. I thought I could slip in and act just as spaced out as the rest of the population. However, the last time I went into a small diner, I was almost caught. A man walked up to me and looked into my eyes. He seemed normal, but he was not. He must have been an informer. He slipped out of the diner quickly. He was making a call on a city pole phone when I hit him with a big stick I found in the parking lot. He went down like a cheap bar-b-que grill. It felt good. I don't think he would have agreed.

Today, I opened my laptop and started to continue my journal. But there was nothing. The file was missing. I numbered this event #1007. I knew right then and there that they were close. I eventually found the file. It was hidden in another document.

You see nothing in the "out world" is black or white. To just get into to your computer and erase the file would be too obvious. And again, completely erasing my book is major torment.

To erase the file would be good for some laughs, but then it would be over. Why not scare the person by causing them to think that the file was gone. Then scare them again and again?

After thinking about this I decided that I would have to redouble my efforts to keep track of as much information as possible. If I didn't make it I would at least plan to put this information somewhere where it could expose this network. Of course, that would not be easy. They would be monitoring every information source. At this point the only thought I had was to create some big disturbance. If I was lucky they would turn their attention to the disturbance and allow me enough time to get this information out over the air waves. But as I saw it, that plan would take some work. For now, I was content to lay low.

This morning, I would work in my lab in the larger room next to the one I was in. I quickly fixed a cup of coffee. I had tied into a power line in the old feeder system for this building. Of course, the building was no longer there, but the basement was. The power was off after the transformer above, but I tied in on the feeder side. (an old Indian trick) So far no one had noticed.

My lab was about 20 feet by 30 feet. It had a 12 ft. ceiling. I had all sorts or material in there. I had just finished running an experiment of what I called "a balanced box". I was trying to prove that a balanced box always falls. The experiment's assumption was that a balanced box was just that; it had equal weight on both sides of the supporting edge it was placed on. But, as I projected, the box fell every time. Now why would that happen? Assuming your average guy brings in a box of glasses and sets it on another box. He happens to place it close to half way on the box below. But wasn't there just as likely a chance that the box would not fall? This got into some mathematics and physics.

I was sitting to the side of the experiment noting all the various factors, but then I realized that I did not have to run any calculations. The box was going to fall. The box fell and broke all the glasses. So you say, what is so unusual about that? You set the box too close to the edge. But . . . ha . . . I tried the same experiment with a box of ping pong balls. If the box fell it would not hurt them. So . . . again I placed the box on the edge of another box below . . . the box did not fall. I tried several times. I would carry the box in from the other room and trying to not think about exactly where I was setting it, I would place it down and wouldn't you know it, the box never fell.

So what was my derivation? Damage will happen when it will be the most destructive result and will not happen when it will not cause any destruction. I am having trouble making this make sense. I stopped a minute and wondered if "they" had managed to emit some sort of mind control or "box" control. I suspect it is much more complicated than that. So even if I got this information down they could manipulate my wording in such a way as to discredit me. I wrote this down under experiment number #1007.

CHAPTER 18

Next after that.

After a quick bite of rancid cheese, I moved on to the next experiment. I moved some boxes out of the way to give me more room. I had several pads used to absorb urine on a bedfast patient's bed. The first pad I poured a small amount of water in the top corner. Total coverage was about 10%. I removed my shoe and sock and kicked the pad with my barefoot just as you would if it were in the way, and you were kicking it into a corner to get it out of the way. The statistics of hitting the water and getting your foot wet were about 1 in 10. So after kicking it a number of times I recorded the data and entered it into my book. No big revelation. I hit the water about every tenth time. Then, after stopping to drink some rain water that I had collected in an old coffee can, I removed the beaker of urine I had stored for this occasion. I poured the same amount of Urine as I had poured water in the top corner of a new absorption pad.

Then dropping it on the floor I again kicked the pad as if to kick it out of the way with my barefoot. I hit urine. It got all over my foot. I washed my foot off and again placed the pad in the floor. I again kicked it. Again I hit Urine. After an hour of data gathering, I recorded a whopping 28 out of 32 times I hit urine. I recorded the information and stared at it as I unwrapped a small hard candy. What could that mean?

Obviously, the kicker was meant to experience a small amount of misery almost every time. Yes, that was it. None of these concepts were meant to bring some "game ending" slug onto the intended victim. But why? I numbered it #1008.

Then after sitting there for a while I decided it might be like a program many war Generals used in inflicting casualties in time of war. If you simply killed your victims, then, you could quickly bury them using a minimum of effort. But if you inflicted some sort of casualty and they didn't die, then it meant tying up hundreds of man hours just keeping them alive. Not to mention the hours of pleasure that could be derived knowing the victim was hurting.

Well, it was just a theory at this point, but I noted the idea in my book. And, how was it controlled? Thinking up a misery trap was one thing, but doing it at the right time was certainly something else. I sat there and pondered this. There were many unanswered questions. I placed the book back in the old safe I had found topside and clicked the hasp shut. Actually I didn't know the combination. I had placed it in a corner and thrown boxes over it hoping to throw anyone off, should they find my hide out.

My head was spinning. I decided to make some fresh coffee. The brewing would have to go very fast. I couldn't afford any coffee brewing smells. So I had hooked the old pot up to a 220 volt line. The power surge was so great that the coffee was almost boiled off before I could unhook it. I figured I had a few months anyway before they started trying to find where the electricity was going to.

A month ago I had rigged a fake short out of the wires next to my shipping container above me. They had fallen for it. Some men in white "Hasmat" suits had showed up with some sort of location device. They had disconnected the wires and hauled off all the material, the conduit and the boxes I had tied together. They would report a small power usage and report the cause as a shorted set of wires tied to an old building that had been removed long ago. The incident would be forgotten.

Today, I would again go into town. I had a plan of attack but it kept changing. The men who fell apart (The digital men) were plaguing my mind. What were they doing? They seemed to be couriers. I could believe that. The internet, phone service and radio waves were too public. Someone who could hand carry private communications would most likely be used. Now days any kids with a dime store computer could mess up the works if he knew some very basic programing moves.

I remembered an address on the leather pouch. It was not in code. Maybe that was my next lead. But, before I took off this morning, I wanted to go check on what I had going on, in an abandoned building near by. I had an "ongoing" experiment running. I started this one about 2 weeks ago. Basically it included the use of three Bums I saw sitting around a camp fire on the north end of the junk yard. I asked them if they would help with a small study. They were of course reluctant. They threw flaming pieces of wood at me and were going to try to take my wallet until I told them that food was involved.

I had found several boxes of canned chili in the same building. The boxes must have been over looked when the last tenant moved out. Anyway, each can contained exactly 1 pound of chili. Now I set up my three test cases with rigid scientific controls. (that's technical talk for taking three bums, giving them each a blanket and a cardboard box to live in and setting them up in the basement of an old building). I don't expect you to follow all of the scientific talk. Anyway, I gave them each 1 can of Chili a day for 14 days. This was actually the 14th day. As far as I could tell, they did not have anything else to eat. I kept the food locked in a box I had found.

I was, of course, checking their weight gain or loss as I fed them a controlled amount of food. I had a theory that needed proving. And you say "But Renn, it's a lot more complicated than that." I look at you funny as if you were trying to explain the laws of physics to me. You say: "To run a scientific study you need to take into account the factors relating to each subject."

There's a short silence, "For example, you would say : "Everyone's metabolism is different." Weight gain and loss can not be explained by any one factor. Some individuals are smaller in stature, some are bigger. Each person has a different calorie requirement. Some subjects will burn calories more rapidly than others. Therefore Renn, you are just "pissing into the wind"."

And I would look back at you and say: "It might get all over my pant leg, but this point is undeniable. And you, maybe you are a product of the system. You line up when the siren wails just like the next person. Your eyes fog over. You have been blinded and you don't even know it . . ." I would stir a stick in the ground as I thought of how to tell you the truth with out completely pissing you off.

Then: "Let me tell you what you have failed to see . . . In this experiment there are only three things that can happen. 1. The subject eats the 1 pound can for 14 days and looses weight. Or 2, the subject eats the 1 pound cans each day and his weight stays the same. Or 3, the subject eats the 1 pound can feeding each day for 14 days and he gains weight. And along with number 3, the worse case scenario is that the subject gains 14 pounds which is the total weight he was fed . . ." I stop to emphasize my point. Then: "Those are the only three possibilities under this strict feeding schedule."

I shake my head as I hold the clip board on experiment # 1110 and look at the results. Bum #1 gained 16 pounds. Bum # 2 gained 18 pounds and Bum #3 gained 19 pounds.

So, I look back at you and say: "Yes there was a fourth possibility. One you over looked. There is one possibility that does not make any sense. Could it be that the subjects gained more weight than we fed them? How can that be? It's impossible isn't it? We water a plant 4 ounces of water over a controlled period and it grows and may weigh twice it's original weight but it grows and produces new cells with the help of the sun through a process we call photosynthesis.

The plant truly does grow by exposure to the sun. But here we have three pasty faced low life individuals. They have not been in the sun, as if it would help them. They have not eaten anything else yet they gained more weight than we fed them. We see overweight people everyday and assume that the weight they gained was never more than what they consumed. Yes, that would be too easy to explain. And of course, that's what you want to believe. But the true result is that man is receiving a very hidden torment. One he can't even see. Yet it's happening every day. A lady eats a cream puff. She loves it. It weighs 2 ounces. Yet the following day she weighs 1 pound more. I look at you as if I am undermining your very core beliefs. I whisper to you: "Oh . . . it's much more than we can conceive. I truly fear for my safety as I tell you this."

CHAPTER 19

The next trip

I stuck my head into the container that held my car. Nothing seemed out of place. I checked the lock. It was still locked on the inside. The outside lock was a fake. It looked like someone had locked the container and then left the whole business for years.

Putting up this ruse gave me some feeling of safety. I opened the container very slowly looking through the crack in the door opening for several minutes. With no movement outside, I pushed the door further and then stepped out of the opening and closed the door. I immediately went into my homeless drunk routine. I pretended to have flies attacking me from all sides. I held the "prop" whiskey bottle in one hand and slapped at the flies with the other. If anyone saw me they would think I was just a drunk leaning against the container. At most, they would yell at me and run me off.

Seconds went by and nothing happened. It looked like the old bastard that ran the junk yard had tied one on last night. When he tied on the "big one", he would sleep until noon.

I quickly pulled out the car and closed the container leaving the fake lock in place. The real way I locked the container was from the outside. It was simple. I ran a rebar though the outside frame to the center door "astragal". It was almost unnoticeable.

I pulled out to the country road still formulating my morning plan. As I started to pull on to the road a car came speeding up. Had I not been looking both ways it would have hit me. I paused to let it get by. I have to admit it had shaken me a little. Now, this incident was something I would note when I got back to the lab. Ok . . . here it is. How many cars would use this road today. I guessed 6 based on watching the traffic on the road for the last 3 months. The road really didn't go anywhere. There were some farm houses down the road about a mile. After that it wandered through the hills until it finally came out at a graveyard south of town. No one would use this road to get somewhere fast. It could have been used by the occupants of the 3 farm houses. But discounting 8 hours of darkness, that meant that there was 16 hours that the road could be used.

If the six car traffic was spread out evenly, that meant that a car came by every 2.6 hours. So, how was it that that the 2.6 hour user of the road came by just as I was pulling out on the road. Yes, you might say: "Leroy or Bill or Tom or whatever your name is, (because I didn't tell you my new name) you are just paranoid. That was just a coincidence. That car could have come by several minutes earlier or several minutes later." But I would answer "Yes, but it didn't. In fact it came by exactly when there would have been a crash had I pulled out." I wrote this in my book as #1111.

So, you would walk off looking back at me and shaking your head with baseball cap slung down over your eyes. And you would continue to take "hits" like this, that you didn't even associate with misery. And maybe you would be part of the group that walked into the cave when the "Warlocks" blew the whistle as we read about in the "Time Machine". Well . . . hell, go ahead. You can lead the group of psycho hypnotized workers. If I go into the cave, it will be because I am carrying a hand grenade. We'll see what they have to say about that.

After noting this incident on a card I carried in my pocket, in code of course, I pulled out toward town. I would transfer the information later. On the way, I hit 13 yellow lights out of 15 possible intersections. They were not yellow far ahead allowing me to prepare to stop nor did they change to yellow after I was in the intersection. No, they changed in what I called the 'panic zone". It would be that time where you had milliseconds to decide if you would proceed ahead or slam on the breaks. Just to let you know, . . . I never stop. Someday I will pay the price. Maybe.

The traffic was light this time of morning. Most people left an hour or so before they had to be at work. It was only six:fifteen. My timing would be good. Except for the rail road tracks this side of downtown. Just as I thought, the one train every 5 hours was crossing as I approached the crossing. The cross bars were down. I was in for a long wait. During this time I was able to reorganize my thoughts and number this one #1112.

The slow travel would give me a chance to stop by and check on an experiment I had running in a closed down assembly line building. I parked the car in a handicap zone, pulled out my fake handicap sign and proceeded around to the back of the building. I pulled myself through and open window and slipped quickly to the main assembly floor.

I suppose that the Company that owned this operation had gone out of business. I found it several weeks ago and hung around for a while to see if it was being watched. It appeared that the building was disserted. I had wired the conveyor belt system directly to a transformer out in the alley. Don't try this at home. On the conveyor I had slices of bread each with peanut butter on them. They proceeded down the line until they reached a point that I called the "intervention zone". I had several devices set up to swing down and interrupt the flow of the bread. Each time an arm would swing down or a brick would fall from a shelf above or a wire would come up. When this happened the bread was pushed off the conveyor. I had a meter set up to record the number of times the bread fell face down with the peanut butter hitting the floor with a splat. The results were staggering. At the moment of my recording I had dropped 10,501 slices of bread. Out of that total, 10,420 slices of bread had fallen face down with peanut butter stuck to the floor. I recorded this as # 1113.

I was about to leave. I scooped up a couple of pieces of bread with peanut butter on them off the line and ate them. I hoped that wouldn't foul up the test results. The bread would be my lunch. As I was leaving I remembered that I had another experiment running in a small room on the second floor. I ran up the stairs and found the room still unlocked. In the room I had placed a number of clean white dress shirts and several black shirts.

In the experiment, each shirt was hanging from a system similar to ones used at Dry Cleaners. I had wired the motor to run very slowly. The shirts were going around this endless loop all day and night. I would guess the mechanism had been running a week or so. At one point in the hanging loop the shirts came close to a big bowl of spaghetti with red sauce. Note the shirts never touched the bowl.

In every case I found that the white shirts had red sauce stains on them. The black shirts were completely clean. I noted this as #1114. It appeared that white shirts attract stains. This would happen, I pictured in my mind, when a young man took his girlfriend out for a nice dinner. It proved what I had expected. My only regret was that I did not have a way to check to see if the stain would occur at the start of a meal instead of the end; thereby causing the wearer of the shirt the maximum amount of this mild torment.

I needed some money. That was true almost all the time. But today seemed worse than most. I had horded a stash of funds in my basement but it was nearly gone. Sometimes I worked odd jobs. I worked at a feed store that would pay me to sweep up. I worked for cash only. Last time I was there I noticed a strange man across the street.

I am sure I saw him talking into his coat sleeve. And, I don't think he had a mouse up his sleeve. I had collected my pay and left the area. The owner of the store seemed oblivious of anything happening outside his store. Sometimes, I got so upset at the peoples general inability to see what was happening all around them, that I almost broke down and told them what I thought.

I said almost . . . It was too risky. I should just move on. But before I completely leave this point I should say that all the new US Currency bills have magnetic stripes embedded in them. Look for yourself. Is this to trace stolen money? Maybe.

Or can they register the money when you draw it out and then keep track of the person drawing the money? (Not an unexplained torment, but one that's happening right now.) Don't be fooled into categorizing torments. That's the easiest way to breed "doubt".

The train cleared and I looked at my other notes. I had seen several of the men in Long Black Coats enter a certain building downtown. I had wanted to check it out but had been busy with my experiments. Today I would at least stick my head in the door. I expected that it could get complicated. It's address coincided with the address on the mystery satchel I had at my lab.

I use to play chess. In chess, you learned to anticipate your opponent's moves. This was no different. I knew that if I just blundered into a situation at this building, I would have no defense, no ability to protect myself. I learned long ago that protecting ones self takes a number of forms. Diversion was a good idea. Surprise on your part, was not.

So, I had brought with me, two cans of gasoline and a roll of string. I had played with gasoline as a kid. It's a wonder that I did not burn myself up. I found out that gasoline when lit burns with a very small blue flame; maybe only a quarter inch above the liquid. If you were not watching closely you might not even see it burning. But you say: "Renn, I thought gasoline was explosive. Don't we see it burst into flames in the movies?"

And I would say back to you, that is what the string is for. The one ingredient that gasoline does not have when confined in a can is air. By the way, don't try this at home. I had a very scientific plan. I would set the cans so that I could jerk them over from a distance. If I didn't need them, well they would just burn out slowly.

CHAPTER **20**

The building

I had parked the car behind the building. I put a jack under the car and jacked up the front wheel so that it would look like it was abandoned. If one of the Men on Black Coats came by, they would not suspect that it was set up to be a get away car. I dressed into my outfit in the back seat of the car. I had some used janitors clothes. As I entered the building I noticed a sign in the pediment above the entry.

It said: "I moaned because I had no shoes until I met a man who had no feet." I was trying to get in without being spotted. But the sign caught me completely off guard. I knelt down by a trash barrel and wrote the words down. I would need to research the meaning of this sign when I had more time.

The building was at least 200 years old. So it appeared to me that because the pediment was put in place at the same time the building was built, the idea of misery was around a long time. The thought of men walking around with feet cut off kept haunting me though I knew that was not the intention of the Author. After reflecting a minute or two I jumped up and ran into the privacy of the entry.

After entering the building, the first opening I came to was a closet with an open door. It was a Janitors closet. I was in luck. Thoughts started to jump out of my mind. Maybe I could manufacture a costume out of some junk. I looked inside. The closet and its' contents were obviously out of use. There were spider webs and dust devils everywhere. Boxes had even fallen off a broken shelf and lay disheveled on the floor. But it had Janitors cart inside.

I put the two cans of gas in the cart along with the string. I was about to leave when I noticed a large sliver tray; the kind that you might use for a larger tea service. It was fairly heavy. I decided to wrap some string around it's handles and tie it to my chest and stomach. If some one shot something at me, it might stop the projectile. You think I'm a dreamer don't you? Well, this all actually comes together in a few minutes. If I got away unnoticed I could sell it for it's silver content. It was of course not solid silver. It was some sort of alloy.

The silver made it look pretty and the alloy made it strong and it sold to a house wife for big bucks even though it just had a shiny coating. I tried to concentrate on my next move but the housewife buying the shiny tray kept coming back to me. Maybe I could write a meaningful saying too. Let's see. Here goes: "Life comes in like a shiny gift but leaves you holding a piece of sheet steel. The luster is gone and the value you thought you had, has slipped through your fingers" Oh . . . There's really no rhyme to it. I decided to make another try later. Meanwhile, I pulled the outfit together.

With my chest piece in place under my Janitors shirt I proceeded to "shuffle" down the hall. I could hear voices around the corner. I slowed. I saw my second closet door. I opened the door slightly and placed the can of gasoline on the top edge of the door. I duct taped it down from one side.

Then the last move was to hook up the string so that it was taped to the can of gasoline and then run it down through the door hinge of the gasoline door and across the hall to a door stop on the other side. I tied it off. Carefully, I lit the gas. It burned with a small blue flame just as I said. Please don't try that at home.

I simply placed the second can on the first step of a stairway opening to the hall about twenty feet down the corridor. I taped it to one side of the step so that the tape would act as a hinge. I taped the string to it. Then I ran the string down the hall in the direction of exit should I need to get out fast. Last move was to very carefully light the gasoline on the step as well. I did so and as I expected, a small blue flame was present just above the liquid.

With my rig set up, I proceeded to make the turn in the hall. I had the janitors broom out and I swept the hall as I got closer to the double doors leading to an area where it sounded like many people talking. As I approached the door a voice came from a dark corner. I jumped back in surprise. My eyes adjusted and I saw a man hung from the wall in some sort of torture device. Blood was running down one arm. He spoke in a slurred voice. He half whispered: "I wouldn't go in there if I were you." He stared at me with dark pool eyes indicating many hours of torture. I reverted back to my Janitors routine trying to show that I was legit and that I had every right to be here. He looked at me for a minute and then said again "Hey buddy. You ain't no Janitor and . . . I wouldn't go in there if I were you." I was amazed at his instant recognition of my plan. I fumbled a little trying to access my possible actions.

I took a rag off the cart and started wiping my hands. Then, I said as if I had not noticed his condition: "Just cleaning up here man. I got to get all the rooms." His response was swift. "If you go in there, they will kill you."

And then after thinking about it, "Actually, they won't kill you, you will only beg to die, but they will just watch you suffer and try different things on you". He chuckled as if he had said something funny. I looked at him unbelieving, but not wanting to make a scene. I adjusted some items on my cart and started to proceed with my plan.

I continued to wipe my hand and then said "Uhh Man. I gott'a clean in there too." He again stared at me. Then he said: "Then you're a fool." He looked down as I prepared to open the door. Then he said: "If you must go in there, put on one of those robes" He pointed at some robes hanging on the opposite wall. I stopped and pondered the situation. He came back after a long silence: "It probably won't work, but maybe they will be too busy to notice you."

I looked over and then noticed the robes hanging on the wall. I took off the janitor's shirt making sure to turn so that the man could not see my silver tray held against my chest and put on the robe complete with a hood. I pulled the hood over my head. I started to open the door and I again heard the man: "Oh, . . . by the way . . . Is there any way you could get me down off this wall?" I looked at him as if I hadn't noticed. Then I said "Hmmm . . . let me do a little clean up in here and I'll get you on the way out".

The man stared at me again as if to say: "You won't be coming out". But then he shook his head looked a little crazy and said

"Ok, it's your funeral". As I left he had reverted back to a face with a frozen scream on it. I wondered how much of it was an act. But then, he seemed to have a "thing" going.

I entered the great hall. The room was much bigger than I thought. The ceiling above had old weathered trusses about 30 feet in the air. The windows high up had been painted to cut the light. There were only a few places that had not been completely painted out, that let small wisps light beams into the hall. Other than that, there were several barrels burning rubber tires placed in the corners. The black smoke intermingled with the window light and made a sort of sickening haze throughout the huge room.

There were figures milling about looking at the contents of different tables. I guess there were at least two hundred tables. Some people were arguing and some were buying items. No one noticed me. The light changed from dim to dimmer as the tires flared up and then faded back as they burned. Also any light was hampered further because each booth had some sort of dark cloth back drop that with the help of long poles, reached close to the ceiling. To make matters worse, two or three of the booths had open flames in fire pits. The resultant smoke and dust, combined to make a dark haze that hung over the whole setting like a bad dream. The only good part of the whole situation was that it would make it harder for me to be noticed. I left the cart and the broom by the door and proceeded to move toward the booths.

I walked to the first booth. The purpose of the booth had me completely confused. There were drawings of the human anatomy: mostly hands, knees and elbows on posters on the back curtain. No one was at the booth except the vendor. He was reading an old book. After letting me stand in front of his table for a few minutes he looked up at me and said "Something special?" I could not see his face because of his hood. A little sneer could be seen on his mouth; the only part not covered by the shadow . . . He chuckled. "Something for a friend?" He "horse laughed" at his own joke. I must have looked confused. His eyes bored into mine. "You like arthritis?"

I stared at him hiding behind the shadow over my eyes from my oversized hood. I responded "What? I ahhhh" He seemed to understand. "Yes . . ." He thought for a long time and then said: "I was thinking the same thing" . . . He looked at me again and started to laugh. #1115. Then as an afterthought: "It's good . . . you'll like it" . . . ha ha ha Then sensing that I was not convinced he said: "If you want a guarantee, buy a TV set". He "horse laughed" again, convinced that he was the funniest man to walk the earth. I shrugged and moved away. As I left he said: "Let you try a little . . . ha ha ha" Again he was his own best audience. I felt all my joints weaken, but then I think it was just my imagination.

I fumbled a little with my robe and headed on to the next table. I was trying to only stop at booths that had no other shoppers. I didn't want to take a chance of being noticed. So, the next one that was empty had a lone hooded figure smoking a water pipe. I looked at his table. There was nothing there except a small book. I must have seemed especially interesting to him because he looked up. He saw the expression on my mouth. He spoke. "What do ya want?" . . . I stood there and said nothing. "You're not from around here?" I stood silently. He looked me up and down. The smoke poured out of the side of his mouth. He spoke again. "It's 45 credits unless you got something to trade."

I stood silently. Then, slowly I said "Whatteya got?" and I pointed at the book. He put down the pipe . . . and fingered the book so as not to lose his place. Then he puts his hand beside his mouth so as to shield the private conversation and whispers: "People's lives." He could see that I did not understand so he raised the one free hand and made a motion as if I would understand. Then: "You know . . . Time" . . . He looked up at me. "With this little device . . ." , pointing to a small matchbox that I had not noticed before, he continued: "you can steal time". Then as if I needed to be "walked" through the whole concept he said: "You know . . . Aunt Elma thought she had at least 75 years to live." Looking at me as if I would now understand . . . He continued: "Well, . . . this little device actually absorbs time." Then he laughed out loud: "The best part is when she realizes that she has overestimated how much time she has left . . . ha ha ha". He laughs a little more and then says: "Time is a funny thing." He stopped and thought for a moment and then continued: "You see people think they and control it . . . They think they can put a measurement on it."

I stammered as if I was completely lost. Then not even noticing me he is deep in thought. He continues: "Time is not a regimented mechanism. You can manipulate it. You can speed it up or slow it down." He continued to think as if he had opened a new way of viewing how our lives are played out. Then he chuckles: "Remember when you were a kid in school and you watched the school clock get close to 3:00 and time to leave?" He was silent as he remembered. Then: "Well, remember how slowly the clock moved as it got closer to the time when schools would be over?" He seemed to go into a trance remembering the deliciousness of how all the little kids were forced to wait 40 to 60 minutes when they should have only had to wait 10 minutes. #1116.

I stood there for a minute . . . He seemed to snap out of his love affair with the past. Then said: "You got anything to trade?" . . . Never at a loss for words, I found myself falling right into the role. I became one of them, at least for a few minutes. Wondering how he would react, I said: "Heart attacks" I waited for a moment. Then, fearing he would not understand; I spoke again: "I got heart attacks". I found myself listening to what I had just said. It is sounded really stupid. But he seemed to take it in stride. He picked the pipe back up and took a long drag.

Then after thinking it over for a few seconds, he spoke: "Not much value." He thought again for a moment. Then: "Too permanent . . . ha ha ha." He seemed to be sitting there thinking about the past. Then: "Not popular anymore." He looked at me for a long time again and then: "You ain't got no Heart Attacks do ya?" He mulled over my outfit looking me up and down and then said: "If you don't want nothin . . . get outa here!" Then, he decided that I was just a free loader and angrily said "Move on!" I glared at him for a minute. I smashed a bug running across his table while still glaring back at him. That would show him. But then, I thought better of it and just walked away. I didn't could have argued, but I didn't want any attention.

The next booth I came to was filled with jars stacked to the ceiling. Many of the jars where balanced on the one below and none of them were all that well grounded.
I could see a big crash coming.

The man at the booth was talking on some sort of communication device. I had never seen anything like it. I over heard the conversation: "Yeah, Yeah, 20 dozen cases. Can you have them here by Friday?" He listened for a second, then: "I've got several buyers. But if your shipment is not here by Monday, they will walk".

There was a silence while he listened to the other side. Then he spoke "Listen Slick! I don't care what your problems are. You have them here by Friday or I'm finding another supplier!" With that he slammed the device down on the table. He looked up at me while scratching his rough beard.

Then "What do YOU want?" I stood in silence. The hood I wore was helping me play my act. Then he spoke looking down almost as an apology. "All we got today and tomorrow are fleas and ticks." He looked in a small manual he had beside him. I'll sell 3 cartons of fleas and 3 cartons of ticks for 20 units. You won't find that every day!" . . . I stood in silence.#1117. Then as if to answer his own question, he stared back at me. "Ok, I know. You want Bed Bugs!" Then, as if to question himself he asked "Bed bugs, Bed Bugs, Bed Bugs! I'm going nuts . . . everybody wants Bed Bugs . . ." He looks back at me. Then "Is that what you want? I know . . . It's the rage!" He waited for me to respond. I didn't. Then: "Well, I don't have any! You'll just have to wait with everyone else." I sneered at him and moved on.

The next booth was funny. The man in a hood leaped over the table to meet me. He says: "Ok buddy, you're my 100th sale of the week. If you buy something, I get an all expense paid trip to Brendmama." I stared at him with out talking but picturing the island paradise. Then apologizing he continued:

"Ok . . . I know they are not very sexy. Some of those boys on rows five and six are selling everything they got. Maybe they got the sex! I don't know. My business is a little slow. But, I say my product is the backbone of mankind! They're what brought us to where we are today!" He was looking at me as if I was still not sold.

Then: "Look I'll be honest with you. I've got to move some of these cases. My ass is on the line." Then, seeing nothing in my face, he came at me from a different direction: "Look, I got a full range. And . . ." as if to make a very important point he whispers: "it passes on." There's silence as if he were waiting for my reaction. He could see that I didn't understand. So he came right to the point. He whispered again as if he wanted to keep it a secret: "Look Buddy, this is the "gift that keeps on giving." He paused as if it was his last effort. Then: "Look . . ." He slowed down and became more animated as if I was some sort of mental case. "Look Fred . . ." He looked around. Then:" One unit can jump to lots of customers." I must have looked completely stupefied. I said: "What do they do?" He now looked at me as if I just climbed out from under a rock. "Look man, it's the flu! I sell the flu!" Then he reflected: "It does a body good" referring to an old advertising quote, except I don't think they were referring to what he was selling. I said: "Hmmmmm?" I started to get the picture. I liked the way he referred to his product as the "gift that keeps on giving" as I thought of all the unfortunate people who would be in bed sick for a week with the flu and then have a stuffed up nose and walk around dopy for another two weeks.

Then he started to lose interest. He could see that I was not buying. He slapped me on the back and gave me a couple of advertising pens. He opened up a small note book and seemed to move back to his pressing thoughts of loosening his job. I started to move away but then he stopped me and tried one last sales pitch. "What about that old "Shingles" man over there?" Looking down his nose at the vendor he pointed out. Then he said: "He can only infect one person at a time. Get these little "gems" pointing to some boxes he had behind the table , he continued: "and you can make a whole town miserable!" He stared at me as if I would see the light and show some sort of understanding. My face remained "vacant". Then he backs away. Then he says: "You're not from the Directors office are you? Look, I'm a fully registered agent. We got top quality products." I continue to stare. Then I slowly move on staring at him all the time. As I moved past several other tables, I could see him talking on his phone and watching me out of the corner of my eye. #1118

CHAPTER **21**

Paranoid thoughts

I was starting to think that I was being watched. Maybe just a paranoid thought, but I might grab a drink at the bar in the corner, look at one more booth, and then head for the hills. I had many questions and very few answers. But I would put all this in my book.

I went over to the bar, but had second thoughts. There were too many hooded figures there. One had a big knife sticking through his robe belt. So slowly I moved on.

The next booth was actually an exhibit with a table at the end for sales. The Company renting this booth had to rent two booth spaces. They needed the room. Behind a plastic screen was a dwarf. He was picking up boxes on the floor and carrying them up a set of steps. Each box had a meter on the box. At the bottom of the stair the box read 40 lbs. As he went up the stairs the box got heavier. Half way up the meter read 60 lbs, and at the top step just before he set the box down, it read 70 lbs. #1119.

Then when the box was placed on the floor of the second level, it went back to 40 lbs. I was in awe. How could they do that? I stood and stared as a second dwarf picked up the 40 lb box on the second level and carried it back down. The same thing happened. The box got much heavier as it was carried down the steps

They even had a video. It showed a poor overworked man standing in a warehouse The poor soul was panting and telling his boss that he was worn out. He said that the boxes seemed heavier than they looked. Later it showed the same man in bed with a hurt back. The crowd standing and watching the video cheered in delight. I backed away in shock. As I was backing away, I bumped into a very shadowy figure. He pushed me away and raged at me: "Hey, watch where you're goin!" I back away and said "What? I'm sorry. Excuse me."

Usually this would have placated most "monster men", but this time it didn't work. I tried to slip into the crowd looking at the works of a headache salesman. The room was fairly dark and I thought I had gotten away. But just as I turned to go for the door, a big meat of a hand grabbed my shoulder from behind. It was "monster man". He whirled me around and stared for a minute. His eyes narrowed. Then "I don't believe we've met! Mister . . . ah Mister . . ." He said, expecting me to fill in the blanks. I looked down and spoke again. "Livermore! My name is Livermore." . . . He stood not giving any ground. His breath smelled like a rendering plant. He spoke again: "Livermore? What the hell, kinda name is that?" I spoke again "Sorry. I'll just get my hat and move on!" . . .

He looked confused, but still glared at me. He looked around at the small crowd that had stopped what they were doing and started to listen to our absurd conversation. Seeing they were watching he felt he had to make me an example. He turned his attention back to me. "You got a better name than that?" He could see that he was losing the interest of the crowd so he started to with draw a very long very sharp knife. He slurred some verbiage out. "I think your playing with me" The knife came out with a "zing". Everyone in the room turned back to look at us.

Our words had not been that loud. But I noticed a hooded figure at a booth near by turning a dial that amplified our sounds. I guess he's the guy that makes things louder than they should be. I remember trying not to wake my mother as I slipped out of the house when I was younger. I had bumped into a table with a fan on the table. The plug and cord were on top of the table. As I bumped the table the cord fell down and struck the floor. It should have just been a small thump. But it's noise volume was 4 times what it should have been. And now that I think about it, a number of happenings start to come back to me. There's the time when I was trying to get a piece of cake without waking up my mother. One plate touched another. Their collision was deafening. I now I start to think: "How could that be?" Or I think about squeaky doors. The sound carries all over the house. It's just a hinge and the noise of two pieces of metal touching each other. That just should not have been that way. #1020. Others jumped into my head and I would write them all down for future study, but maybe not just now. Things were starting to turn ugly.

CHAPTER **22**

Knives

So jumping back to the present, everyone in the room stared on as "Monster Man" drew a big greasy, very sharp, knife. I was about to speak to the crowd. I felt empowered. I would tell them that people of the world should stand up to people like him. I would say that they needed to show his kind that we are not scared easily. But then, I heard a second zinging and felt a knife slashing into my shirt.

I looked down and saw the lower part of my robe fall off. Part of the sliver plate was exposed. The dish had deflected the knife. "Monster man" stood back in disbelief. The last man he cut like that split open like a rotten watermelon. Instead, a shinny glint shown through. The crowd gasped. "Who was this man in a Hoodsman's robe? What was he doing walking among us?" Now, same man I met earlier selling Arthritis, stepped forward from the crowd. He had watched the whole confrontation.

Without further thought he said "This man is an outlander!" The crowd murmured. I back away, but many booths and boxes stood in my way. Then, from his robe "Arthritus Man" pulled out a shining ball of slime and held it in his hand. "No matter" he said . . . "He can help us sell our products. I will highlight him at my booth." He laughed. With that he threw the shining ball at me. "Take this and be crippled my friend. You can have swollen joints and bent fingers for the rest of your life."

But as the ball hit me a funny thing happened. The shinny tray seemed to deflect the force that carried it. You see, there were many malicious inventions shown here at the Bazar, but, only few ways to transport them. I guess throwing was the method of choice. The force had been reflected. As the ball was about to hit me, the force was refocused. In an instant it changed course and hit "Monster Man."

There was a flash. Monster man's eyes bugged opened wide. He stood there for a full minute, just trembling. Then holding his side he doubled over with pain. His hands started to swell. His joints ached. He rolled on the floor. He started screeching and yelling. The Arthritis man was stunned. Never had this happened before. When I saw that the crowd was momentarily frozen, I ran for the door I had come in. They all stood there in disbelief.

I slammed the door behind me and headed down the hall. But then I stopped. Mr. "Wall Hanger" was still back there. Turning and sliding on the floor I scrambled back and un-hooked him from his torture spot. I was unable to get all the rigging off him quickly, so I opened the door to the great hall and grabbed the janitor's basket on wheels. I slung him on it and push the whole mess down the hall. Just as I was about to hit the string I had set across the floor I remember my trap. I looked back worrying that they would be on me like a dirty shirt, but I decided to chance it. I stopped the cart and carefully, I unhooked the string and pushed the cart though.

I pulled the cart though and then, I re-hooked the string. It was not a moment too soon. The doors burst open and a big passel of hooded figures raced out the doors after me. I turned and ran grabbing the second string.

There was a long period where all you heard was cussing and scrambling. Then you heard hundreds of footsteps. The first group hit the string stretched across the hall. There was a big "whoooooooooooooosh!" I fireball shot down the hall. Many screams echoed off the hard corridor walls. Then silence. Then the second group came pouring down the hall.

All this time the tortured man was watching in awe as I counted on my fingers. Then I pulled the second string . . . nothing . . . I swore under my breath . . . Now more running footsteps . . . and there was another fire ball.

But, the fire it wasn't from my can of gas . . . They were throwing everything they had at me. I turned and raced toward the entrance. Just as I opened the front door, a business woman was walking by. She turned and looked at me . . . Then there was a flash in front of me. Something hit her. I could see the anguish in her eyes . . . Arthritis man had missed his target again and hit her instead. Now, I could see her hands curl up and slowly, still starring at me, she crumbled to the ground in pain. I could hardly keep my eyes off her, but a ball of fleas and ticks hit next the door frame next to my head. I raced out the door and was about to turn the corner . . . There was a flash and a ball of energy flashed to my left. This time the ball of energy hit my "hanging man". His eyes grew big. He looked at me in disbelief. Then very slowly, at first, he started to age. By the time I hit the alley he looked like he was 90 years old. Mr. "Old Age Man" had shown us what he had. It was impressive if I don't say so myself.

As I ran, I yelled at him "You ok?" . . . I pushed with everything I had to get this stupid cart through the pot holes in the alley. The car was parked where I left it. I hadn't planned on wheeling a man on top of a janitor's cart, but there was no time to think. I grabbed the jack from the front of the car and pushed the aging man into the back seat with all of his personal torture gear. Then, I jumped behind the wheel just as the group of hooded figures rounded the side of the building.

People were out now going to their businesses as you would expect for a normal business day. The hooded figures stopped and noticed that the business people were starting to notice them. As I peeled out of the parking lot beside the alley, I could see them shrinking back into the shadows. I saw lots of energy forces whirling around the hooded group. They could have inflicted a lot of damage, but now they realized that they would be seen. They slowly retracted back into the vacant building. I was sure that this would not be my last encounter.

I turned to the now little old man. He was still alive. I yelled again over the road noise.

"You ok? . . ." He was jammed into the passengers seat. Slowly he looked up and nodded his head. Somehow, I was going to get us to safety.

CHAPTER 23

The chase

It had not stopped simply with the withdrawal of the hooded figures. It was just the beginning. Of course the yellow lights stopped us at every intersection. There were trains going both ways on every track. Cars that never appeared before, were crossing in my path at every turn. The earth shook . . . Then all hell broke loose. Lightening flashed. Thunder rolled across the city like a bellowing giant. A stink fell over the road I was on and I knew I had little time.

Rain started to pelt the car. The car radio screeched and failed. I looked ahead in the road. Something caught my eye. Little shinny objects all over the road. As I was leaving the inside of the Bazaar I noticed a booth beside the door. The hooded figure had a video to explain his offering. I didn't have much time to look at it, but I remember that he showed ordinary nails laying in the street. #1120 As a car drove over them, they shot into the tire. Yes . . . That's easy enough to explain. When the tire hits the head of the nail, the nail head acts like a small lever arm and causes the nail to turn up into the tire.

But what about the nails without heads. The video showed them puncturing the tire at the same rate as the headed ones. Impossible you say? Well . . . stop reading for a moment and go look in your car tires. It's been happening right in front of your eyes. How could that happen? You never thought it might be part of a bigger plan. It makes me think of the old saying: "He who sleeps through life will eventually wake up and find he has shit on his head." I just made that up. I never told you I was a poet. But then again . . . it seems to fit.

The pavement shook as I drove on. Thousands of nails vibrated on the pavement surface as if under some sort of command had been given. My tires were not exempt. I was stopped at one of the many yellow lights. Like little darts, the nails hit my tires. The tires slowly started to deflate. I leaned out the window and saw what was happening. There was no time to worry about cosmetics. The mag wheels would have to carry the car, if we were to get somewhere safe. I figured that the "Hoodsmen" as I started to call them, would be trying to out do each other. It was a sort of "gloves off" presentation of their wares, with me the recipient. I love getting presents.

The saving grace was that they did not know exactly where I was. But, they were looking. It wouldn't be long. The first time I saw one of the Men in Long Black Coats, it would be over. He would send out the word and the "Vomit of the Devil" would be aimed in my direction. As the common man saw it, "completely explainable" right?

The salvage yard was just over the hill. I had to get there without being seen. The last few minutes seemed to be on my side for once. Maybe the combined forces drew too much energy. They had to rest for a minute or so. There was a crackle in the sky and for a few seconds, all was quiet. I didn't know what was happening. Your guess is as good as mine. I tore up the drive and Mr. "Junk Scale Man" was not in his hut. Or at least he was not sitting. He was probably drunk again and laying on the floor.

I pulled up to my container and setting aside all my "pre-set" tests, I opened the container and drove the car in. With the container door shut, I took my first sigh of relief. They would continue looking until they found me. I had no illusions. But then, I had a few tricks planned myself.

I got some rope and lowered the old man down the shaft to my basement room He had aged even more. I felt I only had a short time to ask him some questions. I laid him on my bed and propped his head up. I lit a small candle and wiped my face with a rag. I stared at him for a moment. Then, "What's your name?" I said . . . He stared at me . . . I fumbled around . . . It looked like he was fading fast . . . "Is there . . ." I stopped. He just stared at me . . . Then I tried again . . . "Is there anything I can get you?" I stammered . . . "I mean you don't look good . . . I'm afraid I don't have any drugs . . ." He stared at me harder . . . Then his mouth moved: "You think, I'm am gonna die?" I looked at the floor and shuffled my feet.
"I've got a full bottle of Coke over there in the frig. Bit, it's not that cold."

Then he looked up at the ceiling and spoke as if to read a prophecy. "I'm not going to die". I looked startled. I said: "What?" He looked back into my eyes. Then he said "Everyone dies . . . But . . . not until they have experienced many great torments . . . and . . ." He stopped and thought about it a minute. Then: "And . . . they are not finished with me" . . . I stammered and said "What do you mean?"

He looked at the door to my lab as if he knew what I had been doing. "It just that simple. You've probably asked yourself what the meaning of life is . . . Well . . . now you know." I recoiled fearing the worst. What did he mean? I thought I was the only one who had a remote idea of what was happening when I experienced theses unexplained minor torments. He closed his eyes and left me wondering what he had meant by his last statement.

I sat on the wooden crate I used as one of my easy chairs and continued to digest what I had been told. Then, I remember my remark about "Heart Attacks". I turned and told him what I had said in what I thought was jest. He was quick to address that remark "Yes . . . that's true . . . they would not have had much interest in "Heart Attacks" . . . He stopped and thought about it. Then he said with a slow almost trance like cadence: "Heart Attacks are too final, . . . Not much value if your main intention is to "torment."

I sat and thought for a long time. He seemed ready to answer more questions, but then when I asked another, he had drifted off to sleep. The night passed without any other events. I slept fitfully on the floor since I didn't have a guest bed. Time passed. Then I woke in the night. I glanced at the digital clock I had found in the junk yard. It wasn't pretty, but it worked. It was the time reading that caught my attention, It said: 5:75. Not that unusual. There's nothing wrong with that. After all we are use to seeing all sorts of numbers. I glanced at it again. It said 5:80. Now I started rubbing my eyes. I looked away and then back again and it said 5:55. I gave a start. I know I saw the clock read 5:75. Yet, there is no such time. So what had happened?

I remembered the Hoodsman selling stolen time on the Bazaar floor. Could I have stumbled in on the very process taking place. Then, when it looked like I might have witnessed something unusual the clock backed up to normal time. I sat there and thought. I was convinced I had seen something that I was not supposed to see. How many times did this happen in an ordinary lifetime. It reminded me of the car wash. When I laid down to sleep, did I expect 6 hours; 360 minutes? Or had the minutes changed into units and the promise I had of 360 minutes would be turned into some other measurement and the actual time I was expecting, slowly stolen away. I resolved to find out more about the time thief. I knew in the depths of my stomach that the "time thieving" was true.#1121.

The whole subject reminded of me when I use to take care of a woman who needed me to get up at night. I would be awakened in a deep sleep. I would get up and glance at the clock as I headed to her room to help her get on the toilet. The clock would say: 2:30am. I would find myself thinking "Oh just 2:30. This will take 5 minutes I will help her and then I will race back to bed. Adding another minute or two to my estimate of how long it would be before I was back in bed, I said it will be 2:38 tops. Everything went as quickly as I expected. I headed back to my bed for the promised four more hours of sleep before I had to get up. But, when I got to the room the clock said 3:15am. Don't deny this hasn't happened to you. You know what I am going to say. We all deny it. I could rant and rave, but I have made note of this and will simply move on, leaving you to question the last few times the same thing happened to you. #1122.

When I awoke later, the time bandits were out of my mind. Now more thoughts of what had happened earlier in the day came racing back. I saw many things. But they all had one thing in common. They were all designed to make man's life more miserable. I could see how some evil being could come up with a "localized" torment. I mean maybe the being could cause someone to get the "Gout" while the inflictor was nearby. But these torments had no bounds. They could reach across large areas. So how was something made from pure evil transported to another location. I beat myself up. I approached the problem for several angles. The result was always the same. I didn't think the hooded men could transport some affliction to a far location. No . . . They had to have help.

I tried to take different angles when looking at the same evidence. But after several hours, I continued down the same line of thinking. This is where it starts to get sticky. My laptop starts to shake as I type this. And I realize, that my thoughts are being monitored. Yes, the only answer I can come up with is that the "Hooded Men" are receiving help. I type this very carefully, because if I am right, my life is in great peril. Why would an "all powerful" being want to be involved with any of this? Is there a benefit? . . . I wiped my eyes and thought . . . Then I started to picture the symbol of the Yin and the Yang.

Without evil there can be no good. So, I worry that if I continue this research I will be struck down. Could life be just a big test and a race through misery? Is this how you are judged. There was no other explanation. I am embarrassed. I hang my head in shame. I see myself as a "being" standing outside a "being". I look at myself and notice my fellow humans going about life not noticing what might be the true purpose for life on earth. "A "test site" for torments."

CHAPTER **24**

Now I understand

From that point on, I resolved to channel my thinking. A few errant thoughts could bring the whole ceiling crashing down. I spent a whole afternoon working on controlling my thoughts. It would have to work on what was in my mind or they would find me even faster than I expected. In fact after some practice I started working on "Misinformation" The term I had learned earlier while studying the art of disappearing. I would concentrate on something important and then modify it slightly. Time would tell if this worked.

The next day I was still thinking about what I had seen. Several questions still hung around: 1. What was the purpose of the Bazaar? 2. If they were selling torments for credits, what could they buy with credits? 3. Why were they so secretive? And 4. Was there a higher power involved? And 5. Was the common population aware of what the "Hoodsmen" were doing? It truly had me confused.

I continued to take care of the "Man on the Hook" as I called him. His aging had stopped. After all if it continued he would have died and ruined the fun his tormentors had designed the treatment for. With the new morning, he was very responsive. I asked questions about his past. He seemed to answer as honestly as he could, given the fact that he had under gone several torments prior to being left on his the hook out side the Bazaar. His name was Charles though I did not prod him for his last name. I kept him from giving me his last name for several reasons. One reason was, because of my privacy beliefs and two, because I was not sure as to whether they could read my thoughts. In any case I called him "Max".

He was unsure of the name at first, but then, it started to sound right after a while. I told him that I would change it in three months anyway. I don't think he ever understood that concept, but I was not concerned.

Today, I had several experiments to do. The first one had to do with plugs with grounded tongs on them. I was running a test to see if I could plug the plug into a wall outlet without looking, like you would if you had to reach behind a sofa and plug a cord in. I found that it was almost impossible to plug the cord in without looking. It seemed to me that the plug could only go in three ways. Those were: grounded tong on the right, grounded tong up and grounded tong to the left. Maybe I was tired from the chase yesterday, but I found that I could not do it all. I recorded 21 tries in the book. I marked this experiment at #1123.

Then I moved on to several other ideas I wanted to check out. I had a number of pieces of lumber in the basement. Mostly I had brought them from the junk yard.

It was a very simple experiment. I grabbed one or two pieces of lumber and moved them from one side of the room to the other. Yes . . . it was what I expected. I had splinters in my hand. Actually several were right in the bend of the finger making them extra painful. I carefully took a needle I had found, and took them out. Then I tried several other pieces of wood lying in the corner. The same thing happened. Please note that this lumber was not any different than you would find anywhere else. All the lumber at one time, had been sold as typical lumber yard lumber, which is cut smooth on all four sides. Yet, I had I gotten splinters in my hand again. I noted this in my book and moved on to my next experiment. I numbered it #1124.

In #1125 I had an ordinary canvas brief case. The briefcase had a number of dividers in it, but no more than any normal brief case. I had several items in it already. The idea was to place something in the briefcase and then 5 minutes later, pull it back out. It sounds very simple doesn't it? I placed a set of keys in the brief case. I just opened it and let them drop in. Then 5 minutes later I opened the briefcase to retrieve the keys. They were not there. I had run this experiment before. My postulate was that the ability to find them quickly, was in direct proportion to the need to find them. For example if you just got off the airplane and were waiting for your bags. You could reach in this brief case and find them after only five to 10 tries and in different locations. But let's say someone was hurt and needed to be taken to the hospital very quickly. You had volunteered your car. Things were moving very rapidly and people were depending on you. Then my postulate was: that the keys in the briefcase would be almost impossible to find. I could not replicate this experiment with out an emergency, though I noted that the keys had been moderately hard to find when I casually opened the bag. With out any further notes I left the entry open for future data.#1126

I had one more experiment to run #1127 before I stopped for a while. I had several paper sacks. In the sacks I was planning to place several different objects. The first experiment I planned was involving several bricks I found outside. The bricks weighed 12 pounds.

I carried them from one side on the basement to the other. The sack held with no problem.

Then I replaced the sack with a new sack, because the strain on the old one might affect the results of my next trial. In the new sack I placed 12 pounds of glass plates that I had found in an old box in the basement. It was exactly the same weight. The sack held half way across the room, but as I was about to place it on an old table, the sack broke. The glass plates fell to the floor and broke in a million pieces. I noted this immediately. It appears that the strength of the sack is directly proportioned to the value of the items it holds. I noted this and set my book aside.

CHAPTER **25**

More experiments

While I was recording data from experiments, I had one that I needed help with. So I decided to ask Max to help. I raised the question with him and he was completely ready to help. So I opened #1128. We would need to sneak into and old building on the edge of the junk yard. It had a basement that appeared to be used for storage, so I never thought about staying there. It was too dangerous. We checked the area for cars. There were none, well at least that ran. ha ha We slipped into the building through a broken window next a the stair to the basement. He moved slowly, but I figured getting out would do him good.

I carried a small plastic container of cat vomit. My experiment was simple. I would ask Max to place some vomit on one of the stair treads going down to the basement. We shoved cardboard in the broken window to cut the light. Then we closed the door at the top of the stairs to make the stair completely dark.

I asked Max to place some vomit on one location known only to him. I then removed my shoes and socks and started down a completely dark stair. Now the amount of vomit I told him to put down was about 3 inches in diameter. I told him to put it on one stair tread in only one location. I measured the stairs first and found that they were 42" wide and 12" deep. That meant that the vomit was only taking up 9 sq inches in 504 sq inches. Taking that further that meant that the vomit covered less than 1/50 of the tread. Now I had already measured my foot. I figured that the part of my foot that would touch the stair was about 3" x 3" or 9 sq inches or about the same size as the vomit would cover. So the question was: How often would the nine square inches of my foot fall on the 9 sq inches of the vomit in a completely dark situation. The results were incredible.

The first time I missed the vomit and I thought the experiment was a bust. Then for the next 25 times I hit it every time. I should point out that after every time, I had Max clean up the Vomit and replace it on a different tread and in a different location on the tread. It was a completely blind test. I was staggered with the results. I made note on my book and took Max back to my basement hole.

I sat on my favorite box and started to think about yesterday. I had thrown the silver platter at them. Ha ha . . . It did nothing as a weapon. But I had used it to deflect the balls of torment they had thrown at me. It was very strange; these hooded men and their Bazaar. They seemed to have incredible powers but yet a shiny platter had deflected the force of their power. I would sit and think about this for a while.

I was about to get up and check on "Max" soon, when I saw another box in the corner. It held an old pair of jogging pants and hooded sweat shirt. I would put this somewhere close. I might have a use for outfit later. I sipped my cold coffee and thought. There was something in the back of my mind. It just wouldn't come forward. Then it hit me; the old mirror in the basement room where I slept. I had mounted it on the wall but I had just thought of another use. I checked on Max. He appeared to be asleep. So, I took the jogging outfit, the mirror and a brick and one of the paper sacks and went back to my lab. I grabbed a bottle of glue that I had stashed away and the materials for the project were complete.

I had decided to limit the information I gave Max until I could determine what his particular "colors" were. Even then, that is if I decided to trust him, I might want to keep information to myself. I worked most of the day on my new project. I intended to go back to the Hoodsmen's convention. I thought I might have a thing or two to talk over with them. I am sure they would take it a little too seriously, but that's business.

CHAPTER **26**

Evening

Evening came. It was still light. I was going to leave Max to sleep. He looked about 90 years old now. But then, at the last minute, I decided to take him with me. I don't know, it was just a feeling I had. Maybe he could help. I shook him and asked him to accompany me. He sleepily agreed. So, after loading him in the car, I quickly pulled out of the shipping container using caution, but with a purpose. I was wearing my little experiment under a grey rain coat. The rain coat was handy because it had stayed dark and had begun again to drop water from the sky by the bucket load. After almost hitting a car on the lonely road by the junk yard; the one that shouldn't have come for another 3 hours, I arrived at the same parking lot on the back side of the old building that housed the Bazaar. I sat there for a minute running the whole scenario through my head.

Maybe I mentioned before, maybe I didn't, but the game of chess is very interesting. It is not a game of moves but a game of "future projections" of moves. What do you think your opponent will do if you do this? Or if he does that, what will you do? I never was that good at it, but I liked the theory. So I said to myself "Self? What if they are waiting for you?" . . . I thought for a minute and then: "These are not stupid men. They will be on the look out."

So, getting out of the car I searched for a "counter measure". There was nothing much in the parking lot. Most everyone had already gone home. A few paper boxes blew though the black topped lot. It had lots of holes in it. But, that seemed to be the norm now days. It was a "hall mark" of Cities gone broke. I was about to give up, when I looked at the lot next door. It was about 150 feet away. It was at least 20 feet higher than my parking lot. There was a chain link fence at the top of a bank of grass. The grass had a gradual slope towards the lot I was in. It was a secure parking area for school busses. Without hesitation, I grabbed the rope I had in the trunk and headed up the slope.

I had an idea that might just add a twist to a possible chase situation. If it didn't work, well, they would have me and Max hanging from the wall with spring loaded clamps on our private parts. The idea gave me a chill. I came back and grabbed Max. I whispered into his ear. He looked up the hill, nodded and took the rope. I was hoping old Max would come through if it came to that.

Several minutes later I entered the condemned Convention Center. Nothing much was different. The halls were empty and the buzz of voices was still reverberating off the sad paint peeling hallways. Several more "Max types" were hanging on the wall in front of the double doors leading to the Convention Center auditorium. All three of the poor souls were asleep or unconscious. I really didn't stop to check. There were different devices on each man; clamps, needles, syrup with ants eating it off one's forehead. I didn't look at them long. Instead, I grabbed another hood, dropped my raincoat and entered the dark smoky room.

The large hall was lit about the same way as it had been before except there was a stage with some lights pointed at it. The Lights pointing at the stage were not lit as I entered. I acted disinterested and moved seamlessly between the booths. The first one that caught my eye was a small booth with no advertising. The man was asleep. A sign in front said: "Eye Glasses" 4 credits each. I stood there looking trying figure out why anyone in here would want eye glasses.

A small man with hood completely covering his face brushed in front of me. He was eating an orange which drizzled down his mange like beard. He said "Scuse me Harry . . . I'm behind on my assignments."

I looked at him and backed back a pace. The little man shook the merchant. "Hey, Simond, I got hard units here . . . Geme 20 of those Eye Glasses."#1129 The sleeping man raised his head and just pointed at a box on the corner of the table. The small man quickly pulled out a wad of units and shoved them into the box. He then stepped behind the table and lifted a box of glasses. He retrieved twenty pair, turned looked at me whistling as he moved. He then stopped whistling, sniffed at me and was gone.

Now the salesman was awake. He looked at me. "Ok Jack." he said sneering a little. "How many pair?" I thought for a minute and then said "What do they do?" He looked closer at me as if to say: "You fool, either you have been asleep for the last twenty years or you're two bricks short of a load." But then, he let his head drop. "Listen Jack" he complained. I've been here since 6:00 am."

He thought for a minute, then: "You really don't know what these glasses do?"

He paused, waiting for me to respond. Then: "Well . . . The "Guineas" buy them and take them home. No problem. They use them for a day or so and then . . . Then the glasses disappear . . ." He thought a minute "Ha Ha! It makes them crazy" Then he continued: "But the best part is that the "Guineas" go out and buy another pair and "Bingo! The glasses show up again." He smiled as if he could picture the whole thing. "They are so happy to find the glasses. They forget they just bought another pair?" He paused and then he added: "Then you know what happens?" He waited for me to respond. I thought for a minute.

Then I added: "You show up with a bag of Christmas presents?" The vendor was aghast! "No you fool!" He whirled his eyes looking at me again to see if I was kidding or if I was just about as smart as a loaf of bread. But then, wanting to make a point, he quickly added "No! Both pairs disappear! . . . It makes the "Guineas" super crazy! Ha ha ha" He laughed out loud as if he had told the funniest joke known to man. I let him laugh a little and then said that they were on my list, but that I would be back after I checked on a few other items.

I was about to leave when another hand grabbed my shoulder. I turned half expecting the see the man with the big knife, you know Mr. "Monster Man", but instead it was a pleasant enough, unshaven, chap looking at me. He smiled and opened his mouth to show that he had no tongue. I stepped back a little startled, but he just smiled and pointed to some nice looking mechanical pencils he was selling out of a sack on his back. The pencils had diagrams on the cardboard packaging.

On the cardboard backing holding each pencil, it showed no matter how lightly you tried to write with them, the lead always broke. He laughed when he saw I understood what he was selling. Some white goo dripped out of one side of his mouth. I motioned to him that I was moving on and made a throat cutting motion with my hand. His shrugged back in fear. The cringe on his face slowly disappeared and he quickly slipped back into the crowd.#1130.

I was just starting to look at a display showing how a device could be put under a car that would cause it to rain when ever the car was washed #1131. I was intrigued. What an ingenious devise. It had rained so many times right after I had washed my car. I was about to ask the hooded figure about it when there was a screeching sound. There was a mike "feedback" and a tapping and testing of a PA system. The level of the lights on the corner stage started to come up. The hall noise started to lower.

Then there was a complete silence. I tall skinny hooded figure came to the mike and stood for a long minute, looking out at the audience. Several booth vendors rushed for the chairs in front of the stage. A fat man was hurrying from his booth when he hit the midget who had been carrying the variable weight boxes the day before. The dwarf went flying into several other chairs, turning them over as he hit them. The dwarf surprised everyone buy grabbing a metal folding chair and screaming back at the fat man. There was a loud crack and the fat man fell to the floor. No one seemed to care. People continued to flood the area with chairs sometimes walking over the fat man's body.

The speaker laughing at the scene stepped forward unhooked the mike started to speak. "Greeting Hoodsman!" and there was a loud cheer from all over the Convention Hall. The sounds reverberated from the walls. He continued on the tail of the cheer. "We are here to SELL and to WORK!" and there was another big roar. Then the figure continued holding up his hand to silence the crowd. Then, almost yelling he spoke: "What is the code?" The crowd cheered back": "Don't kill the Guineas!" . . . The leader laughed in pride "Yes! And what is our Creed?" and the Hooded figures yelled back as loud as they could this time. "There can be no good with out bad." They grew silent and then almost a religious chant rumbled from the depth of the group. "It is good that good needs bad. It is good that good needs bad. It is good that good needs bad."

The speaker sensed the romance of the verse that had just been said and stood there in meditation . . . Then, he looked up and said: "Thank you all for working this hard." He reflected at what he had said, expecting reverence from the group.

Then: "Yes, I am here to tell you that this month's goal has been met. We have done "his bidding" and we will be rewarded!" The crowd yelled and whistled. Several guns went off in the background. The speaker raised his hand to quiet the group and then continued. "I will let you get back to your bargaining and trading, but first, tonight, we have a special event. We have been pulling your "chits" together for a "drawing." He waited for his words to sink in. Then: "We're going to have a "door prize" today!" The crowd went wild. Someone from the chair section yelled "What is it?" An old bat of a man in the back of the room yelled back "It's your sister, Mac!" The man in the front whirled around and pulled out another very big knife. The speaker, not wanting to loose his audience said quickly "No! No! No! . . . It's much better than that!" The crowd grew silent again. Then the speaker spoke as if he was giving away box of gold. He spoke again: "It's something that you all want!" Some one else yelled "Is it, free cow stomachs?" The crowd again yelled and whistled.

The speaker held up his hand to calm the crowd, he said "No! it's not!" But the crowd still thinking about cow stomachs yelled "MMMMMMMM" like it was the best delicacy they had ever heard of. But the speaker still wanting all the credit said" Wait!" And they all stopped.

CHAPTER **27**

The door prize

"Someone here will get the "door prize." and as a further comment the speaker said: "It's extra special". The crowd went: "ahhhhhhhhhhh!" Then the speaker continued. "I have pulled all your "chits". Mebble" . . . He pointed to a hairy looking gorilla of a man, "has most of your names on little pieces of paper." Someone in the back yells: "Mines not in there!" The Speaker continues "Oh . . . don't worry, we got enough."

Then the speaker feeling a little bad: "Hey Jim" give him a couple of credit books." Then the whole crowd started saying: "Mine's not in there either, mine's not in there . . ." Someone else say: "Hey . . . it's rigged!" The speaker quickly raises a gun and fires it into the air. He sneers "It ain't . . . that . . . big . . . a . . . deal!"

The crowd falls into a quick silence. He turns to the dwarf that had had the fight earlier and says "Ok Melvin, reach in there!" He stops a moment. The jar is too high. Then: "Mebble you big lug, let him reach in there!" Mebble grins a kind of very stupid grin and leans way over to allow the dwarf to get access the slips of paper. Melvin raises the winning slip of paper out. The speaker grabs it looks around the room as if the announcement would rack the audience back on it's heals. He reads it quickly "Hark Ballwood!" There's a jeering from the crowd as a skinny man in a hood steps forward.

He looks around at the jeering audience. Then with slumped shoulders, he walks up on the stage. He looks dazed. He's still a little taken back, but he says quickly "Ok . . . what'd I get" The speaker now wanting to make a big show, motions to three hooded figures with trumpets. There's a screeching non harmonious wail as the trumpeters herald the coming announcement. The trumpeters stop.

The speaker raises his arms as if to emphasize the coming announcement and says pointing in my direction: "You get . . . an honest to goodness . . . (wait for it) . . . an honest to goodness "Outlander!" He looks around as if he has brought back "sliced bread". Then: "You get the Outlander for you very own slave!" There was a silence and some murmuring. Then quickly the flood lights were turned on me!

I froze as every eye in the hall was focused on me! At first I tried to act like it was the hooded figure behind me. I almost pulled it off. I turned and grabbed the man's arm behind me. He shrank back in fear. The huge bear of a man to his side hammered his fist into the surprised man's face. The man staggered and fell. The crowd hissed in appreciation.

"Bear" man grabbed the man's burlap hood and both fell to the ground fighting. The speaker laughed, but then said "No! You fools! It's the man next to him!" They all turned and faced me. I knew the jig was up. Feverously, I looked for an escape route. Nothing! Would this be the end? With this many Hoodsmen, they could simply pound me to death. It looked bad. Then, I spied the heavy PA cable running to a large speaker on a stand raised up beside me about 10 feet off the convention floor.

Using my cat like skills, I jumped up the rungs on the speaker stand to the base that held the speaker. I grabbed the cable and jumped out holding on to the cable trying to swing out over the crowd.

Opps! The cable held and I smashed back to the speaker. I thought it would be just like you see in the Errol Flynn movies. But it looked more like the "three stooges". I hung there like an over stuffed sausage. My whole life passed before me. I guess I thought it really was over when a big knife came slashing by me and hit the cable. The knife was meant for me, but it cut my bonds instead. The cable was cut and hung loose. Quickly, I jumped out again. The cable held. I would mark this down to my good luck (which there really isn't any). I began to swing out over the crowd. The hooded figures in the audience pointed at me and laughed. Some smoked drugged cigarettes and just watched in awe.

But some were raging mad. They would show this "Outlander" what pain without death was really about. Have you ever been in a situation where, well you know, you're "out gunned" one hundred to one. I had a dream once. I was on the tee with Tiger Woods. Tiger hit first. It was a beautiful shot. The crowd roared with delight. Then there was silence when this awkward looking unknown "goof ball" steps up to the Tee. (That's me) There's a short silence while everyone prepared to write my epitaph. "Here lies Butt Face, who flubbed the big one, in front of everyone." Then, there's this loop to loop, ugly swing. There's some question about whether the club will even hit the ball. But then the ball screams off the Tee. The crowd is completely stunned. My ball hits Tiger's and causes his to spit into the woods. I look around at everyone who had made fun of me. Things would be changing. I would show then. I rest my case!

CHAPTER 28

Real World

But, let us go back to the real world. I'm swinging in the air over a bunch of over confident goons. You think it's the end for old Bram. I forgot to tell you, I changed my name again.

Suddenly, the flea and tick man steps up first. He fields a great pulsating ball of insects out of his backpack. He compacts the ball in his hand for more aerodynamics. But at the same time "Shingles man" steps forward and rolls up his sleeve. I looked at him from above thinking that would really make me miserable for a long time. But there are other movements in the crowd and Mr. "Old age" pushes everyone away and pulls out a packet of wickedness.

All this time I am climbing the cable and swinging at the same time. They all rear back to throw all of their torments at me when what should happen? . . . I drop the rain coat. The crowd is startled. Now swinging across the room is a man in a sweat suit covered with little mirror bits glued to the suit. The odd light in the hall casts funny rays of light onto my outfit. The crowd is stunned. They slowly murmur. "Ewhhhhhhh!"

I think that since no one in the audience has the wit to come up with my name, I yell it out: "It's Mirror Man!" Then I thought "No not really, but it does sort of roll off your tongue."

The fleas and ticks hit me first and quickly are reflected to someone is the chair section.

There's a sound of falling chairs. We hear a "Ahhhhhhhhhhhhh!!!" A big lug of a man stumbles through the chairs and falls to the floor with bugs crawling all over him.

Then "Rash Man", who was sitting watching the whole thing from the stage jumps up sending the chair he is sitting on into the crowd below. He pays no attention to what the other spoilers are doing, but carefully pulls out a sack that starts to pulsate as it were alive. With out another thought, he swings it heftily and it spews toward me. It also hits and mirror and it reflected back directly at the thrower. The man is hit with what appears to be a dust cloud. Then, he slowly turns red and starts to scratch. We loose focus on the man as "Old Age Man" takes a turn. But just as "Old Age Man" is rearing back Rash man screams and falls off the stage.

Now I have gained quite a momentum in my swing and with one or two more swings back and forth, I am able to hit the "cat walk" above the stage. Quickly, I scramble onto the relative safety of the "cat walk". A huge mass of fleas and ticks hits just next to me. There's a banner hanging over the rail that I am now standing behind that says: "Welcome Hoodsmen!" on it. The crowd by now has started to buzz like a hornets nest. I see an exit way at the end of the cat walk but, I have one more issue I want to take up with these "Pro's from Dover". I rise up from behind the banner and yell at the top on my lungs: "Wait! I bring you a message!" They all stop surprised that I have the guts to talk at them. But then, curiosity takes over and they all stop, wanting to know what this "Outlander' has to say. They hold their actions momentarily. I make a motion that says "wait a minute". I duck behind the banner and then: I drop my pants and hang my gleaming white bare ass over the rail!

They crowd is dumb struck. They are awed. They are confused! They stare in silence. You could have heard a pin drop. Actually it was a machete. But who cares at this point. Time seems stopped for a moment. The Hoodsmen below are yelling, but their sounds are sucked up by some time warp. Then there is a slowing noise as we return to normal. Someone in the back yells "get that son of a bitch!" and the chase is on.

I hit the exit door on the fire escape cat walk. I open it and rush through, nearly falling down the fire ladder to the pavement. I am feeling good. I have beat them again . . . ha ha ha. But then, a dumpster in the corner of the parking lot erupts with all sorts of hooded figures all carrying sharp knives. I had been correct. They were smarter than I had given them credit for. They might get me this time. I started to run but I could see that they would out flank me. Then it was time for my next chess move. That's when I raised my arm and signaled Max.

The group stopped to look at me and to question why I had raised my arm instead of heading for the hills. They turned and looked up the hill but nothing happened. I thought "Max! Max, where are you my man? . . . Max!" There's another long silence. Then, the first bus starts to slowly roll forward hitting the fence. It looked like the fence would hold it in place, but that was correct until the second one hit the fence.

By the time the third one hit the fence it was laid flat and here came about six busses right at the group. Several figures in the first group screamed and ran back toward the dumpster hoping for some protection. Just as they got to the Dumpster a School Bus hit a bump in the down slope and ramps into the air.

There was a whizzing sound and then a short silence. Then, there was the sound of metal hitting metal. Another short deathly silence filled the air. At the same time two more buses barreled toward the rest of the hooded figures. There was a lot of pushing and shoving as the white faced figures scrambled to get out of the way.

The last bus down carried a red faced old man named Max. He slammed on the brakes just as it reached my car. A big cloud of dust swallowed us up as the great machine came to a rest, not 5 feet from my car. I rushed to the door and helped Max out. He had a cut on his forehead from the sudden stop, but otherwise, he was able to help me haul his very "old" body into my car.

CHAPTER **29**

The Parade

As he was climbing in he looked up and said: "I like a parade! . . . ha ha ha" and then he slumped over in silence. I slammed his door and jumped though the driver's door. As I drove off I could see the hooded leader staring at my car from the balcony that I had escaped from; high above the parking lot. I am not sure how happy he was. But then, what did he say? Was it?: "There is no good with out bad."

Well, I guess he got a taste of the bad . . . ha ha and the good was that I was good. Good and gone. Ha ha ha I like my jokes. I should just sit around and tell them to myself.

As I drove off the sky blackened. Lightening shot sideways out of the clouds. Great gusts of wind billowed toward me as if called from below to bring news of terrible events to come. I knew I better get lost quick. It rained all night as if the weather had been a partner with the Hoodsmen. I slept fitfully as if at any minute the slime bags would burst into my basement. True I had had a good time out of what could have been a disaster, but some day my risky behavior is going to catch up with me. Maybe.

They knew I was at the Convention Center from the start. They were so sure of themselves, that they ran the convention floor as usual knowing that they could reach out at any time and smash me like a Nat flying around them. Well. The fly swatter flew by and believe it or not, it missed me.

The next day Max was still asleep. I had hung the mirror suit in the corner. It had earned its way. I am sure that at least six deflections had raised havoc with the Hoodsmen. They were not happy today. In fact I could feel it. It had rained all night and it was still raining this morning. The snarling creatures that I had seen once and heard many times seemed to be crossing my area more often last night. It had been scary, but as far as I could tell, I had no breaching in my security system; an elaborate very scientific set of tin cans tied to a long string.

And leaks, I had leaks. I had placed buckets in five places, but I had eight leaks. So I had everything up on bricks. Max seemed to take strength from the bad weather and slept all the harder. I on the other hand, had a head ache. I would rest today although I now wanted to find out more about the disappearing men. I wanted to make a quick appearance at the train station but had decided against it. Maybe tonight should see less activity.

While I waited, I played with an old under counter refrigerator. I didn't work. I guess the coils were burned out. But it was the magnetic catch that I was interested in. I had my book open to experiment #1132. The idea was to reach in and grab a soda and then close the door. It sounds simple. I tried walking by and reaching in. I tried walking directly up to it and retrieving a soda. The refrigerator seal was rubber with magnets behind it. It was simple. I said that. The magnets would hold the rubber seal against the door frame and keep cold air form leaking out. I didn't have any cold air but that was beside the point. What happened was this. If you were not paying attention, the door would close and bounce off the door frame. You would expect that even in that situation the magnets were strong enough to pull the door shut and complete the seal. The results were astounding. Eighteen out of twenty tries the door bounced off the door frame and did not seal.

So I said: "Why? What was the purpose?" If you had a $100.00 electric bill and the next month you had a $200.00 electric bill courtesy of the refrigerator, then you might not notice. However, your bills were $100. more than last month. Following that same line of reasoning, if your bills went up, you would have to work all that much harder.

If this was part of a plan, what did it mean? If several items like that made your fiancés tight that month when they really shouldn't have, it put you though another torment. Not a big one, although some bills can be very big. But, was the point to make it just bad enough to add an additional load for you to carry on your back? Was this meant to break you down?

I was reminded of an acting class I took one time. In order to be a good actor the instructor, at least in his opinion, needed to break you down. He wanted to break down all your inhibitions. Once he had you with no self respect or hopes for the future, he would build you up and there by make you a better actor. I thought it was insane. But, following that reasoning, are we all in acting class?

Do we have to have the props knocked out from under us only to have someone build us back, better than we were before; "in order to be a better person?" As I said in Renn's law earlier, if we broke our leg could it be reasoned that the leg would heal, but in doing so, we would face adversity and win, thus making us a better person. This whole concept had bothered me before and continued to worry me now. I would continue to reflect on this. I closed the book and put it away.

Evening came and I decided to slip out with out Max. I was packing my knap sack with several items including my mirror suit when Max raised up and look at me with some reservation. "You're going out?" I nodded as if it was obvious. "If you have to, I want to go. I think I can help"

I looked at him with disbelief. Then: "Max, I appreciate your helping yesterday, but I am concerned that if I get in a jam, you might not be able to keep up." He looked down at his hands which appeared to be old and not too useful and then said: "I know where the Warehouse is". I looked a moment at him. Was he telling me the truth? I said: "What Warehouse?" He looked at me with fear in his eyes. He continued: "I was dragged through there when they took me from my normal life. They went though several experiments before they decided what torment to try on me. I saw a lot more than they thought I saw."

I studied him for a while. Then: "Max . . . I am concerned about your health." Max shook his head. Then: "No . . . I am only a grade two . . . They have a lot more work to do on me" He raised himself up and looked at me. Then "You've got to see this." He let himself fall into a sitting position. I decided to let him go with some reservation.

CHAPTER **30**

The Warehouse

The trip to the warehouse district went on with out interruption. Max hardly spoke. When he wanted me to turn, he simply motioned in the direction he wanted me to go in. I was still not completely sold on Max's benefits, but he certainly seemed sincere. He had helped out in the parking lot at the old Convention Center. That took a lot of moxie. But, I couldn't be too careful.

We drove for a while in silence. Then, at the end of a rise in the highway I saw a big block like building. There were no cars or trucks around it, so it appeared to be closed up. As soon as I had stopped the car, Max was out looking in windows. He turned and said: "They had me in here for several weeks." . . . he paused and then: "I am not sure what all is in here, I just know that they had me hooked up to some sort of monitoring device."

Without another word, Max picks up and old rebar laying in the grass next to the building and starts working on the nearest locked door. After a few tries he succeeded in working in the steel rod to between the door and frame. There was a loud squeak, a shutter and the door swung open. Max dropped the bar. He gingerly stepped in. He seemed to go into some sort of trance. We found ourselves in a cluttered hall way. It had several offices on one side. We could look through the glass window beside each door. No one was working. The offices had one desk and a back table all strewn with papers. Before I knew it, Max was climbing some stairs. I whispered "Max! Slow down. We've got to be careful." Max didn't know it, but I did have my Mirror suit on hidden under my jogging suit. All I had to do, for complete protection, was pull off my hood and pants. He was already at the top of the stairs and had the steel door at the top opened. I rushed after him.

We were again in a hall way but this time it was much wider. There were rooms on each side with glass window walls opening to the hall. This time the rooms also had nicer furniture and general office fixtures. The offices appeared to all be empty. I was about to ask Max to move on, when I saw in a corner of one of the windows a small "pixcelization" mark. I stopped and looked carefully. Yes, it was in the glass. I could not figure it out until Max touched the glass. There must have been some static electricity in Maxes his finger. It caused the pixels to jump a little to another part of the glass nearby.

I stepped back in wonderment. Could the window simply be a screen. The screen showed whatever the occupants of the office wanted to show. I rubbed a piece of fur I carried in my pocket as a good luck charm against my pant leg and then placed it on the glass. Sure enough, several pixels moved in the screen and then the small area in the glass screen went back to normal. I was astounded.

I had seen glass a few years earlier that went opaque when a charge was run through it. But, I had never seen glass that displayed what looked like a 3D image. I opened the door to the Janitor's closet next to the windows and found a ordinary extension cord. I took out a small pocket knife and cut one end of the cord exposing bare wires.

Then using some duct tape from the closet I taped the wires on the glass at two points about 2 feet apart.

When I plugged in the extension cord the glass immediately lost its image qualities and became clear, at least from my side. Inside I saw several hooded figures watching a video screen on the back wall. I was guessing that the glass was one way from the other side because they did not notice that Max and I were watching them.

On the video screen was a video from a surveillance camera in a large parking lot. We could see your average person get out of his car and walk through the large lot to a retail store. As soon as the person was inside the store several dwarfs came out of a metal box at one end of the lot. They some how started the subject's car and then . . . moved it. The hooded figures were sitting in desk chairs that rocked back. As the subject comes out and tries to find his car they started to laugh. One said: "Hey guys . . . watch this one!" . . . They all watched intently as the subject tries to find his car. They slapped their legs and roared with laughter.

The scene changed a little later. The leader said: "You think that first part was good , watch this one!" One hooded figure reached for his beer and missed it. His arm hit the mug and spilled it on the floor. The mug splashed the beer all over everyone. Several Hoodsmen yelled: "Hey! Watch it!" But the leader was rolling on the floor. He said: "You gotta see this one again. "The "Guineas" are soooooo stupid!" A man is seen searching for his car for 15 minutes. He remembers that he parked it in a general area but the car is no where to be found. He walks isles of cars. Pretty soon people in the parking lot start to look at him as if he were going to break into one of the cars. He feels very awkward. Maybe he is getting too old to move in this young peoples world. He even takes out his keys and hits the alarm button on the key ring. Nothing. We see him walking out with a store clerk. Finally they find it. The man thinks he is loosing his mind, but never, and I repeat, never, attributes the unexplained event to outside intervention. His reasoning was that he must be getting old and can't remember where he parked his car. I number this one #1125.

We unhook our extension cord and tape device and move on down the hall. The next window was not close enough to a wall outlet so we moved on. The next window showed another office a little different but basically the same set up as the first one. Again we taped our special cord to the window and plugged it in. The scene was similar to the first one. Four hooded figures were rocking back on office chairs and watching another video.

This time it must have been from a video camera with night vision that they had hidden at the torment site. We see a man in his bed clothes get up and without turning on the light and head for the bathroom. He is in there for several minutes. Then we see him come back out and head for bed.

But just as he is near the bed, he stubs his toe. "Whack!!!!" We see him jump holding his foot and hear him yelling "Ahhhhhhhhhhhh". The hooded figures whail in laughter. A big beefy hooded goon slaps his knee and says : "Huh huh . . . Hey Fouugle, that's a good one." Max and I stand there wondering how they fit into that torment program. Maybe they were the "maintenance" crew for a much larger elaborate plan.

Then they rewind the camera and zoom in closer using more enhanced twilight night vision technology. The bed support is seen moving on some sort of swivel. It has a mechanical device the actually moves the support out in front of the subjects bare foot as the subject moves by. Of course, the subject never suspected that there would be outside manipulation. No, it was the subjects fault. He would rethink the predicament and say to himself: "I should have never walked through a dark room with out turning on the lights." I marked this down as #1126.

Again, we unhooked our electric cord device and moved down the hall. The next window was also very similar to the first two. When the current was run through the window, the glass went clear and we could see a darkened room. In the room were two Hoodsman working on what must have been an "Outlander" on a gurney. The "Guinea" was hooked up to some sort of shocking device. They would place a long tongue under the subject's back and turn it on. The subject arched into the air as far as his restraints would allow. Then he seemed to loose consciousness.

Max backed away. I could see that he knew about what was happening. Max talked with a wail: "Ohhhhhh" . . . he stopped and watched a minute. I turned and looked at Max. "Max, what is it?" . . . He murmured: "Ohhhhh" and seemed to start rocking back and forth on the balls of his feet. I knew we had stumbled on something far worse than the stupid Hoodsman's afternoon video. Max finally said something: "That's what they did to me." He stammered. "It's part of the "intake process" . . . They break you down . . . then they run experiments on you." The man on the gurney was now flipping like a fish. We could just hear him through the glass. "Ahhhh Ah Ahhhhhhhh . . . Ahhhhhh"

We slowly backed away and moved on. This time a simple door with no window waited for us. The door was unlocked. We opened the door and peered in. There was a class In progress. They had the lights turned down low so it made it easier to slip to the back row. Everyone had the standard hood on, but I could see underneath they had some sort of uniform on. Maybe, it was a fast food uniform. I couldn't tell for sure. The hooded teacher talking had just switched slides on a huge screen and was shuffling some papers and clearing his throat to speak.

CHAPTER **31**

The class

He spoke: "Yes students, if you'll look on page 43, it clearly shows you how to perform a simple soft drink "routine". You see we allow the Guineas to drive up and order drinks at your standard drive through restaurant." Raising his head for a second and looking over the class. "Yes, this is very easy. You see, you take a 12 ounce cup or a 16 ounce cup and fill them with 1 ounce more drink than the cup can hold. We have devised special cups for this process. Then you put on the lid. You hand the drink cup back to them and most of the extra 1 ounce spills in their lap." Looking up again, the instructor spoke: "Class? You see this? This is one of the Directors favorite offerings." Looking back at his papers, he continues. "Then as an added twist we have been working with drink cup lid manufacturers. The top of the cup will also hold an extra ½ ounce of liquid.

So after the initial spill, the indention on the cup lid will hold more liquid to spill upon raising the cup to the Guineas mouth." #1124. He looks up. "You all have this?" The students make marks in their manuals and murmur approval. A hooded figure raises his hand to ask a question. The instructor looks up and waves the student off. "Sorry, we have a lot to cover. I will answer questions at the end of the class." Then he turns his manual to the next page and addresses the class again.

"Now if you will turn to page 44, we will talk about airplane seats." He looks up again showing a hairy but be speckled face. He speaks: "I know this is a jump, but this is what they gave me to teach today, so you will have to bear with me." He looks at his watch. Then "On Page 44 we show how to cross the seat belts on an airplane. Note, that it appears they are trying to be neat. So, in this process, none of the "Guineas" catches on.

The real purpose is as follows." He switches on a video. It shows a man with bags in both hands coming down the airplane aisle. He has a number of passengers behind him so he moves out of the aisle and stands in front of his seat. He then sits. Places the bag under his seat and what ever he has in his other hand in his lap. Now we see that the seating is fairly tight, so it is a little awkward when the stewardess comes by and asks everyone to put on their seat belts. He realizes the he is sitting on his seat belt. He raises up a little and reaches under his legs. Now the crossing of the belt causes extra effort, because they get caught as he is trying to retrieve them from under his seat. He leans forward and everything in his lap falls on the floor. Finally, he is able to pull the seat belt latches out from under his legs. We see a passenger tugging and pulling. The instructor interjects. "It's fairly straight forward.

As an extra added treat, we try to work it so that the passenger has had to run to catch the flight. Then when he runs into the "belt cross" as we call it, we see his "Vector" go through the ceiling. Yes class, as you know, that's what it's all about." #1125. I marked down the word "Vector" for further study later.

Now the instructor told the class to turn to page 45. "This one is a little larger scale, so we need to get this trick in the works from the very beginning. It's actually two "treats" in one. We work directly with the Airlines. On a two leg flight, basically we try to never have the arriving gate in the same building as the departure gate. It's a matter of devising schedules well in advance. The Director is holding our feet to the fire on this one." He looks up again. He sees someone on the front row sleeping. He slaps the manual against the podium.

"Hey son . . . if your gonna sleep, it won't be in my class!" The sorry student on the first row snaps to attention. The instructor glares at him for a long minute. Then, as if feeling pressure to continue, the instructor again turns the page. He speaks again now in a more hum drum voice. "Now this next "treat" is very simple. We again work with the Airlines to make sure that the gate the passenger is gong to, is the farthest gate in the terminal. Usually we just see them struggling down a long corridor." An image flashes on the screen of a passenger over loaded with carry-on's sweating and shaking as he struggles down to the very end of the building. The instructor laughs: "One of our favorites, is to set up say gate 24 as the departure gate for a "Guinea". We see the passenger stop at Gate 23. He drops his bags and rests on a seat nearby seeing that gate 24 must just be around the corner. He, of course, wastes time resting. When he finally gets up to go around the corner to gate 24, he finds that there is a long corridor complete with a people moving walk way. Gate Number 24 is at least 4000 yards down the corridor. He will have to rush to catch his plane." We look at the video and see the man stumbling down the corridor. The man jumps on one of the people moving belts. He tries to run on the belt but quickly runs into people standing on the wrong side of the belt.

We see our man stop in complete resignation. He drops his bags and leans on the moving rail with a hand over his face. The instructor interjects "We have a "walking belt sitters" class tomorrow if any of you would like to take it." Then the instructor looks out at the class. Then: "It's good for extra points." No one is listening.

He looks at his notes and speaks again: "Now, moving on". Then as an after thought "Oh I forgot. I was supposed to show you the new plastic bags we have come up with. The passengers are given peanut bags for a snack. He fumbles with the video projector. "Yes here it is." We see an industrial plant. All the workers have burlap hoods on, but industrial uniforms underneath. We see a long production line with big machines turning out miles of bag material. "Yes, plastic bags have come a long way." Says the Instructor. He continues: "After much research, we came up with a plastic that was so strong that the Guineas can't open it."#1126

We look up at the screen and see several people sitting in airplane seats trying to open a bag of peanuts. The bag resists every effort. The instructor laughs and as an after thought he says: "Oh that reminds me, they have one other plastic bag. You should see it." He flips through some slides and then "Here, this one. It's different." We again look up at a small video. It shows a passenger on an airplane trying to open another candy bag. After much pulling the bag splits down the middle and spills the entire contents all over the passengers lap and continues to pour on the floor. "You see, they have developed a bag as an alternative to the non opening bag." He looks up at the screen as if they would see exactly what he was talking about. Then, "You see, the "Guineas" pull hard on the edge of the bag so that they can open a small opening and slowly pour out the candy. But what they don't know is that we have set up a tear point in the middle." He looks up and we see the bag split down the middle to the passenger's dismay. We see candy spill everywhere. #1127 Then: "You get the picture"

The Instructor looks at his watch. He speaks: "Class, take a few minutes, and finalize your notes. Then please exit to the copy room." Quickly, we took this opportunity to slip out without being seen. I made note of the term "Copy room". It was an interesting term; one that might shed some light of the Men in Black, but we decided to get the hell out of Dodge.

When we got back in the hall we noticed that the building ended here and was connected to a much larger building next to it, maybe 100 feet away, by a small raised and conditioned walk way. Both doors at the entrance and exit were unlocked. We slowly and carefully moved to the next building. It was much taller. The walls along this corridor were even higher than the other halls. It appeared to be some sort of lab. There were exposed bar joists in the ceiling. The whole flavor was that of a "utilitarian" opperation. The air reeked with mold.

We again saw a window in the hall, this time just acting as a mirror in its un-electrified state. The window was only about 4' by 4'. I had a little time stretching the electric cord from the wall outlet and taping it to the window. The glass reflected our images as we worked to connect the cord. When I finally plugged in the cord the glass went clear. I stared for a minute and backed away. I was aghast! I was shocked. I could not believe my eyes. When the glass turned clear I was looking at millions of cock roaches. They were writhing and wiggling in layers held up by large clear glass shelves. I suppose the shelves were there to keep the sheer weight of the bugs from crushing the ones on the lower levels.

CHAPTER 32

More Bugs

The room was 40 or 50 feet tall and extended downward maybe the same amount. There was an opening in the center where a railed pedestal with a mechanical arm and pedestal on the arm stood. The arm moved up and down and left to right silently through the hungry brood on insects.

On the pedestal arm platform were our friends from the Convention Center; the dwarf and his friend the fat man. Hanging on in the back, appeared to be a friend of the dwarfs.

They all had hoses attached to the platform. They were spraying some green liquid all over the cock roaches. The platform arm seemed to be on some sort of programmed movement. It would rise to the full height of the room and then slowly sink to the lowest point. Then with some vibration, it would move forward and repeat the process.

The dwarf's friend was eating something on a stick and didn't seem to be interested in his duties and a "spray technician". The first dwarf, the one with a temper turned and saw that the second dwarf was not looking after his assignments. Dwarf one hauls off and socks the 2nd one in the face and then points at the hose draped over the safety rail. The second dwarf raises his arm to protect his face and slinks back to the rail. He then picks up his hose and half heartedly starts spraying. When the head dwarf has turned away we see the second dwarf give him the finger.

I stood there for several minutes. I did not know what to think of the whole scene. I looked at Max. He was just as wide eyed as me. He shrugged indicating that he did not know what was going on either. Max kept looking back at the one window where we had seen the intake process starting. I am not sure Max was really with us much after seeing that. But sensing that we short for time, we moved on.

There was not another window until we got a least half way down the hall. The window was again "mirror like" at rest. It was the same as the first window, also about 4' x 4'. I found another electrical outlet and again hooked up my cord and tape system. This time I thought I was ready for what I was about to see, but I have to tell you, I was not.

When the glass went clear we were staring at thousands of clear containers stacked 40 feet high, filled with fleas and ticks. A number of fleas and ticks had gotten out and were crawling on the inside of the glass. Most of the containers had small signs on them indicating what species they were. Just as we were taking in the scene, our friends on the mechanical arm started into this section.

The arm must have been on some sort of track that allowed it to move through several areas. The arm stopped at a hatch which the fat man opened. Inside, were medium size crates of what appeared to be raw meat. There were also green blocks of different sizes mixed in. As the last of about 16 crates were loaded on the platform, I was able to look at the contents of the crates a little more carefully. It was not just meat as I had suspected, but something else very familiar.

I could not place the type of meat until one piece fell and hit the window we were looking though. It wedged itself against some crates just below our view port. It was a human arm with a green block attached to it. I stared in disbelief. The crates held human body parts. An arm, with fingers still in place, hung out of one of the crates. The fat man reached over and grabbed it. He roughly shoved it back into the feed basket. One of the green blocks that seemed to be attached to the arms and legs dislodged and fell 40' down to the floor on the first level. There was a scraping noise as the insects below fought for the morsel. I was in complete shock.

Then to make matters worse, the dwarfs started fighting over who would throw out the pieces of human body parts to be sucked on by this swarm of insects. The dwarf with the temper raged at the other one who seemed to cower back, but all the time hiding a body part behind his back that he intended to throw out to the insects. I pulled back in revulsion. Max stood paralyzed by the abject gruesomeness of the scene. I shook him, but he only partially responded. "Max! Snap out of it. We've got to get out of here. Finally, he focused on me and I knew I could get him moving. After a little more coaxing, he seemed to come back to reality. We headed down the stairs and into the parking lot. The car was where we left it. Nothing seemed out of place except for two or three more cars in the lot, parked close to ours. I was in a hurry and didn't think much about it.

I shoved Max in the passenger door and was moving around to my door when I looked at the car closest to us again. It seemed very normal except for the back bumper. The back bumper was only partly there. It was pixilated, the like the man's briefcase I saw at the train station. I stared for a few seconds, but then realizing our danger, jumped into my car and drove off.

Max was silent as we drove home. I sat there stopped at the 40th yellow light and finally could not help myself. "Max! What did we just see?" He sat there staring ahead in silence. I hoped he could shed some light on the situation after I got him calmed down a little. He just sat there and stammered: "I . . . I . . ." But then he stopped and just closed his eyes. My mind was racing trying to make sense of what we had just seen. I would have to try to sit down and put the various elements together. For now, I decided to just let my brain go into neutral.

I was driving home and would have almost been there, except I remembered something else. I had moved some Bums. I had them running a small experiment in a building we would pass as we moved out of town. I really didn't want to stop. I wanted to go home and sleep this whole thing off. But the Bums had no food and I couldn't just let them sit there. So, I stopped the car behind the old warehouse building and asked Max to stay put. It would only take a few seconds. I had my very qualified "researchers" working on the second floor. I had started a very simple experiment. It had to do with pant sizes. I had the bums find a pair of pants that fit them. I had gotten them started the other day while it was still light.

CHAPTER **33**

My name is Thaub

I asked them if they had a pair that was comfortable and seemed to fit ok. They each found one and the experiment was started. The pants weren't new. They were part of a stash of old clothes I had found in another building. Anyway, under very strict scientific conditions, I had them wear the pants all day, take them off at night and then put them back on the next day.

So you say: "Renn you have finally flipped. What on earth could you show by having Bums take off and put on pants again?" First of all, I would tell you that I do not know a "Renn". My name is "Thaub". (I changed my name again.) Anyway I took notes each day as the Bums got up. They marked the pants with some sort of mark that only they could identify, so we would not get the Bums "crossed panted". (very bad joke)

The notes I took were astounding. Each Bum had trouble putting on the pants in the morning. The waist was severely tight. I could not believe it if had I not been there. The same pair of pants at night seemed to have changed sizes in the morning. I suppose if I am now catching on a little, the purpose is to make the "Guineas" think they are gaining weight because they were not able to control themselves and of course, ate too much.

But it did not end there. I had the Bums try on shirts too. They seemed a little tighter but not like the pants. I thought for a while on this. Then it hit me. There are a lot more body organs below the belt that would be affected by the extreme pressure of the tight pants.

The rib cage would protect the upper body organs. Thus the pants were the easiest way to make the Guineas feel uncomfortable as well as making them feel ashamed that they had eaten too much or eaten too many fattening foods. After all these years of worrying about what to eat, I found it out. You are supposed to feel that you are not taking care of yourself. In the end, no matter what you ate, you would still feel that you are not good example, not able to control yourself and thus you are not worthy of much. I marked these thoughts in my book #1028. Tossed a couple of cans of Chili to each Bum and headed back to the car.

We arrived several minutes later at the salvage yard and again the "booze master" was not sitting at his seat at the entrance to the junk yard. No telling where he was. We rolled right through and slid into the shipping container without so much as a squeak. When we got below I could see that Max needed some rest. I let him take my bed again and I sat on the old chair I had rescued. I had almost forgotten about the men with the missing pixels. Now I had cars with the same diagnoses.

So, putting on my scientist's hat, I made some notes. I guess I had been on the run for 6 months. During the first 3 months, I had seen;

1. The Men in Black over Coats. I think there are the sentries.
2. I had seen the men and women with pixelating parts. Maybe they were the couriers.
3. The zombie ghouls like the one that stumbled into my basement.
4. The "normal" workers.

Now this last 3 months I have seen:

1. The Hoodsman. The Bazaar sellers.
2. The Dwarfs. I thought they might be the workers.
3. The "worker Hoodsman", Brood keepers like the one running the feeding device.
4. The "teacher Hoodsman", the teachers and students.
5. The white sheeted Directors assistants.
6. The Director (Whoever he was)
7. The pixelating cars.

What did this all mean? And the name "Guinea", I had heard that term a lot. Even I had used it. But what did it mean? Max stirred a little and I took a shot. "Hey Max, you know what "Guinea' means?" There was a silence and I had just moved on to thinking about the next question when he replied. "Guinea" means "Guinea Pig". I sat there for a minute thinking. Then: "What?" Max again mumbled a repeat of what he had said: "Guinea, means Guinea pig." I had a feeling about that. Were the "Outlanders" the Guinea Pigs? But how were they Guinea Pigs? I had seen how the "Hoodsmen" were developing "torments" for mankind. Maybe that was it. How many were there and what was the purpose? And why were little torments better than big torments? All questions that I would have to answer.

I grabbed an hour of sleep and decided to do some exploring down by the train station. This time I would for sure leave Max. He had been helpful, but he still could slow me down in a chase situation. So after two hours I left. Then with 45 minutes sitting at 14 yellow lights and waiting for at least 12 trains, I arrived back near the train station. I had just started walking with no real purpose. The area was very upscale shopping area.

There were many display windows with mannequins in the windows dressed in very expensive clothes. I normally paid no attention to these store dummies. But one dummy caught my eye. It stood motionless with a very "eye-catching" dress on and waist length Mink coat draped over it's shoulders. I looked and then I looked again. I was staggered. I was awed. The mannequin looked exactly like Anna. I dropped the bag I was carrying and just stared. The likeness was unmistakable. I pressed against the store window, but it truly was a dummy.

I was about to go in when I noticed a man in a Long Black Coat looking at me at the end of the street. I would mark the address and return later. I walked slowly the other direction hoping that we were not in for a foot race. He did not follow. I turned a corner and went back into an alley and sat down behind a trash dumpster. I could hardly believe it. The store dummy was an exact likeness of Anna. It had been a long time since I had seen her, but I could not have been surer about it. I was about to get back up and pull myself together when I saw the paper sign blowing across the alley.

It said: "Fight night, Friday night." I grabbed it and looked it over. It said: Winner will get 20,000 credits. I was no fighter. But the credits did catch my attention.

If the type of fighting that I imagined was going to take place, I might have a chance, or least "Mirror Man" might have a chance. I folded the paper flyer, put it in my pocket and pulled myself up on the trash container. No sign of the man in a Long Black Coat. So, I slunk on down the street. I should have remained sitting behind the trash can. I could just picture myself jumping from cage wall to cage wall evading the grasp of a giant Hoodsman. I had my mirror suit on but it didn't seem to deter him. The scene faded out as a blast of cold air hit me in the face. Back in reality I continued down the alley. I was in hoping not to be spotted.

CHAPTER **34**

The Capture

I had not noticed the man in the Long Black Coat was close by.

I turned the corner and they were waiting for me. They didn't seem worried about catching me. Of course I turned to run. But to my astonishment, there were cage bars in the way. So I turned to the right and as quickly as I turned, I ran into another cage wall. I turned left and the same thing happened. Then, as I stood bewildered, little white bars seemed to generate as I watched running horizontally from column to column. I was stupefied. I was in some sort of green blob cage that was generating itself as I watched.

The man with the Long Black Coat never even came over to see me. He just said a few more comments into his coat sleeve and walked away. I was left all trussed up in some sort of futuristic security box. Shortly after he left, a small truck with forks on the front pulled up and lifted me into the air. I was in for a cold ride in my prison to parts unknown. I jarred against the sides of my cell as the truck sped through the streets.

The sides of the cage were as hard a rock. They seemed to be some sort of silica held together with green resin. I suppose a very big man could have broken out, but not without a lot of effort. The next thing I can remember was the hard walls of a dungeon cell. My silicon cage had been removed. Somewhere along the way they slipped me a "mickey". What ever it was still made my head throb. I had been here several hours I guess. I pulled myself up to sitting position against the moldy smelly back wall and stared at the steel door that secured my prison.

To my surprise, the cell door opened as if they had been watching me. Two burly hooded figures came in and jerked me off the ground. They looked at me for a second and then started hauling me out of the cell and down the hall. I said in sarcasm: "I can walk if you like." They did not respond. They just gripped me harder. I smirked: "Ok. I'll ride, but just watch my coat I just had it cleaned." They smirked and continued on. I was led down several halls, up a flight of stairs and through a court yard. Finally I was pulled into a large tapestry laden room with Gothic paintings adorning the walls. A small man was sitting at a very official looking King Louis the V desk.

The guards placed me in a chair in front of him and stepped back one step. I moved slightly and was reminded that the guards were still there and I should stay still. I received a little "love" tap from one of the guard directly behind me. The force of the hit caused me to fall forward and hit the small man's desk with my head. He didn't look up, but surprisingly, produced a rag and wiped the area where my head had hit. A different voice was clearing its throat came from behind me. The guards had been replaced with a tall thin man in a white robe.

With the guards gone I gave some thought to springing from my seat and running. In fact I pushed on the arm rests to spring out of the chair except I hit some clear bars just inches above my head. I was actually in some sort of cage generated around the chair. The bars again were, I guess, silica. The bars were generated in the same way that the cage bars had been generated on the cage they first captured me in.

The small official man spoke first: "You'll find that you are secured to the chair. There's no need to struggle." With that he again started reading his document. He had a small writing device and continued to make notes in the side columns of the document. The man behind me spoke: "This is the one sir." The small official man still not looking up said "Yes, I know."

CHAPTER **35**

Outrage

The leader spoke again but very slowly. "What's his Slot Number?" There was a long silence and then: "We don't know sir." The leader seemed engrossed in his work, but then looked up at the thin man and spoke angrily: "Everyone's got a slot number." Then again even slower "I said, what is this man's slot number?" There was a long silence. The thin man shuffled some papers and then quietly said: "We can find no Vector on this man".

The leader looked up and said: "Mr. Spade . . . Everyone's got a Vector. If you can't pull it from Central Control, I will." . . . Then the thin man said as if to explain why they had no more information: "We marked him with detectable ink the last time he was at the Bazaar. But, he has evaded us since then." The small official man continued to read the document without looking up. "Yes . . . you imbeciles!" There was a long silence as the thin man tried to decide if he should speak. Then the small man spoke again: "What does he know?" The thin man ruffled through some papers and then said: "We don't know for sure. No one has been able to follow him. Most of the marker ink was reflected. There was just enough left on his clothes to allow us to detect him in the alley."

The small man raised a communication device to his face and spoke something in to it, then put it back on the table. For the first time looking up and directly at me he spoke with an angry slur: "You think you're pretty smart." He was waiting for his comment to take effect. Then: "I heard what you did at the Bazaar." A long silence and then he almost spit out the words: "You are very resourceful . . ." A long silence. Then: "Well, we have some surprises for you too . . ." He stopped short of saying what he wanted to say. Then, dismissing everyone, he said: "Get him out of my office . . ." He was looking up as if he was very upset about someone to taking him away from the reading of his document. "Take him to the cell and get the shock therapy room ready. We'll see how funny he thinks that is."

What that, he waved one hand to dismiss everyone. The guards reappeared. The cage melted away and I was carried off. I was thrown back into my cell wondering how long I had before I was flipping on a gurney like the man we saw earlier. I found myself biting on my tongue imagining what it might feel like to have 24 volts shot through me.

I started to formulate a plan. When they brought me in late last night they had thrown me into this cell with out taking my back pack. I suppose they went through it looking for weapons, but there was just a warm up suit with mirrors glued to it, some running shoes and socks and a couple of apples. After they left, I had taken out the suit and lodged it behind a pipe in the ceiling. Later that night, almost as an afterthought, they came back and took the back pack. But my suit was still in the cell.

I napped for a few minutes before I heard them coming down the hall. If my idea was correct, "Mirror Man" would again make a showing. I had just enough time to pull my plan together. The cell door opened and the guards not suspecting anything, walked in. Then, with the light from the upper cell window behind him, "Mirror Man" stood up all puffed up, as a great mass of muscle. The outfit now had a face mask as well. I had worked on it right after I got back from the last trip to the Bazaar. I had filled a small paper bag with dust from the floor. As they entered the cell, I threw the bag at my feet.

The dust rose catching a small shaft of light for the high cell window producing a threatening glow all around me. I completed the illusion by yelling something ridiculous at them: "BOOORRRRRRRRAAAAACCCCCKKKKKKKKK!!!!!
!!!!!!!!"

The guards were shocked. Their faces went white. They stood wide eyed and then backed away a few steps. Then, one of the guards drew a funny looking pistol and quickly fired it at the "monster" in front of them. A ball of fire came roaring at me, but as before it was reflected back. It missed both guards on the reflection but bounced off the front wall and hit one of them in the back. The stricken guard yelled and crumbled to the ground. The other guard looked at the first guard and then at me, thinking I had crushed the man with my thoughts. He squeeled a little "EEEEEEEEEEEEEEE" as he stood there frozen in place. A dark stain appeared spreading across the crotch of his pants. He backed off and hit the wall behind him. He quickly looked a saw that he has missed the door by several feet. He corrected his position and jumped through the door. I could here the low moaning of fear as he and ran down the hall.

"Ahhhhhhhhhhhhhmmmmmmmmmmmmm!!!!!" Shortly after he was gone, an alarm horn sounded. I knew soon "Mirror Man" would be out matched. I had little time.

The iron door had been left open in the second guard's haste. I was able to get out before it automatically locked back down again. I tore through several doors, not knowing where I was going. I ran for several minutes. Then to my surprise, I found myself back in the hall that Max and I had visited earlier. I tried the hall doors again but they were all locked. I looked up and saw a camera monitoring my position.

They knew exactly where I was. In fact, I could hear a whole mass of running boots coming my way. They would be on me very shortly and it wouldn't be pretty. I turned and looked for something to fight with, all the time knowing that I would be no match for these crack troops. I was about to give up and fall to my knees in resignation when I saw the extension cord that we had used to reverse the charge fields earlier on the hall windows. I grabbed the cord, but this time I twisted the wires together.

Then just as the hall door, not 30 feet away was bursting open, I plugged the cord into a wall socket. There was a snap and a spark and all the windows went clear. I tried the doors again and this time they were open. They had been on electro-magnetic locks. The guards were closing in on me. I saw three troops with sharp knives raised to strike me. I don't think they planned any kind of interrogation this time.

I had one move left. I found the door with the fleas and ticks. I pulled on it. It opened. But nothing came flying out. So as a last resort I grabbed the first rack and pulled it out in the hall in front of the on coming guards. I rack teetered and fell right in front of the onrush. But nothing really happened until the first guard hit the rack and fell.

Surprisingly, it had been secured to two more racks in the feeding room with it. The second and third followed the first one. The racks fell on top of the first guard. Just then the rest of the rushing troops hit the pile up. I backed away as a saw a mass of black insects pour over the guards. At first there was no sound from the guards as they tried to figure out what this mass of crawling and jumping things were. Then: "Eeeeeeeeeehhh!!" Then: "Aheeeeeeeeee!!!!!!" Then several guards rolled on the floor to the side of the racks coughing and spitting and scratching. They yelled: "Help!!!!!" and: "Help us!!!!!" One guard got to his feet holding his collar and ran against the wall. Then fell as the mass seemed to completely engulf him. I backed away looking in disbelief. Then with out another thought, I turned and continued my exit as the wailing and scratching grew louder.

I tore out the first door I found open. The door had a fire escape stair connected to it. I grabbed the rail and slid down at mock speed. I slipped behind a trash Dumpster and waited for the guards to pour down the fire escape. Nothing happened. I sat there trying to figure out what to do. I wondered if they had my car under surveillance. I sat in silence for a few minutes. Then suddenly I heard and big panel type truck coming. I quickly slipped back behind my protection. The truck came rumbling by. I rose up to see if I could get any hint of what to do next. The Truck was filled with dummies standing straight up. What an unusual sight. I was about to look away when it hit me. The dummies looked familiar. "No" I said to myself. The dummies were all exact replicas of Anna. I shrank back and sat against the building in shock. I sat silent for a long time. Somehow, I would make sense of all this.

It started to rain. Big blocks of clouds moved in as if following the lines of an evil story. Lightening arched over the horizon as if saying that there would be no escape. I was soaking wet, lying in my spot next to the trash Dumpster, but then the lateral rain blowing at 50 mph seemed to offer some protection.

The blur of water and wind would allow me to slip out of the building compound. This time I had to get back down town. I had left my car by the train station. A Bum friend was pushing a grocery cart down the street. He offerd me a ride. It took 20 minutes, but he got me to my destination. I had one can of Chili in my bag. I gave it to him and he was ecstatic. Then, running in low position, I ran for the car. I tore open the door and sat huddled in the front seat. I sat there for several long minutes expecting a rush of guards that might have followed us. But, strangely, nothing happened. So I started the car and slowly pulled out of the train station parking lot. I drove out of the area with my light off. I had a lot of questions for Max. He probably didn't know much, but he was all I had.

The Rat ran across the floor and stopped to smell my nose. Maybe it was a gesture to show me that he had no fear of me. I had dropped into my lair after pulling into the shipping container. I had been awake for a few minutes and I chose to just let him show his prowess. He deserved it. After all, I was the one who almost ended up like fried bacon on some "Directors" plate. He was the smart one sitting here in the protection of the basement and he wanted me to know it. He was here safe eating all my food. He had the run of the place.

I was the one laying on the floor wet and half dead. I would make a note of that for consideration later.

After another hour, I stirred again. I slowly raised myself and walked over to Max. He was still asleep. I would need to put some thought into what had happened in the last few days. But for now, after thinking about everything that had happened lately, I decided to trash the whole thing and sneak back to my sleeping chair. It could all wait for a little while. Maybe it would solve itself while I slept.

CHAPTER **36**

Early the next day

I lay completely rigid in the ditch for what seemed to be hours. I had found an old grey suit coat and pants complete with a white shirt and tie. The pants didn't match the coat but I figured the fashion police would not be out this early and the general public wouldn't care. My face was stiff. My expression was meaningless. The mistake I made was to think I could lie in a ditch for a long time and not get chilled. I shivered several times but tried to think of other things. I should have thrown this out as a hair brained scheme, but now I was committed.

A bird flew down and walked in front of me; as if to taunt me. I held the brief case firmly and considered "beaning it", but I didn't move. The bird moved closer and started to peck on my head. No, I misspoke he was pulling my hair out. It really hurt. I moved slightly and that scared him. I guess he thought I was dead. Maybe I was and didn't know it. Actually death seemed to have some peaceful protection that life couldn't offer. But then, I snapped out of it. I was here and this was now and I was going to eventually kick some butts!

The bird screeched and flew a few feet to my left side. Actually, I was grilling myself as to why I had made such a stupid move like laying in the ditch. The ground was cold and wet. I guess maybe my whole left side now soaking wet. But then, maybe the soaking wet clothes added to the ruse. To be honest, I had searched my sources and plied my memory.

I had reenacted the past several days. I had reread my notes. I even got Max awake for several minutes. But nothing jumped out. For the life of me I could not figure out where they were keeping the "pixilated" people. So I had come up with this "imbecilic" scheme and figured I would join them; that is if some City Control vehicle would pick me up.

I lay there for another 30 minutes before a Van pulled up. Two men sat there staring at me for a few minutes. Then both doors opened at once. I could just barely hear them at first. The big one said: "There's another one over there." The short stocky one just winced and said: "Wow, that's a big one and he sure is ugly." I was immediately offended. I begged to differ with him, but I stayed rigid. Then he continued: "I think they are having more and more trouble with the "walker units." Then the big one said: "Who cares. Not our job." Then staring at me on my side: "Let's get him in the Van and take him back to the lab. They are probably looking for him." They threw me roughly into the back of the Van and drove off.

The drive was uneventful except for one stop they made. I was not ready for the back door to open. I had changed position and I worried that they would notice. So as I said, the door opened and "Wham!" they threw another "walker unit" in on top of me. "Watch it!" I thought, but decided not to make my point right now. The "Mirror Man" suit was in the brief case freshly washed in my rain water tub. I expected that it would see some action later in the day.

Finally, they pulled up to what must have been a dock. The Van stopped. I expected them to get out and open the door, but instead there was a long silence. Then, the sweet smell of Hemp grass filtered into the back of the van. After several minutes I heard the conversation from up front. "Yeah . . . You see those Hornets Friday night?" A long silence took the men over except for some slow inhaling. Then: "Quiet about that. You know at our level, we aren't allowed to watch sports events."

The other speaks: "Ah shit Al, I don't give a rats ass." There was another long silence. Then: "You'll think rat's ass, if they give you a shock treatment" Another long silence "Well, they'll just have to catch me." The short stocky one continues: "Give me another hit." There's another long silence. Then: "You see Buster the other day?" The conversation was so interesting, I have to admit, I fell asleep. I was awakened later when they grabbed the "walking unit" on top of me. Then a minute later they grabbed me. Both me, and the "walker Unit" were loaded on some sort of drivable cart. The small stocky one was driving. I could see the tall worker slip back into the Van for another quick drag.

We rode in the cart for several minutes before we turned a corner and went though a large double door. We were in what appeared to be a large rusty airplane hangar. There were stacks of "walker units" everywhere. The stocky man hit the break and pulled on some sort of lever. There was a loud squeak and seconds later they threw me on top of a big pile of dummies. I lay there acting the part for a while until the man drove off.

Our pile was right next to an office with a large view window. Inside were several Hoodsmen. They were watching another video. One spoke: I could just hear him. "Here it is. It's the Director's new catalog." The other Hoodsmen sat and clapped almost like little kids. A female voice came on. "And now it's a new V3 toaster" One Hoodsman spoke up . . . "Oh I know this one" A second one spoke: "Shad up! . . . maybe they got it workin better." The female voice came on again. "It's a toaster that never toasts bread on the first toasting no matter how long you set the timer for . . ." There's a silence while the woman holds the toaster in her hand, as if it were some sort of device that could change the world.

"Yes" she says, "No matter how long you wait, it never toasts the bread." She pauses to let us completely understand what she is saying. "But" she says with gleaming eyes. "Push the toast down a second time . . ." There's a pause as if we will miss something.

She continues: "Then push the toast down a second time" (repeating herself as if she were talking to third graders, "and as soon as the Guniea turns his back," She shows a little sensor at the base of the unit. "Yes, as soon as they turn their back, it absolutely "chars" the toast." And, as an afterthought: "It's good for 3 vector points. And if you use this unit, you'll be doing your reporting area a whole lot of good." With that the video fades to another clip. I took out my smaller travel book and noted the torment as #1128. I would enter it into my big book when I got back or should I say "if" I got back.

The Hoodsman laughed and slapped each other on the backs as they started drinking some kind of liquor. One speaks up: "Yeah we had several of the old toasters." He took a swig of dark foaming drink and then continued. "The trouble with the old ones is that they came on so strong that during the "second toasting" that they caused fires. Several Guineas were killed in house fires. The Director was very upset." The other shook their heads too. One said "Yeah, your "reporting area" loses Vector credits among other things, when that happens." Then, as if to make light of it he said, looking at the wall as if it were the door to someone's office with the power to change everything: "Yeah, you can't torment someone if he is dead". The group emits a little laugh in wariness, but a smaller Hoodsman already had the video controller and was flipping the new catalog item. Then he said "Here! This is a good one."

A woman is seen looking for something. She looks everywhere in her house. She gets up on a small ladder and looks in cabinets in the kitchen. She looks under the bed and in the bathroom. Then a small Hoodman in the back speaks up. "Oh . . . I seen this one." The others hit each other as if to say that the half wit in the back doesn't know anything. As he sees that they are making fun of him, he speaks up even louder: "Hey, I seen this one!" and as if to prove it he says: "It's the one about the disappearing driver's license."

A bigger Hoodsman in front says; "That's right George, now shut up!" Then, the big Hoodsman looks around to see if everyone is enjoying the taunting. We see the lady completely frustrated looking in the car seat. She can't find the missing license anywhere. Then the leader, feeling that they might be being too hard on George continues: "Yes, it's the disappearing license" a pause then: "We have been using it for years. But there is one "new' feature."

We see the woman standing in line at the Drivers License Bureau. She is seen waiting for hours and then buying a new license. The leader starts in again: "As soon as the woman buys a new license and gets home . . ." He looks at the group as if to emphasize the point; "Guess what?" There's a long pause. He continues: "The old one shows back up again!" The group claps their hands together in excitement and raises their liquor mugs in a toast. One says "Yeah , we used it the other day. My Guineas went wild! One got so mad he threw up! . . . ha ha. It made my day!" They all laughed and joked. I marked this one as #1129.

I was just putting my black book back in my pocket when I heard a door open. Several Hoodsman walked into where I was laying with clip boards. They seem to be checking the different piles. One speaks up: "Put the A types over by the converter." He continued: "We'll try to get to them this afternoon." They didn't start on my pile, so I slowly belly crawled off the pile and opposite where the Hoodsmen were working. I slithered across the floor and into a smaller room next to the main hangar space. The room was dark.

I saw that it had no windows, so I felt that I could turn on the light and not arouse suspicion. I slipped off the suit coat and stood near where the light switch was. I flipped it on. At first, my eyes were having trouble adjusting to the bright light. Then, to my complete amazement, there stood Anna along with a number of other walking units. There was one small detail however; she was as still as a statue. In fact she was a statue or at least a digitized version of the woman I knew. I couldn't help myself. I touched her hand. It felt real. Then her eyes moved and met mine. I stepped back in awe. She spoke: "I am walking unit number 2235. May I help you?"

I stepped back further in wonderment. I stuttered and I stammered, but finally I said: "Anna? Is that you?" Knowing it was not, but I was never good at quick come backs. I figured she might give me some information that would help me find the real Anna. The walking unit brightened a little and then said: "I have refreshments for everyone". I stammered and stuttered. Then: "But you look just like a woman I knew once." The unit looked to each side and then said: "Will it be Coke or Pepsi?" I stepped back and just looked at her. She was beautiful, but also not real. Maybe I could fall in love with a dummy. Just joking.

I turned and tried to reason with this machine. "I have to find Anna! Can you help me?" Not expecting to get any more out of the "walking unit" I turned and started for the door.
Just as I passed through the door frame I heard from behind me: "Try Building 7, Room #23." I turned and my mouth dropped open. I said: "What?" But the walking unit appeared more removed than ever. Its eyes stared right through me. Then it spoke again. "Coke or Pepsi?"

I turned and headed out. I heard the Hoodsman in the big room next door, but they were working at the other end. I could easily slip out. The numbers 7 and 23 were burned into my mind. I would find that location if it was the last thing I did. As it turned out . . . It almost was. I ran out of the Hangar and headed toward a group of buildings. There were no numbers, so I just had to take a chance at the first building. It turned out to be building # 4. With much haste, I raced on. Building #7 was just in front of me. I could not believe my luck. I tore through the main door and looked down a series of halls. Room #23 was not to be found.

A guard was sitting at a desk in front of a double door that led down a hall I had not seen when I first entered the building. He quickly got up as I approached with his weapon drawn. I had my mirror suit in my back pack but there would not be enough time to put it on. He spoke: "Hold it right there buddy". I stopped and tried to figure out a plan. He spoke again: "There's no public access down here." He stood firm with the gun lowered but ready to fire. I stammered: "I was here for the window washing job."

He looked at me and then raised a small clip board. He looked at it all the time watching my every move. Then: "Sorry, I don't have you down. Besides, here's no administration down this wing. You must have some wrong information." I stammered again and then with resolve said: "Yeah, I guess so. But is room #23 down there?" He brightened a little but then said: "Yes, but there's no public access. Now move on." I stood there for a few seconds trying to figure out any other move, but none came to mind.

I turned and said as I was turning: "I just was trying to find Anna". There was a long silence as I was completing the turn when he spoke again: "Wait. Uh . . ." He now stammered. Then: "Are you Brad?" The question shocked me. I stopped and turned: "Yes . . . I mean, yes, I am Brad." The guard looked around to see if anyone was within earshot. Then he motioned: "Come with me."

CHAPTER **37**

The Ruse

I was amazed. I thought my trip to this building was a complete "bust". He opened the door to office #23 and ushered me in. He quickly pulled the door shut from the hall and was gone before I knew it. There, in the room were many digital models of different people. They were labeled and placed in crates holding 9 per crate. I was dejected. Here I had been directed by one dummy to a room full of more dummies. We could have a dummy convention and I would be lead dummy. I could see it now, (my imagination sometimes runs wild especially when I am disappointed) I would have a tall drum majors hat on along with a marching outfit. I would raise my head in pride and I high stepped to the band. Behind me would be a dwarf pulling a rack of nine dummies . . .

The crowd would cheer as we set a new record in synchronized marching. The dream faded out. I turned to go. I walked back to the door and reached for the knob when I heard from behind me: "Brad?" I turned and saw her for the first time in 2 years. She was still very beautiful. We stood looking at each other for what seemed like several minutes. Then she ran to me and we embraced. I pulled away long enough to look at her. I touched her skin. Yes it was real. At least, I think it was.

She stopped for a moment and said: "I thought you would never find me." I backed up enough to look into her eyes. "Is it really you . . . I mean Anna? Is it you? . . ." She laughed and shook her head and said "Yes Silly . . . it is really me." I looked at the floor for a short minute and then said: "I was devastated when you left." She raised her finger to her mouth as if to tell me to not even bring it up. Then she started to cry. She spoke again: "I know. I felt the same way. It was a terrible time. But, I had to go with them. They had my father." I stammered again: "What?" She looked into my eyes and said again: "They had my father and they would have killed him if I had told anyone where they were taking me." I was at a loss.

I looked at the floor trying to figure out what had happened. Then: "But you left so quickly . . . I . . . I . . . I didn't know what to do. I mean . . ." She cut me off. "I know sweetie. But it was very serious. It was life or death." We embraced again and then we collapsed to the floor.

I was still in shock. I blurted out: "But what did they want you for?" She looked at me with complete honesty and said: "I'll tell you what I know. But you may have to fill in most of the broken parts. They did not tell us anything."

She stopped to look at me to see if I was beginning to understand. Then: "Everything I know I was witnessed. Some things make sense and some do not." She grabbed my hand. Then: "Sweetie, We have a few hours before there are workers in this office. Let's rest. Before long, I will have to be in the great Hall for Check In." She smiled and said" After that, we can hide deeper in the complex." I said: "But, what do you mean?" She put her hand over my mouth and then I looked at her and realized that she meant what she said. I pulled her close and we slept.

Several hours later she touched my arm. I was instantly awake. She looked at me and said: "We've got to move soon" She smiled again: "I have to be at check out." Then: "If I'm not there, they will come looking for me." We got up and moved down the hall. The guard was not there now. I assumed that the building was shut down for the night.

She stopped at a closet before two double doors and pulled out a Hoodsman's outfit. Then: "Put this on and stay back in the corner. Here take this clip board. They won't approach you if they think you are reporting to someone big." Then: "Act like you are making a report on how well the Check In is going". She turned and was out the door. I ran after her as soon as I got the hood on.

The room was very big. It must have been some sort of hangar, very similar to the last one I was in earlier. This time there were no piles of dummy parts. It was completely empty. The floor was polished concrete. It glistened from the bright lights above. I moved into a corner and acted like I was taking notes. Shortly after I reached the corner, there was a noise and the far end and a tractor like vehicle came in pulling two large wagons. The first one was filled with what were obviously dummies. They vibrated as the vehicle came to a stop.

The second one had people on it dressed similar to what Anna had been wearing. When the tractor came to the dead center of the hangar it stopped. Immediately a mechanical arm came down from the ceiling. The arm supported a railed platform. On the platform were several men dressed in white coats like scientists. In the back was a dwarf who seemed to be guiding the contraption. The platform stopped in front of the two trailers. There was a long silence as the white coated men checked their clip boards. While they checked the clipboards, a laser light from anther part of the arm danced around each persons ID tag. Then it moved to the dummies and did the same thing. At last a man in a white coat said "014-15 . . . Check!" With that the dwarf sprung back into action deftly guiding the arm back into the ceiling. The tractor started up again and slowly rumbled off. The lights slowly went off in the hangar. I stood there acting onerous. As if I knew how to do such a thing.

There was a long deafening silence. Maybe it's the kind where you know you've been there before. I should have heeded that feeling right then, but no, not Mr. Wrong way Basketball. I stood there not knowing what to do. I guessed that Anna would make her way back to me. I was about to move out of my corner when a hand touched me from behind. I was surprised because I thought I was in a protected corner. But, it had been dark and I didn't see a small hallway to my right. Anyway I almost wet my pants. To my relief, it was Anna. I turned and threw my arms around her. We embraced for several minutes before she said: "We've got to move from here. There will be "walkers" in here soon."

We moved down the dark hallway that she had come through. She found a door at the end of the corridor and she motioned me to follow. The door shut, and we found ourselves alone again. We fell to the floor in the corner behind some boxes.

I hugged her. We sat there for a long time and then I said: "Tell me what you know. I have a lot of pieces floating around in my head." She looked at me a little funny. Then she sat there for a long time trying to decide what to tell me. Then she spoke: "You are in great danger here. They know you are here." I looked at the floor and said: "It won't be the first time" Then I said: "But what are they after?" I sat for a second more then: "I mean they have gone to so much trouble." She was silent for a long time and then: "Power, control, supreme recognition, absolute obedience.

It's really a lot simpler than it seems." She sat there thinking and then: "But I should not have said that." she stammered: "If they found out I helped you or gave you any information . . . well . . . I don't know . . . I mean, I have seen several others go into the "cleaning room" and not come out . . ." She thought and then: "I can't say any more" I looked at her a little closer this time.

Several rays of light were shining on her beautiful face. Then I spoke with deliberation: "Your not Anna are you?" There was a long silence. She started to argue, but then she sensed that I would not be fooled. She spoke: "How did you know?" I looked at the floor again. "I don't know. Maybe its how you carry yourself." I stammered: "I was so excited when I thought I had found her." And then: "So if your not Anna . . . what are you?" She bit her lip almost like Anna would have and then whispered to me: "I am Anna in a lot of ways." But then she recanted: "I am what they copied of Anna." Then: "But I am not programmed to lie . . . I can't lie to you." I sat there for a long time and then said: "But is Anna alive . . . is she here?" The semi human touched my arm and looked into my eyes and then said: "Yes" Then she stammered as if a dummy could have feelings: "She's alive but she is in the "Holding block." I looked back at her and then: "The Holding Block? What is that?"

She spoke now in a more monotone voice as if some switch had gone off inside her: "The Holding Block" She stared straight ahead as if going into a trance; "The holding block is where they . . ." She stopped and seemed to be fighting something inside, as if she was not authorized to give out this information.

Then as if she had thrown back some internal doors she blurted out: "The Holding Block is where the keep "originals", people they have copied." Then as if still fighting with some sort of internal control: "The "originals" can never leave". There was a stark silence as I took in this information. I was elated and crushed all at the same time. To be told the love of my life was alive was joyful. But to be told that I would never get her out was defeating. Then, I regained my resolve and said: "I will get her out one way or another." The dummy just looked at me as if it had gone back to neutral mode. I got up to leave. I looked back as the dummy stared ahead.

I opened the door and was about to close it silently when the dummy spoke one more time: "They want your book." I closed the door and stood there dumb struck. I thought they might know of my book, but this was the first time I was assured that my suspicions were correct.

I ran to a dark area in the big hangar. There were no "walkers" out yet. I leaned against the wall and slipped to the floor. I sat there for a long time thinking. How did they know about my book? Had I said something? No. Had someone broken in to my basement while I was out? No. I had several safeguards. Then I thought a minute. I slammed my fist to the floor. Then I spoke out loud: "Max!"

CHAPTER **38**

Trust

I had been so trusting. He seemed too innocent. I started to get a headache. My eyes blurred. But, I had to reason this out. Had he been planted? Surely not! No way! Or was there a way? I mulled the idea over several times until I was shocked back into reality. The lights went on in the hangar. Almost instantaneously the "walkers" came out marching in three rows. It was hard to see from my corner. They had come into the hangar from the other side.

From my distant location I could still imagine how their eyes must have been. They might have been glazed over and they marched as if that had no souls. I knew I had only minutes before they would be close enough to see me. I slipped back down the hall where the Anna look alike was. I had seen an exit door further down the hall. I was out the door before I remembered something very important. I quickly slipped back inside the door and back to the room where the Anna Dummy was. I opened the door quickly and whispered: "Where is the Holding Block?" The dummy just stared back at me. It must have been taken out of commission. It was easy to see that I would not get anything more. I waited a minute hoping for some change, but none came. So, I turned and still in full stride I raced back to the outside and slipped behind some large crates before you could say "rat me out". It was time to rework my plan.

I thought and thought. If Max was one of them, then I was in big trouble, bigger than "yo mama"; a nervous joke. I just hopped that my contingency plan had worked. If they had come to my basement with or without Max's help, they might find out where I had hidden my book but it would not be that easy. I had found a black book in the junk yard and placed it in the safe. It had no lock on it so I hoped that they would just take it and go. The real book was on top of some pipes hanging just inches below the basement ceiling. It was a move I made as I left this morning. You never can be too careful.

Throwing all caution to the wind, I decided if the jig was up. Then, I thought, who gives a shit about being seen. I grabbed a box and threw it over my shoulder. I started walking toward the car. If anyone were to see me, they might think I was a worker. But the truth was I didn't care. I was going to find out what was going on with Max and my book if I had to take twenty "Hoodsmen" with me.

Well, nothing happened. I set the box by the car and jumped in. In a few minutes I was on the road and headed back to the junk yard. On the seat was a pack of three thick ham slices I had traded a restaurant owner for in return some heavy sweeping. Maybe the meat was still ok, but sitting in the car had not helped it. I was very upset and I decided that the meat could help me out if I needed it in a few minutes.

As I drove into the junk yard I noticed "Mr. Booze man" was sitting bushy tailed and waiting for business. He saw me coming and raised the booth window to yell at me when I hit him square in the face with a slab of ham. "Splat!". "Booze man" fell back with a muffled yell and must have hit the booth floor. He could spend a little time thinking about that one. It was just part of the pressure I felt building up inside. If Max had turned on me, I would take the other two slices and tie them to his head.

We'd see what an old man looked like with ham ear muffs. I tore through the yard and stopped at my container slowing just a little so as not to add to the two hundred scratches I already had on my car. With the container door shut and feeling like Booze Man had not seen my hide out, I slid down the fireman's rail to the basement. The place was in shambles. Boxes were strewn everywhere. Max was no where to be found. I checked the safe. The "bait" book was gone. Then glancing up to the pipes in the ceiling my heart leaped for joy. My real report book was still in hiding. I don't think Max knew it was up there. I had been very careful to screen what information I gave him. But then, where was Max?

Had he gone off with the intruders? What ever happened, I figured I had only a few hours to clear out. It's wouldn't be long before they discovered that they had some kid's diary. I can see it now. They would open the book with several of those robed managers sitting in some over stuffed chairs, with their legs crosses, looking expectantly at the book. After clearing his throat a "Hoodsman" would start reading about Jennie's date with the eighteen year oversexed older boy. Though it might be a little steamy, it was not what they were looking for. There would be some screaming and swearing. The Hoodsman would be thrown out with the large steel door slamming behind them. They'd be told not to come back alive without the real book.

I looked around at the "digs". A tear came to my eye, or maybe it was a piece of rat fesses. With everything being moved around, there was lots of "stuff" in the air.

I was hoping for the tear, but you know how that goes. It would take some time to find another place like this, and I just finished the plumbing . . . ha ha I grabbed some clothes. Checked the refrigerator, but wished I hadn't done that. If food could walk, I would have had a track team.

I had a few boxes packed with clothes and a few of my scientific instruments like a wooden spoon and hammer and some left over mirror pieces and of course my black book. I found no trace of Max and expected he was now sitting in some small room eating a piece of grilled meat and drinking a bottle of the Director's finest. He'd have his feet propped up and ready to receive more salutations, well, until they found out he gave them a "bum" wrap. And the word "bum" fits in here in a number of ways.

Oh . . . thinking of Bum, just made me remember. I would have to stop by another old building on the way to my new hideout where ever that might be. I had completely forgotten. I had another "Bum" experiment running. I opened the container door and backed the car out. No sign off Mr. "Booze man". Maybe the slap in the face with the ham slice was enough adventure for him for one day. I'm sure his next adventure was to the bottom of a whiskey bottle.

I tore trough the gate and again had to stop and wait for the one car a day that came by the junk yard. Had I not been paying attention, I would have run into it. I arrived at the old building several minutes later. I only had to stop at four yellow lights and wait for three trains to pass. I had a lot on my mind and had determined to have a meeting with myself right after I checked on #1128. I had the three bums on the second floor of another abandoned building. I found a room that was out of any drafts. This one needed my most accurate measurements. I had each bum lying on the floor. One bum was on a wood floor, one was on carpet and one was on a tile floor. I had given them several cans of chili and a can opener. Their job was to determine which surface was the least comfortable. Of course you say Renn or Thaub or whatever your name is now, we all know that the tile will be the coldest and thus the Bum #2, on the tile, will be the most uncomfortable. And I would say: "Thank you, thank you. Of course you are right. But how right are you? That's the question.

By the way I changed my name again. It's now "Dark." So if the tile is the coldest, then it must be room temperature. If the room is 55 degrees, sorry but it's cold in here. You weren't expecting shirt sleeve temperatures were you? So, I check the temperature of the tile and you back up a little and say "Well . . . maybe it's a little cooler since a little air is moving across the surface." So I say , "Ok, if it's 55 degrees then maybe the tile is 53?" We measure it by placing our very scientific and calibrated hand on it. It's colder than that. "But wait!" I say. How can that be? I take out a surface thermometer I have stuck in my pocket. It's 42 degrees. How can that be? Ok, so I didn't have a surface thermometer. But just go touch some tile in your house. It's very cold. So when a guy gets up to go to the bathroom in the middle of the night he freezes his feet. It's much colder than physics will allow. Yet, no one notices and no one complains. They just carry the big stones on in life. It's just another torment. But I am sorry to say it's true. I am not making this up. Go try it if you don't believe me. You can run your own experiment tonight. I'll buy the Pizza afterwards.

I threw another couple of cans of Chili to the Bums and walked out of the room. I was in full disgust. I would go to the diner that I had eaten at before. It was the one where they didn't seem to stare at me. I would mull this whole few days over. But first, I had to find a new "hole". I was already working on an idea. After a few odd turns in the car to see if I was being followed, I decided it was safe enough to go check it out. There were some caves north of town. I explored one once. If I could get the car into one, it would become my new "Mirror Man World Headquarters"

Sure enough, after driving for five minutes down a dirt road I found some heavy brush blocking a cave entrance that opened at an angle so it was not seen from the dirt road. The area seemed remote enough. The cave walls and cciling would block any "look down" radar. But, the brush needed to stay in place to carry off the whole "secrecy" thing. So, I sat there and thought and thought. How could I keep brush growing but be able to move it when I wanted in or out of the cave? That was the question. The answer finally came forward. "Pots" I would go get every container I could find in the old junk yard. I would "repot" all the brush and taking care as an attentive gardener, I would nurture the brush along with just the right amount of water.

The pots in place and my bags and sacks and boxes out of the car I went back to the café for some hard thinking. I was now a man of "property" again. I sat in the café booth and reveled in my good fortune. I ordered turkey and gravy and biscuits. I was staring at the plate of food in front of me, not really hungry. I just had a lot on my mind. The food looked tasty enough. The gravy was a little thin and ran around the interior rim of the plate. I was in deep thought. The woman

I loved had been close to me but maybe now, not so much. I had lost my hide out. The old man I trusted had turned me in. I had been in jail and chased by guards. I had been in line to get the piss shocked out of me. I was at my wits end. I stared and stared at the plate and found myself pushing the biscuit from one edge of the plate to the other almost unconsciously. If I wanted soaked biscuits I would have dropped the biscuit into the gravy.

I was actually thinking of putting some butter on it and how good a dry biscuit would taste with butter. I moved the biscuit again to keep it from getting soaked by the gravy. But everywhere I moved it, the gravy followed. I moved it onto some turkey thinking that the space between the plate and the biscuit would be separated by the turkey. But the gravy seemed to creep up the sides of the turkey slab and head for the biscuit.

I moved the biscuit to the very edge of the plate, but the gravy seemed to build up at that end of the plate and slowly flow toward the biscuit. It seemed that someone or something or entity was determined to ruin my biscuit. #1130. Try this at home, you'll be surprised. That's when I lost it. I could go no further without coming to some sort of reckoning.

A guy should be able to go through life without having to face such mundane torments. But no, it was, I guess, part of a bigger plan. No one was exempt. Everyone should bare the burden. I was incensed! Well, I resolved right then that I might not stop it all, but I was going to foul up as many torments as I could. The "gloves" were off! No more Mister nice "Mirror" guy!

CHAPTER **39**

A New Direction

The night was in the small restless hours. The house sat among many other entry level homes in the area. The sounds were normal for that time of night except for the creaking of a laundry room window. Slowly it rose. A small dwarf leg slipped out and then a second one. The dwarf sat on the sill and waited for his helper. They had been in the house stealing sock mates. When the home owner (he he) finished drying the clothes tomorrow he or she would not be able to match any socks. They smirked at their genius as they sat there savoring the moment. It drove the "Guineas" crazy. The Guineas always thought it was their fault. They had just not paid any attention. Or they were just not good house keepers. But in truth, it was just another wonderful torment. "Oh, this one was always good they thought." The Dwarfs smirked as they re-hashed what they had just done. The Director thought of everything. They each slipped a candy in their mouths and turned their attention to dropping to the dark ground beneath them.

They crawled slowly down the side of the house with the sack of stolen sock mates. They hit the ground, but something was not right. Yes, it was for sure not right. They were in a trash barrel. They looked up to see "Mirror Man" reach in a grab their sack of socks. One dwarf screamed at the sight of the shining "protector of mankind".

But, the other was indignant. He saw what was happening. Their little trip of torments had been foiled. He raged at the figure looking down at them. "You fool . . . You can't fight the system!" To their surprise the figure above spoke: "I might not get you all, but I am going to certainly throw a wrench in the gears." With that, mirror man pours a jar of honey over their heads. The bigger dwarf yelled back: "Uwweeee, what is this? . . ." Shaking his arms as the sticky liquid flowed into every fold of his clothes. He raged: "You won't get away with this!" He raised his fist as if to represent the wrath that would surly come down.

I threw the socks back through the laundry room window and ran out of the yard. But you say: "Dark, why didn't you give them a bigger punishment?" And I would say back to you: "I'm going to fight the same way they do. It's the little torments that will come back to them!" With that the great shining "purveyor of good" disappears into the urban foliage. The night returned to its naked silence.

The cross arm was about to come down and a young couple had to decide if they could make it before the train came by. The deck was of course "stacked against them". But wait! A bum steps out with a sign. It says "it's ok. We'll slow down the train." The bum motions to another bum at a control box. The train has slowed and finally stopped. The young couple drives through.

A man is driving his son to a soccer game. They are late and will just make the start of the game. Then the green light does that thing where you know it will change before you get there. It will cause them a significant amount of torment. Except this time a bum is standing by the stop light with a sign. It says:

"Go on through. We'll handle it" Next to him is another Bum with the traffic control box open. They wink at each other.

A man was seen coming out of his office and preparing to get into his car. He had his hands full. He had a brief case and a computer cord, a note written to himself about items to pick up on the way home, his keys to open the car and three plastic travel cups. Two of the cups were stone dry. One had some old syrupy liquid in it. As he reached to unlock the door while still holding everything in place, something fell. Can you guess? (He he!) You're starting to catch on. The cup with liquid fell. The idea was that not only would the cup break, but the liquid would splash up his legs to his crotch. It was a double hit. He would lose his best cup and then find himself trying to explain what the large wet spot was all over his crotch and the diner party he was heading to.

No matter what he said, people would think he had wet his pants. Everything was set perfectly, except for one thing. A large "meat hook" of a hand reached out from under the car just as the cup was falling and caught the cup. A bum pulled himself out from under the car and handed the man the cup.

Several dwarfs had crept into a man's closet late at night. They had a big jar of mustard. They were preparing to meticulously paint mustard stains on the man's ties, when the closet door burst open and a large net was thrown over the dwarfs.

A man has just gotten on an airplane and was placing his bag in the overhead bin when to his surprise his pants ripped. Not just a small rip that he could easily hide as he departed on his 5 hour plane ride, but a rip from the front of his crotch to the back. The man sits there with his underwear hanging out. A

Bum was sitting next to him with a new pair of pants ready for the event, but after looking at the man's exposed hairy thighs the Bum mumbles something and looks straight ahead. The man with the ripped pants turns and asks the Bum what he said. The Bum after realizing he will have to fumble around the man's crotch to put the new pants on him, says: "Looks good to me". And he starts to read a magazine.

An older couple was seen at the airport, each carrying two large heavy bags. They were ripe for the "last gate" torment. Sensors were going off in hidden boxes in the terminal.
The men in white robes had just poured coffee and were settling down to watch the whole scene on closed circuit TV. The Old couple looked down the long hall and set their bags down in dismay. How could it be that every gate they went to was this far away? The woman took out a handkerchief and wiped her forehead. But all of a sudden there a honk from behind and it was the Bums dressed in clown outfits in a golf cart. The brazenness of the move was startling. They quickly put bags and the old couple in the cart and whisked them to their gate.

An Airline Stewardess was seen carefully crossing seat belts in each seat before the passengers got on board the plane. But close behind her, unnoticed was a Bum dressed in an Airline Captains uniform looking not too official, following behind and throwing each seat belt to the side. Had anyone been watching, they would have seen that from behind the properly dressed Captain had an old pair of jeans on with the back of the Captains coat partially ripped out. The Pilot actually had a scraggly Bum's beard. At first glance he seemed almost sophisticated.

A fast food waitress was just putting the last ½ ounce of 12 ½ ounces of soda in a 12 ounce cup making sure that the last ½ ounce would spill all over the patron. She also had included the special lid that would allow some spillage but then hold some of the liquid until they actually took a drink. Then the rest would spill on the customer's lap. This was of course after the patron saw the first ½ ounce spill on his car seat.

She passed the overfilled cup out to the car and a hand took the cup. But it wasn't the customer's hand. It was a Bum's hand. Quickly he took off the lid and poured out 1 ounce of liquid and replaced the lid and handed it to the surprised patron. The patron and the waitress looked in shock as the Bum gave them a big toothless smile.

By this time the men in white robes had put down their coffee and were pointing at the screen as several "counter-events" took place. One higher ranking white robed man was seen yelling and throwing some reports at the other robed men. They all jumped up and rushed out of the room, most likely rushing back to "shore up" their areas of responsibility. They would easily put down this small uprising.

But, by now word was spreading. Mirror Man and the Mirror Man organization of Bums were making themselves known. This was just the start. For the last few days Mirror Man had met with several Bum lieutenants. A small but growing "Bum" organization was spreading across the Country. Several cities had already formed Bum Groups. An MM representative had given a presentation to each group. Charts and graphs were shown. The Bums were interested, but not so much for the good deeds they would be doing, but for the cans of Chili that the MM organization promised.

Bum teams were taking to the streets. They were helping little old ladies cross streets. They were standing in front of water splashed from cars as it was targeted at elderly couples, waiting to cross the street. They were fixing flat tires for helpless women. A little boy's sucker that fell in the dirt was quickly replaced by a nearby Bum. The Bums were on site when a woman's laundry blew off the line and fell into the mud. All the clothes were quickly whisked into a large sudsy laundry tub on wheels that they had in the alley. The tub was pulled by two small dogs. All this was being monitored by the Directors staff. Ratings were not just down, they were in the "crapper".

The Director's staff had received several memos threatening eternal tormentation if the staff didn't correct the situation. Several white robed men were sitting in a room with large monitors on the walls. All the monitors showed downward graphs. We can't understand exactly what they referred to, but let it suffice to say that the trends weren't good.

One of the head men in white robes was seen bursting into the room and screaming at the other white robed men. He then turned to leave but as an after thought, he turns again and kicks over some folding chairs. Other white robed underlings were seen scurrying to pick up the chairs.

Several days ago the MM organization met with the owners of a Chili factory. It turns out that the owner was very upset about Chili almost always "jumping" into crackers on a bowl of chili and crackers. It just wasn't right. People should be able to eat Chili without having soggy crackers. No one had ever stood up for this idea before. Everyone just sat there and accepted it. And when the MM Organization returned all the

Chili factories wife's "mateless" socks, he was really convinced to join the group. From that point on the MM organization had trucks going to a number of cities spreading the word and of course, chili for all the Bums.

But, the "tormentors" acting through GREMIS were a large professional organization. They had seen resistance come and go. They went ahead with business as usual. No small "upstart" group would affect their way of bringing torments to the common man. They even expanded their research. They continued to propagate new and fiendish torments. The Hoodsman continued to run Bazaars in several cities. The Director had moved in and sent several men in white robes who he thought to be slackers, to the dungeon. He was personally calling all the shots.

Then GREMIS struck back with a vengeance. A whole city came down with the flu. People were seen hanging out windows of their houses, throwing up, faces red with fever.
Special styles of hot coffee cups had been infused into the system. The patron would hold the cup and take the first drink of Hot Coffee. But after that, the next time the cup was raised to the customer's lips, the cup would bend and send hot coffee all over the customer. A paper cup still in research was rushed through. Hoodsmen showed up at the research facility and grabbed the products. The scientists rushed out yelling: "Wait! It's still under study!" But the burley "Hoodsmen" pushed them aside and carried out boxes of cups. The cups had just enough wax to keep the product in while it was being consumed. But many times the cup was left on someone's desk with ½ the liquid still in it. This is where the "genius" came in. As soon as the person left, the cup lost its ability to hold liquid and let the contents seep all over the desk. Maybe you

have already had the pleasure of testing this product. Don't say you haven't or we'll be seeing you tonight.

A large overhead door opened at the GREMIS headquarters. People stood back in shock as two hundred men in Long Black Coats marched out. Right behind them came another two hundred of the pixelated men and women all carrying briefcases. The neighbors all backed away as this snarling mass of semi humanity marched forward.

Dogs put their tails between their legs and scurried off. At some unheard command, the pixilated army split into three columns and headed off the property. Then there was a rumbling sound as a number of large trucks rumbled out. Each truck was packed with Hoodsmen all wielding clubs. There would be hell to pay tonight in River City.

The white robed men watched their monitors with smiling smirks, as the columns of tormentors filed out. Another white robed man of lesser in rank was seen showing him material on a clip board. The results he was showing, were obviously what he wanted to see. They both raised their fists in triumph. But, maybe their celebration might have been premature. The MM organization was just gearing up.

Several large boxes arrived at the Bazaar. Three dwarfs manhandled the boxes onto the loading dock. A second group of dwarfs read the tags on the boxes and hauled them into the hangar like bazaar floor. Right behind them came a very short dwarf on a fork lift. He lifted all the boxes onto the stage. The boxes obviously had been sent to the Bazaar leader. The tall, skinny, but very stately man rose up from his coffee cup laden table and jumped onto the stage as the gifts were placed at his feet. He raised his arms as the Hoodsmen in the large Arena roared in pleasure. They were running their businesses as though no one had challenged them. After all, who was this Mirror Man? He was more of an idea than a real threat.

The leader again raised his arms as if the first roar had not been loud enough. Actually the "attention" is what he lived for. Goose bumps rose on his skin. He was, as they all knew, the human representation of what they all aspired to. His long flowing robe hung over the stage in glorious display as he looked into the eyes of his admirers.

Never without soul lifting words, he was about to speak when a dwarf jumped onto the stage and started to unwrap the packages. The Speaker looked down: "Thank you Tom. I think these are from the Director. We have "truly" been recognized!" The crowd roared so loud the stage vibrated. Soon, everyone will sharing in the gifts!" The crowd rumbled in deliriousness. But, at that moment, something in the wrapping paper crackled. "Snap!"

The dwarf backed off. Something under the wrapping paper had started burning. The crowd grew silent as they watched smoke rise from each of the boxes. Then, there was a small "pop" and one of the boxes broke open spilling . . . what? (he he) Ticks and fleas and bed bugs! In a flash, they were all over the stage. The second box was similar but with a small exception. It had an explosive charge in it. There was another pop and this time fleas, ticks and bed bugs flew everywhere. But you say: "Dark, that's scary and all that, but we've seen fleas and ticks before." But then I would say to you: "Have you seen "Deer Ticks?" I'm not making this up. They are really out there. Who would be so "viperous" as to devise an insect so small yet so intense. The insect actually burrows into the skin. It lives there and lays eggs there for years. Years later bumps are still present on the skin. I know personally. I have them.

The first black swarm of Fleas and Ticks hits the leader. He grabbed his throat as they flowed like liquid over him. He retches as he tries to call for help. The dwarf was next. He rolled on the stage clutching his head. A black mass almost consumed him. The Hoodsmen onlookers at first started to laugh. This must be a prank of some sort. There will be a big birthday cake in the third box and the Leader will raise his hands again showing us he has played a trick on us. They would revel in the "prowess" of their kind. After all, they were the leaders of "anguish". They were the soldiers of misfortune. They were here now licking their lips with man's struggles. But how could this be? The leader stumbled and fell off the stage. Then third box exploded and a fine back mist of insects flew into the far reaches of the hangar.

Deer ticks (my favorite) were everywhere. Everyone in the Hangar started scratching and itching. This was not what was planned. This was not how it was suppose to be. But was this a crack in the armor of GREMIS?

CHAPTER **40**

Tit for Tat.

I was exhausted. I had almost worn out my Mirror man outfit. But it was a symbol for the Bums. I had to put it on every time I talked to a group. I had Bums in twenty States now. I had bums at the airports and bums at the fast food restaurants. Several surprise boxes had been delivered to Bazaars in other States with the same results. Bums were monitoring stop lights and train crossings allowing easy access to intersections.

Bums were hiding behind houses and bagging up dwarfs as they tried to steal "sock mates". The grocery stores were almost out of honey. Bums were putting extra reading glasses on tables in houses when the "disappearing" ones vanished. The Guineas never knew. Bums were replacing wet absorption pads before the "Guinea" knew it was wet and kicked it. Bums were slipping in and fixing bed posts during the day.

A little "guerilla glue" went a long way toward gumming up the swiveling bed posts from causing the hundreds of "stubbed" toes. Bums were wiping up vomit before the Guineas could walk into it barefoot. Boxes that that weighed 40 pounds on the ground were replaced with 20 pound boxes. Then when the box got heavier, it really only weighed what it was supposed to weigh in the first place.

The fever of fighting torments raged on, but the Guinea's never knew. And the fact that the targets of the hundreds of torments never saw the torement, upset the white robed men all the more. People were actually getting happier. This was terrible. It was against the laws of the universe. Man was made to toil and struggle. How could mere men know happiness? It was War! They would stamp out theses "upstarts!"

But, at the same time I noticed a chilling event. GREMIS was closing all the coffee shops. It turns out the most of the coffee shops were using ceramic coffee mugs and not the trick paper cups supplied free from GAG (Government Action Group) a retail processing arm of GREMIS charged with supplying torments to the retail community. The effect of no torments in the coffee shops meant that the general population was actually enjoying itself. GREMIS had determined that this was bad for business. Thus, when I strolled around the corner to my favorite café, there was a giant Hoodsman standing in front of the door. A sign on it read: "Closed for health issues". I wondered whose health they were talking about.

But, the Director and his plans were relentless. Gimmicks were placed on the market that obviously had not completed their design. Straws that had holes in them were made available. The net effect was that the person trying to suck some liquid through the straw also took in a lot of air too. This little trick caused the person to belch up air for the next few hours.

Gutters were sold for houses that didn't "gut". Upon the first rain the gutter would deflect and hold extra water until finally causing it to fall ripping off the fascia of the house. Special heating systems were sold that actually funneled cold air onto the first 6 inches of the floor. The occupant felt warm except for his feet. They were very cold. But the occupants always thought: "Oh, it's just me. My body's circulation system is not what it used to be."

Plastic cups were sold that made extremely loud noises when held under a refrigerator ice dispenser. Thus a person taking care of a sick person would sneak into the kitchen to get a glass of ice. Pressing the ice dispenser on the refrigerator door, he would be shocked to hear the tremendous crashing of the ice cubes as they fell into the cup. The sick person sleeping in the other room was almost certain to be awakened.

Trash truck crews were sent to special school. They were shown and expected to use scientific techniques to increase the noise level while collecting trash. Signs were placed on highways that read "bridge ices before the road". The "Guineas" just read the sign and drove on not knowing that special cooling coils had been placed under the bridge to heighten the possibilities of "black ice". If they wrecked they would always say: "It was my fault. I should have slowed down.

The hundreds of GREMIS troops were also taking their toll. Guineas were being rounded up and placed in plastic extruded cages. Mass experiments were taking place. Questions that had remained unanswered up to now, because of the GREMIS secrecy policy, were in the process of evaluation.

How would man hold up to 120 decibels over an extended period? What about intense heat? What about intense cold? Not physically, that was, of course, known. But how would the Guineas hold up mentally? How many torments did it take to drive a "Guineas" insane? If it was 109,257 could the Guineas be brought to 109,256?

Since the gloves were off, many questions that couldn't easily have been answered before, seemed close to being solved. Formulas were being developed that would bring a resident close to insanity, but not take him over the edge. After all, it was almost like death, how can you make an insane person's life miserable? Would the insane person know that you were tormenting him? The thought of that the idea made the Directors mouth water in anticipation. It was a whole new market. Several special labs had been set up just to see if you could torment a crazy man. The Director was very through. No effort to make sane people or insane people feel bad or inadequate was considered too small.

Then after several days to intense pressure, the troops disappeared. Everything went quiet. Even the torments slowed down. The Director, of course, could not bear to stop them all together. The rain increased and lightening filled the sky. The earth shook and people sat at their windows waiting to see what would happen next. Then the storm stopped. The rain dribbled out and the lightening ceased. A fresh smell of clean grass and clean concrete sidewalks filled the air. But, in the City Center a big banner had been unraveled. The banner was as big as the building it was on. It read: "Mirror Man. Let's negotiate. We can all live together. Man was meant to struggle. Meet us tomorrow night at the City Square. 8:00pm. You won't want to miss it. Someone wants to see you." Signed: "The Director."

Several of the Bums came to get me. We all rode in my car to a point they had picked so that I could read the sign. We stared at it for a long time. No one said anything. We restarted the car and came back to the Cave. Plans needed to be made. The Chess game was on. After saying some condolences at the MM

World Headquarters, the Bums made their way back to their various camps. The weather remained calm as if preparing for its role in a great battle.

Later that afternoon, I sat on my new high tech patio outside the Cave. I had fashioned two tree trunks for seats. A third one served as a patio table. Ordinarily, I would not have gone to this meeting. After all, we were dealing with not just a "mad man", but someone who thought they had "divine" permission to bring the struggle to man. I would make some tea and reflect on it. I thought and thought. Everything followed the Company line except the last sentence. "Someone wants to see you." If Max were there, I would guess he wouldn't want to see me. Who else might want to see me? They were using it as a "lure". I thought most of the afternoon.

Then it came to me. It could only mean one thing. They had Anna! Max could have told them about her. I might have ranted and raved in my sleep about her while he lived with me. It was the only answer. I decided then and there that Mirror Man would make another appearance. But how? There were just too many of them. Frankly a lot of them were "undercover". You would not be able to tell the good guys from the Company goons. Plans would have to me made. I picked up my cell phone and called the Chili Company owner. Maybe I could call in a few favors.

Later that night several trucks arrived at the cave. I got busy unloading the materials. There were a number of boxes of broom sticks and still more rolls of wire. Also in the shipment was burlap, the kind that the Hoodsmen made their clothes out of. Last but not least, was a box of broken mirror pieces? After several hours of unloading, I whipped up a special Frito

Chili pie for the driver and told him to thank the Chili owner for his help. Minutes later the trucks were leaving dust as they rumbled down the dark dirt road. If my plan worked it might be the chance I was looking for to get Anna back. If it didn't, well . . . I just might be doing hard labor for the rest of my life. Aw, we were doing hard labor now. What's the difference?

We started in right away. I had several Bums come from outlying camps to help. We split several cans of Chili, their favorite, fixed some Saw Grass tea and commenced to work. The work lasted most of the night. When I finally finished I noticed that I was the only one still awake. Well, they had earned the rest. I would catch a cat nap myself and then, prepare for this evenings events. It looked like most everything was done.

At 6:00 pm I had several Bums report in. One spoke: "Chief, it's tighter than a nickel balloon." The second Bum looked at him and said: "Hey Bullace, how is a nickel balloon tight?" Bullace just hunched his shoulders and said: Hey I ain't no word smitty . . . I just mean it's crawling with Hoodmen." The smaller Bum piped it: "Yeah, I seen it. You couldn't get a slice of string cheese in there if they didn't want you too." I sat there thinking. Something's not right. How do they expect me to feel secure enough to even step into their trap. It would take some thought. I noticed that the first batch of Saw Grass tea had started fermenting. Maybe a little Saw Grass wine might put a new light on things.

We stayed to our plan. The first group of Bums went in dressed as Hoodsman. The second group of Bums stayed dresses in third normal street clothes except they all had small back packs on. I also had a "Hoodsmens" outfit on. The outfits were part of what we spent the last night working on. I had a couple of tricks up my sleeve should the meeting turn ugly. The night was calm as we approached the City Square except for lightening in the distance to the north.

CHAPTER **41**

Town meeting

There were all sorts of people gathered to hear the Director speak. He would of course, not be there. His image had never been actually seen, but his voice was unmistakable. The Men in White Robes would bring the Directors word to the people. I was surprised to see a number of towns people dressed shabbily. Most of the time they lived a normal life and accepted what ever was dealt them. They dressed for work each day and were prepared to accept life's twists and turns with out question. But some of them looked like they had been pushed to the limit. One man sat on a blanket with his wife. His coat was ripped. His hair was disheveled and his face swollen. He raised his arm as we walked by. "Sir, help us." He stood up. "We have been pushed to the limit. We can't take it anymore! They have taken our house and our jobs. They have brought every kind of malice known to mankind upon us." I stopped for a moment and looked into the man's hollow eyes. He started to speak again, but four small arms grabbed him from behind and pulled him into a rolling trash cart. It was the Dwarfs.

They were running field interference for the Director. It was one thing to take the torments, it was something else to point them out. I had first hand knowledge of that. The wife rose seeing her husband being carried off. She started to scream but before she could, a third dwarf came out of the crowd and sprayed her face with some sort of calming chemical. She smiled and sat back down on the ground as if nothing had happened. Another similar man was seen running through the crowd. His coat was also ripped. He passed a rolling trash bin and before he knew it, the top popped open three dwarfs had pulled him into the trash bin. The top closed and I was surprised to see no resistance. I would have to make a note of that.

As I got closer to the City Square the crowds of people got thicker. Finally when I got to the square it was wall to wall citizens. There were families sitting on mail boxes. There was a square dance group sitting on a street curb still in garish costumes waiting to hear the speech. There were firemen and cowboys. There were teachers and librarians. And, of course, there were Hoodsmen everywhere. There were also several large billboard trucks parked in well placed locations. The billboards had sayings from the Director. The boards were lit, allowing the people to read the well placed words. One said: "There is no good without bad". Or, "Tribulation makes us stronger!" and other words of wisdom. The gathering seemed like a cross between a company picnic and a hanging.

The storm was moving in closer now and lightening flashed every few seconds. White Robed men sat in chairs on the stage. Two speakers stood in shadows as the crowd quieted down. The first speaker came to a podium on a stage that must have been 10 feet in the air. On either side of the stage were the Emblems of GREMIS emblazoned in red neon lights. The lights we so bright, that it made it hard to see the speaker. But when he spoke I knew I recognized the voice. To my surprise the Bazaar leader stepped forward.

He had tan colored bandages covering part of his face and neck. Anyone just making a quick glance wouldn't see all the bites. But, I knew they were there. I wondered if he would offer some explanation. He appeared to be here to promote a higher cause. After all, men needed leading didn't they? He raised his hands, but the roar in the crowd was weak. However, not faltering he started to speak: "Greetings River City!" Still no screams and yells in reverence. He seemed disappointed. He adjusted several of the bandages. They make up artists had all the bites looking pretty good. Everything was cleaned up, but I think the Deer Ticks were still there burrowing deeper into his skin as we speak. I personally loved it. Then bowing his head he continued. "We are here to come together." The crowd did seem to fall into some sort of trance.

Then lights on the stage flashed and spot lights twirled and he yelled as loud as he could: "What is our creed?" and the crowd now completely transfixed talked in monotone back to him: "There can be no good without bad". Lightening flashed now only ½ mile or so away. Thunder followed and even the frame of the stage creaked as the sound waves hit it.

As if on some sort of cue, Hoodsmen started passing through the audience looking for someone, I think maybe it was me. Dense fog poured in from the river and filled the low areas around the stage. As the crowd was trying to awake from the forced spell that came over them another voice took over. The voice was more hoarse. It was sort of gravely, but I recognized it before he stepped into the spot light. It was, of course, your friend and mine, the total scum bag "Max". I looked up and saw that he had my favorite coat on. I had wondered where that went.

I hope it gets caught on a door knob and strangles him to death. Opps, I forgot, that would not allow for the maximum number torments. Maybe just a broken neck that he could live with from now on. Someone would have to feed him soup every day. He looked out over the audience without speaking as if he were looking into each Citizens soul.

After a moment of shuffling some papers, he spoke almost as if the thought took him over. "I was lost and now I am found." The flashing stopped and the crowd got silent as the presentation got serious. He continued: "I lived among you." There was silence. Then: "I feel your trials and tribulations" The crowd grew restless, but you could tell that they had been treated this way before and that they would respond when asked to. They were still under some sort of trance. Max yelled this time: "I feel your pain!" a murmur was heard in the crowd. He looked out now reaching for crowd contact. "I lived in a camp by the river." He stopped as if to compose himself. Then: "We lived, but we could not see." He lifted a handkerchief to his mouth as if overcome in sadness. "You see, we had nothing to live for. It was a day to day struggle with no direction." Now, he was wiping an eye. "But GREMIS . . ." He stopped as if to decide if it was too personal to tell the crowd. Then: "Yes . . . GREMIS came along and showed me how the bad side of life could be good!"

At that point all the Hoodsman stopped what they were doing all turning toward the stage and in lock step and in unison proclaimed the Creed: "You can not have good without bad!" The Citizens all stood there as if questioning the honesty of the speaker. Max saw the confusion and decided that he was pushing the Directors concepts too quickly. So he took the mike off the stand and stepped forward fearing he would lose the contact he had with the audience. Then: "But wait!" the crowd was in complete silence. Then he spoke again: "I bring you greetings and salutations from the Director."

The crowd gave a respectful whisper to each other. "He sends you his complete love." A huge organ sound roared above the crowd. Lights flashed. Thunder rolled. Max continues in the vain of a well healed orator. "Yes, give the Director your soul, and he will give you happiness through struggle and tribulation." The crowd murmured.I cringed in anger. I seethed with indignation. Had I not been one step ahead of Max, the Director would have my black book right now and of course that would have been the end of it. I had patched his wounds. I had given him rancid bread. Well, that's not so important. Ok, so it was bad bread. So, sue me. But, I had helped him and this was what I got in return!

A man in the audience stands up and yells out: "But what about my home. It was all we had!" Max looked down at him and referred to a paper he had. Then: "You are Smith, John at 125 Appian Way?" The man stepped back is surprise. "Yes . . . but how did you know?" Max waves him off and starts in: "Everyone of us needs to toil in life." He stopped to let it sink in. Then: "You took too much for granite. Your life was too easy."

Max got a tear in his eye and continued: "You were happy. Sometimes we need to set Citizens back." Max rechecked his papers and then as if to emphasize a point: "You were to be an example." Max paused and then as if pleading to the man: "But now don't you see? Your life is clearer. You have become stronger. You can make your way knowing you can over come anything!" Max raised his arms as if to receive thanks from the crowd but only received silence.

At the same time I saw another man running from some Hoodsmen. One Hoodsman talked into his sleeve as the man slipped and fell. Shortly after that, several other Hooded thugs came barreling around a corner. They were driving some sort of odd cart with a long arm on front. There were quite a few people between me and where the action was taking place, so it was hard to tell exactly want was going on. But, to my surprise, not more than a minute from when the man started making noise, he was being lifter above the crowd like a captured bird.

A mechanical arm held him fast as he flailed and screamed about 15 feet above the concrete below. The cart quickly backed up, made some sort of whirring noise and then disappeared behind a nearby building. Not wanting to call attention to the silencing of another crowd member, Max raised the papers he held and said: "Don't pay any mind to that," looking to see if anyone heard. Then: "We are living the life!" He waited for a response from the crowd, but none came. Then: Then realizing he had lost the attention of the crowd, he changed subjects and then: "You will see!" Then he went into the business end of the talk and said: "We have passed out reports on various sectors of the City" The crowd was still entranced in the mechanical arm incident. Max rapped his papers on the podium.

Then: "UHHHmmmm. Excuse me, I know we all have other duties to attend to, so if we can have your attention for just a moment more." Then seeing he still didn't have their attention he finally said: "Well, just take the hand outs home. The Director wants the Communities cooperation."

He then laid the papers down on the podium and stared at the audience for a long time as if trying to decide what to say. This was to be the "punch" the Director had asked for. Finally after looking one more time at a clipboard he carried, he spoke again: "But Friends listen." He held up the handkerchief again and wiped his mouth. Then: "It pains me to say this" There was a short silence. Then: "Not all is good in River City tonight!" There was complete silence. Max looked at the clip board again as if to check what he was to say. Then "There is a rebel among you." No sound. Suddenly several sound speakers hummed on in front of the stage. The first sound was a low beep. Most everyone in the audience stopped what they were doing and looked directly at the stage as if in a trance.

Then a voice came out of the speakers. "You will respond to the Director's attaché." The audience quickly responded in complete sequence. "Yes. We will respond." Max continued: "There is a man among you who is working against us." Max had been waiting for the response and quickly fanned the flames. "He does not have your best interest at heart." He looks out over the crowd as if to see weakness. Then: "He is just like you and just like me, except he does not believe in man's struggle!" There was a long silence. All of a sudden a picture of me is projected on the screen behind the speaker's podium. It's a little old, but you could see that GREMIS had been doing their homework. I stepped back a little out of fear. "Yes, this man may be here. If you see him, we want to meet with him and give him our unconditional love." I doubted that. Maybe love at the end of a shocking pad.

Max spoke again: "We know he is working among you. We could, of course, find him, but we decided that we could reach his heart another way." There's a long silence. I thought for a moment and added in my own version of what they might be thinking: "Reach his heart with a three foot cattle prod." Then he continued: "We want to be his friend."

CHAPTER **42**

The cage

With that, a cage was rolled forward with a canvas covering on it. It had sat at one end of the stage the whole time, but with the "ruckus" going on at stage front, I had not even noticed. Two dwarfs pulled out a step ladder. One was the mean one from the insect feeding room. Just as the second dwarf had gotten about half way up the ladder, the mean one reaches the other dwarfs belt and pulls him off the ladder.

There's a crash as the dwarf hits the stage floor. The dwarf lying on the floor yells some obscenity, but is quickly carried off by some Hoodsman providing security on the stage.

The mean dwarf gets to the top of the ladder and flourishing his short arms as if doing a magicians trick, quickly removes the canvas cover. Standing in a brass cage was a beautiful woman. I stared closer. I could not believe my eyes.

I stumbled and fell back. I caught myself on a brick ledge. I was in shock. It was Anna. I stared and stared. I had been fooled before. I worked my way closer, all the time watching the Hoodsmen who were watching the crowd. I looked for movements that might indicate that the figure in the cage was a dummy. But I could see none. My eye sight started to fade on me. I could not hold back my emotions.

I yelled at the top of my lungs: "ANNA!" Then, I wished I hadn't. The Hoodsmen started making their way towards me. The Dwarfs on the stage rushed out to try to see me. Max still holding the microphone tried to continue his "good Samaritan act." He held the mike close to his mouth. "Dark . . . Or Renn or Thaub, whatever your name is. We don't want to hurt you. We just want to talk." I would believe that right after I bought the biggest investors share to the Golden Gate Bridge.

I looked up at Anna, held in the cage and something inside of me "snapped". I broke out in a sweat. I started shaking. I pushed several onlookers away and lunged for the stage.

At the same time, three burley Hoodsmen reached me. I saw them coming, but I grabbed the bars to the cage anyway. The leap exposed my midsection. In a flash they were throwing punches. The air left me for a few seconds. Another severe blow came to my back. I saw stars as they tugged at me to pull me from the cage bars. Someone in the crowd yelled: "Hey, let him go!" But I thought the threat was an empty one with all the Hoodsmen around. In fact, I think the man was whisked off never to be heard of again.

I still held the bars after receiving several more blows. I pulled myself closer to the beautiful woman in the cage. Anna got down on her knees and looked back. She had tears flowing from her eyes. She looked at me as if to apologize. Then looking even closer into my eyes she spoke: Oh Brad. I missed you so much." She looked at the Hoodsman holding my legs and said: "But, you've got to let them take you. There are too many of them." I looked back at her as I received two more severe strikes to my midsection. I spoke very clearly. My whole body started to shake: "Never!" Another blow hit me. She got down even closer to me and whispered: "I'm scared".

I looked back with the most intent stare I have ever done, while trying to keep my body and mind from coming apart and whispered back: "I'm scared too." I looked around at the huge Hoodsman holding my leg and then at the top of my lungs yelled: "I'm scared too!" A silent moment and then I said: "Scared they won't give me a good enough fight!" With that I brought my right leg back close to my body and let out a tremendous yell as I shot the leg forward and hit the leader of the Hoodsmen right in the face.

He yelled "OFFFhhhh!" And fell back. At the same time I pulled whistle out of my jacket and blew it. The signal was instantaneous. My first group of Bums located all through the audience pulled off their Hoodsmens outfits and displayed the all new and improved Mirror Man suits. There were at least fifty mirror men. People backed up as they looked at the oddly dressed Bums. Now my right leg came back into lunging position and shot out and struck a second Hoodsmen. He fell to the side as well.

I was almost free. Everyone was watching the Mirror Men and my struggle on the stage when another signal came, this time from the leader of the Hoodsmen.

There was silence for several beats and then with a loud banging noise all of the billboard fronts on the portable billboards located throughout the crowd, fell down. There was a huge rush of dust as the huge panels came down. One or two men in the audience were caught under the swing of the billboard fronts. There was a muffled screaming. But the crowd was in complete shock. Inside the structure that held the billboard were squads Men in Long Black Coats. They stood there as if waiting for a command. Someone in the audience yelled "Look out!", but it was too late. The command came quickly and all Men in Black Coats marched out of all four locations and into the crowd. Several men got in the way of the first group. The men tried to form a wall that would hold the Men in Black Coats back. But at the same time the Men in Black Coats pulled small weapons and pointed them at the "rogue" members of the crowd.

There was an electric flash and all four of the "would be protectors" fell to the ground. The citizens backed off in fear. One of the Dwarfs yelled still on the stage: "Here come the good guys!" Another one jumped up and down and turned several back flips. Another Dwarf started juggling some light weight bowling pins. But the Men in Black Coats were hardly the good guys. They started rounding up people and putting plastic handcuffs on them. The Citizens were then marched back to the billboard frames and shoved into holding cells built into the structures frame. The portable billboard would also double as a portable jail. When they got it full, the unfortunate citizens would be transported to who knows where.

Finally, I kicked the last Hoodsman loose and scrambled to the stage. For a moment I was free. The crowd saw me and roared approval. I raised my fist as if to show that we would fight to the last Bum. Lightening flashed as if to challenge whatever I had planned. I paid no attention. I had one more trick to perform. I blew the whistle two times and this time the second group of Bums, the ones with the back packs on, pulled off their backpack covers and raised the connected broom sticks in salute. They were now . . . (wait for it) "Electric Super Bums!"

But, they had something else with them. They had a battery on their back and, they each held a broomstick. The broom stick had two terminals at the tip. The terminals were tied back to the battery. When someone was touched by the tip of the broomstick it would complete the circuit and allow a charge from the battery to flow into the victim. I worked on this most of last night with my Bum helpers.

My theory was that the Men in Black Coats were just like the men with briefcases and just like the glass in the hallways of the GREMIS buildings. An electric charge affected the function of the glass. I was hoping this might also work on the Men in Black Coats.

Lightening flashed again and this time the huge thunder clap following it vibrated my chest. It was followed by another huge rap of thunder. The Electric Super Bums moved in on the Men in Black Coats. There was a clash and sound of sticks hitting people and then the first Bum touched a Man in Black. It was amazing. The charge shot through. There was a static sound, the man turned and faced his attacker, and then the man just turned to dust. I could not believe my eyes. The crowd watched in disbelief. A second Man in Black raced forward toward the Bum who hit the first Man in Black.

He ran into the stick and also received a little jolt of love. He stopped and raised his arm as if to strike down the Bum but instead crumbled to dust on the pavement.

Then, the storm started to move in. The small pile of dust that was once a very threatening Man in a Black Coat, blew away. The dwarfs of the stage pointed at the scene and yelled: "Look out for the Bums!" All the Hoodsman stopped and watched what was happening. Someone yelled some obscenities. Then, all hell broke loose. At the same time the Hoodsmen were pulling out items from their bag of torments, the storm hit with full force. Lightening flashed and thunder roared. Balls of fire crossed in heavy streams as the Hoodsmen rained down horror on the Mirror Bums. The torments were reflected by the Mirror Bums and as before and the balls of torments flew in every direction. The bums who had no mirrors, the Electric Super Bums, didn't fare so well. A man and his family were trying to get out of the way. They had made it to an alley and were just ducking behind a dumpster when a huge ball of Boils hit him and his wife. They buckled in pain. Parts of their necks started to swell. We could just hear their screams above the waves of slashing rain.

A dwarf had been eyeing me and Anna. He picked up a folding chair and rushed at us. I was still trying to reflect balls of flu and balls of ticks and fleas. The dwarf jumped to the top of one chair and raised the second chair as a weapon. Wielding the folding chair, he screamed at the top of his lungs as he dove for us. I deflected several blows and finally pushed the small man into several others. They all went down like bowling pins.

I had a rod from one of the stages supports and was in the middle of prying Anna loose from the brass cage. A ball of "shingles" whizzed by me and hit one of the white robed men. The man fell to the stage floor in agony. One of the dwarfs saw what had happened and yelled out: "Hey! Watch where you're throwing those things!" He turned and watched the white robed man roll on the stage floor.

Quickly he turned back where the ball of fire had come from and yelled out: "Now, look, what you've done!" Several more balls of fire hit near him. He scrambled under a vacated chair and held it over his head. The brass cage bars started to yield and before I knew it Anna was in my arms. It was definitely not a digital copy. We hugged tightly for a minute but it was not to last. Several balls for Fleas and Ticks hit at our feet. We jumped back, trying to evade the crawling insects. Another ball of the flu hit close by. I knew we were sitting ducks if we stayed on the stage. I grabbed her arm and headed for the back of the stage. The men in white robes were long gone except for the one still rolling on the floor of the stage. Now the wind was at full force and the stage shook with each monstrous gust. We stepped around two dwarfs. They were both rolling on the stage in pain. I laughed a little, thinking that they were reaping what they had sewed. I looked down at one of them as we quickly skirted by and said: "It couldn't happen to a more deserving guy!"

CHAPTER 43

Max

Anna grabbed my arm and motioned me to keep moving. Suddenly a bolt of lightening hit part of the stage frame. The metal on the stage glowed with white heat as the electricity from the lightning bolt flowed through the metal supports. The electrical charge running through the stage frame must have weaken a weld in the stage supports because the top cross bars started to break loose under the pressure from the wind. I knew it would be like a house of cards. We had to get off the stage fast. There was a second flash of lightening. The thunder that followed was so loud we could not communicate. Rain slashed at us now running completely horizontal and hitting us like little needles. But at the same time, I was mesmerized by the absolute war going on below us in the town square.

Anna pulled on my hand again as I watched the melee in the streets. The Bums with the mirror suits were holding their own. But the Bums with the electric sticks were taking a sever beating. It was true that every time they touched one of the Men in Black Coats, the Men in Black fell in a pile of dust. But Bums had no way to fend off the balls of torment.

We found a back stair and were heading away from the battle. We turned a corner and Anna tripped. I reached down to help her up when a voice from a hidden corner whispered at us:

"Wait, I can help!" it said. I turned and saw the very beat up face of your friend and mine, the one and only . . . Max. I was stunned. I stepped back trying to find some sort of explanation why such a low life, slime ball would come offer to help us. Was it a set up? Then my blood pressure started to rise to a boiling point. I raised my fist to smash in his worthless face when he blurted out: "They forced me to do it!"

I looked at Anna and then back at him. He quickly raised his hands in protection and then said again: "I couldn't help it. It was what they wanted me to do." He waited to see what I would do, but then figured he only had a short time before he started taking in shots from a guy that out weighed him by 80 lbs. He continued: "I swear . . . They told me that they would hurt Anna!" I was looking at Anna as if she could help explain. Anna shook her heard in agreement. She spoke: "Yes, Max met me for a short time." She was looking at me to emphasize the point. "I told him about you. And I guess it was all part of a plot to bring you in."

I looked back at Max and said: "But what happened at my basement hideout?" Then with out stopping: "You mean to tell me that you just decided to go with the intruders?" Max shook his head and waved his arms like a mad man. Then: "No, No, No, it wasn't like that. I was sleeping on the bed, and next thing I know, I am staring into the business end of an electric charge pistol." He looked at me and then at Anna. Shaking his head he continued: "Believe me, there was no reasoning with them." He looked behind us as if he had heard some noises.

Then, changing the subject, he said: "Look, you need to go with me on this one." He stopped and held his arms around himself as if to keep himself warm. Then he continued: "If you can just cut me some slack, for just a few minutes, I will explain everything I have seen. But for now . . ." He started looking around with wild eyes. "We gotta get out a here!" I looked back. I heard some noises, but I could tell for sure if it was Hoodsman running down the corridor or the fighting on the outside. I turned and looked at Anna to help me decide. In the end, I guessed we had no choice. I nodded at Max and he took off down a dark corridor.

CHAPTER **44**

Nostalgia

This is where it gets a little sketchy. One minute I was running down a corridor with my beloved Anna and the "Skank" Max, and the next minute I was lying on a floor smelling a flower that had been freshly cut and laid by my nose. It seemed strange, or maybe not. I couldn't remember for sure. I started to rise up and pick up the flower, but I found that even though I felt fine, I couldn't raise my arm. It was so very strange. Everything seemed just "peachy." I was lying in this nice room smelling a flower. But wait! No, maybe I was mistaken. The last coherent thoughts I had were: "What we would do as we ran down this dark corridor." Now I am feeling fine except I think there might have been a little time "glip" in the last few minutes or hours.

It all seemed to run together. Yes. There was something strange going on. I raised my hand to scratch my eyebrow except that, it didn't raise. I thought it was very funny. It must be a dream. I tried again. Well, what do you know? Neither of my arms will move forward. The whole idea seemed like a joke. I stopped and had a chuckle. In fact everything seemed a little funny.

But, I felt I had to take inventory of my faculties. Funny, I would have never said it like that in the past. Then it hit me. I was secured by something and I was lying on the floor. The funny part of the situation must have come from some sort of drug. So laying there didn't seem too bad. But my mind kept sending out a warning. It was saying "No you fool, everything is not ok!" And I would send some thoughts back: "Oh . . . I feel ok. What's the big deal?" And my mind shot back. "Your bound and lying on the floor Monkey brains. And what's worse, you don't know what they have planned for you."

And then, after a few seconds my mind, who at this point, had turned into another person that I didn't like very well, started rocking the boat even more. So this other insulting person (my mind) continued. "Hey Spinach for Brains, have you looked around?" and I answered: "Yes . . . it's not so bad . . . in fact I might just take a little nap." And now my mind was mad. "Look "toothbrush face", you are in a bad situation and in case you haven't noticed, Anna and Max are gone." I slowly looked around and sure enough both Anna and Max were not in the room. Slowly, my "real self" started to come out of the fog that the drugs had induced.

Everything didn't come back all at once. In fact, at one point, I guess I relapsed. I started thinking about the nap again. I spoke to that stupid blob in my head. This time I meant business. "Hey, who ever you are . . . I'm going to take a nap and forget about this whole inane business." But my mind just kept hitting at me: "Look, Sherlock, it doesn't take a genius to figure out what has happened to you. If you don't try to come up with a way out of this, you are going to wind up being "fish food". At that point, I had had all I could take. I spoke softly but directly to my brain: "I am going to take this nap if I have to pour butter over Rome . . ." I relaxed my head back to the floor and prepared for a nice summer long sleep.

But then, I started to come back to consciousness. "Well . . . Maybe I could try to get up" But the nap still sounded good. With my muscles fighting against the material bonding my wrists, blood started to flow back. I came back to the present. One wrist was not as secure as the other. I worked and worked. Finally the bond gave way and I had one hand free. I brought the material around from behind me and saw it for the first time. It was some sort of green plastic formed into a rectangular box. It appeared as if it had been poured over my wrists. The green block looked familiar, but I couldn't place it. Somewhere in the last few days I had seen the same material.

I was just working my hand out of the second block when the door opened and a man in sandals and a white robe walked in. Quickly I put my hands behind my back closed my eyes and laid still. The sandaled feet approached me and stood there for several minutes. A second helper followed the man in a white robe. He spoke slowly: "Is this the man?" The helper checked the board then pulled out a small device and clicked on an area near my neck. The device beeped and registered a serial number. The helper checked the serial number against his clip board.

Then: "Yes Sir. This is the man. #4037756123." The man in a white robe just stood there for several minutes. Then: "You've got all his "aged affects?" The man checked the clip board and then looked around the room. Then: "Yes sir. Archives started working last night. They say it's everything they have." The man in the Robe took the clip board and signed it. Then handed it back to the helper and then said: "Very well. Send him to the grinder. With that, the man with the sandals; the helper following close behind, turned and walked out. The door shut and I lay in silence.

I was in full control of my faculties now. I slowly moved my head to allow me to view the room more fully. There were a number of piles of items in the room. I had not noticed them before mainly because I was still arguing with my stupid brain. At first, I could not focus on what was in the piles. But sometime later, I started to come out of it and, I found I could see. One pile had just eye glasses. One pile had single socks. One had a broken bicycle chain. One had a number of mechanical pencils. A strange pile in one corner had traffic lights stuck on yellow.

I pulled off the block on my wrist and raised myself to a walking position. Then, slowly I stepped over to examine the piles of materials. My first thought was that some of these things look familiar, but I kept checking the boxes and baskets for more clues. There was a big vat with cat vomit in it. Next to it was a pile of socks soiled with cat vomit. I remember stepping in a lot of that. I saw a number of shirts with ink stains at the pocket where someone had put a pen in a pocket with the pen point still out.

There were white shirts with spaghetti spills on them. There were cheap reading glasses that had all come apart. There was bicycle chain that had broken and I'm sure someone had a nice bump with that one. You know I remember that happening to me when I was a kid. I almost had a rupture. Then, something very odd caught my eye. A pile 6 feet tall of used toilet paper. I couldn't believe it. (You won't read this kind of thing from other Authors) Why would that be in here? It smelled to high heaven. I looked closer. I moved several clumps with a rod I found near by.

The one thing in common, that all the toilet paper clumps had, was that there was a hole in the middle of each clump as if some one was using the toilet paper clump and it had broken causing the persons fingers to plunge into . . . well you know where. I know that has happened to me hundreds of times.

Anyway . . . I moved on. There was a door at the end of the room that I had not noticed before. I slowly crept up to the door and peered around the corner. In the room were racks of more odd items. I saw some skates and a dog leash lying together. I remembered when I took my dog for a run while I had skates on. The dog had pulled just fine until we came to a down slopping hill. I got going too fast and tried to stop using the toe runner as a break. I, of course, had gone head over heals down the hill. I hurt myself a number of places.

Then, more shirts with stains. I noted they were all my size. Then my old soap box racer. I couldn't believe it. It was the one that I had run into a concrete block wall with. I knew it was mine because it was all crumpled up in the front. Then it hit me! I had to stop and catch my breath.

These were all mine. They were from my past. Oh my God! Every item in both rooms was from my past. One other link, they all represented something that had failed or gone wrong in my life. Then that was it. This place was a museum of my past torments. Someone had meticulously kept everything that had caused me pain or suffering, from the mechanical pencils that always broke the lead to the Yellow Malibu car from my college days. The car was in the corner with a smashed in passenger side just as it had happened. I was stunned. I had to sit on the floor and gaze at the odd assortment. There was the skate board that had been hanging on the garage wall of the house I bought after I first got married. It had hung on the garage wall for 6 months. I never touched it. But there was that one Saturday morning when I just could not stop myself.

I had placed one foot on and as I raised my other foot to find my true fame in the world. I had instead, found the concrete drive at about 20 miles an hour. Then of course, this was just the invitation to pain. For eight months after that, I had a pain spiraling down my right leg. After a while it went away. Looking back it does beg the question: "How can you get the most bang out of someone who is already hurt?" I would find out later that true torment is taking someone from completely fit to unimaginable pain and then back to normal life.

I looked further. There were old rubber bands that had snapped and stung my fingers. The Bee that had stung me as I rode on a boat in the middle of the lake was mounted in a little box. There was an x-ray of my hurt knee that still bothers me today.

There was my old travel bag that once you put something in, you never found it again. And, of course there was a computer in the corner with my mysteriously shrinking bank account. Money put in that account, vanished slowly, so that you would not notice until of course you needed the money. Maybe it had all been part of a much larger plan.

CHAPTER **45**

High school memories

I had just opened a set of log books with entries from my High school days. There were pictures of my good guy friends who had been killed. The pain of the loss was still there. There was a picture of me with a cast on my foot. Bill Brunner had come down on my foot when we were playing touch football in the gym. And there was a picture of the rock that had hit me in the middle of the forehead when I was in a rock fight as a 6th grader. And, there was the BB gun that shot my thumb as I foolishly dropped a BB down the barrel. Oh . . . and there was the football helmet that I threw up in on my first football trip. I got car sick on the bus. I had to wear the helmet for the whole game.

Suddenly the door opened and the man with the sandals and white robe came in. I had no time to put on a sleep act. They probably were watching me the whole time. He spat out his words: "Yes, you guessed it, Mr Reed, these are all your torments." He looked around the room and continued his sneer. Then: "A meager collection. You are getting off easy." I backed up a little. He looked at me again and did a funny thing with his mouth as he spoke: "Yes, if I were calling the shots, we would have gotten a lot more CT's out of you."

He looked at me as if he knew my question. Then, as if I was a compete idiot he spoke louder in case the drool from my buck teeth had caused me to loose part of my hearing. He yelled: "CONTROLLED TORMENTS!" Then: "You know Mr Reed, we have been with you for a long time." He reflected a minute. Then" We did get many "JLASEM's" out of your life. He looked at me again as if to help a complete mental cripple. Then he helped me with the acronym: "Joyful laughter at someone else's misfortune". He stopped a minute then: "But don't blame us. It was a training lesson for you." I thought a moment then I said: "You mean you really loved me and wanted to help me and the way you did it was through my misfortune?" He stopped a minute taken back by my insightfulness. Then: "Yes" Still in surprise. "Yes, how did you guess?" I looked down and kicked the floor. I was going to say more but thought better of it. I held my temper and spoke softly: "Oh, I think I read the classic comic book." He quickly came out of the love trance he had been in and continued with the business at hand.

He turned and faced me. He looked very angry. He continued almost yelling: "I said your getting off easy . . . You only had 24678 Vectors. Most people have twice that when they are taken out of service.' He spat on the ground and then said: "You must have made someone really mad!" I just stood there stammering. It was all I could do to whisper: "Where are my friends?" He kicked something on the floor. I think it might have been some of the gutters on my first house that did not carry any water. All they did was fill up with water and then bend in the middle letting the water flow over the side like a water fall. He was not listening to me at all now. Then: "We have followed you for a long time. And, we know why you are here?"

Never at a loss for words, I jumped into the middle with: "You mean the ice cream franchise." I put my hands in my pockets and then: "Yes, I was here to get permission to set up four kiosks in your main mall area." The man stared at me and then he started shaking: "Don't Bullshit me!" Then: "You know how much trouble you have caused this District? The Director is irate and I'm not much better!" He seemed to calm down a little, but he was still red in the face. Then resolved, he said: "You know what Mr Reed, it will all be over soon anyway." He checked his clip board. Then: "You'll meet up with your friend on the conveyor belt."

With that he threw the clip board in a trash can near by as if figured he didn't need to keep records on my case anymore and headed for the door. As a last thought he turned and said: "We tired to reason with you." He stopped and put his hand on the door frame as if to steady himself. Then with a very emotional tone he said: "Man was made to endure hardships." He thought for a moment and then: "We just help him find the right ones." He almost had a tear in his eye. He thought a moment and then: "Some day you would have understood, but now that day will never come."

I jumped in: "A sort of fraternity." Then I narrowed it a little: "A Fraternity of "victims".

He hissed at me for a few seconds and then as an afterthought he said: "That may have been true, but you have a different function now." He turned and slammed the door behind him. I couldn't help it. I had to put one more comment in as I yelled at the closed door: "My names not Reed either!" I stood there thinking, but nothing else came to mind. I said to myself: "Ok, Mr. Mind. Where are you now, when I really need some help? What, the cat got your tongue?" There was a complete silence. Well Mr. Brain, where are you? Are you on a siesta? No help when I really need it? I thought so. Well, without any other thoughts, I rushed the door. But it was locked. This was another predicament I would have to think myself out of.

I sat down on the floor and leaned against the wall. I was angry, upset and sad all at the same time. I would have to work out a plan. I knew Anna was in peril as well. I was not about to let these pompous self appointed jerks guide my life or as he just said, end it. But then it hit me. The slug that had just been in here said "Friend". That was singular. That had to mean that the "Skank" Max was working with them. I knew it all along. If I ever see that "garbage sack" again, I will take that artificial age he has going, and make it real.

I was deep in thought when I noticed that a machine that looked kind of like a large soda machine was moving toward me. I thought that very odd. I reached into my pocket to get some change. Then I decided it might not have the kind of pop I liked. It whirred a little and then moved forward a little and then stopped. A few seconds would go by and it would go through the same procedure. The only thing that bothered me was that it was headed straight for me. I got up as it approached me. I was about to move out of the way when it shot out a green jelly. The jelly sprayed all over me. I said "Hey! Watch it! I just got this shirt cleaned!"

But, before I could put in another insult, the jelly had hardened and I was frozen in place. I tried to kick. I tried to flex my arms, but I was stuck in some sort of green block. As the block completely hardened, it hit me. This was the same stuff I had on my wrists when I was thrown in here. I flexed all my muscles one more time but instead of helping I only rocked the block I was bound in enough to cause it to fall on it's side. I lay there looking like a hard "Jello" salad, and I was the fruit.

My feet were sticking out and two hands which I placed forward at the last minute and my head were sticking out, but the rest of my "beat up" body was trussed up hard. Things had gone from bad to worse. I lay there like a package ready for pick up.

And sure enough, the door opened again and in came a fork lift driven by a Dwarf sitting on a wooden box. He had an Aviator's hat on to signify his rank among the lesser dwarfs. These guys were not fooling around at least the management wasn't. I don't think the Dwarf gave a shit. He was eating a giant chicken leg with one hand and deftly wheeling the big machine with the other. He never even glanced at me, but accurately placed the lifting bars under my green block and raised me into the air. Then, with a shift of gears, he backed up and headed for the hall way. The door opened automatically. Once in the hall we jumped into high gear and were rumbling down the hall. My feet were close to being ground off by rough textured wall. After several minutes, we approached a double door and again the doors open automatically.

The room we charged into was another hangar sized room. I could not move my head much, but I could see that the corner we were headed for had hundreds of green blocks. I found myself singing a little melody with the words. I think it was: "It's all over but the shouting." All joking aside, it looked like the whole pile was set to be "ground up" for bug food. I always knew I had been selected for a higher calling.

Another fork lift entered the room this time driven by the another Dwarf on the feeding arm. It was obvious that these two little people did not like each other. As the forklifts passed the one with the chicken leg threw it at the other. It hit him in the face and caused him to swerve. The swerve caused his machine to brush against sides of the first machine. When this happened, the Dwarf that through chicken leg shrieked in anger. He dropped me on the pile and quickly whirled around to face his attacker. Then with blinding speed he placed his machine in gear and raced toward the other fork lift at ramming speed.

A group of Dwarf workers had just finished a work shift and were walking back through the larger hangar like room, when they saw the stand off of the fork lifts. Quickly they pulled boxes off a shelf nearby and formed a make shift bleachers. One dark headed one on the top row yelled: "Go papa Jake!" Papa Jake was the favorite. He was facing off against a younger man called "Winner Bill", who usually lived up to his name. Winner Bill was never happy with anything and now he had had it with Papa Jake. WB was some what of a mechanic and had already "souped" up his fork lift. He reached behind the seat and adjusted the "Governor Cable" running to the large electric motor. The cable had already been tinkered with, so unscrewing the governor stop was not much of a problem.

CHAPTER **46**

The joust

With the governor cable loose, WB's machine seemed to become the monster it had only dreamed of becoming before. WB sat there looking at Papa Jake out of the corner of his eye as he "reved" the giant electric motor. At the same time he had slammed on the front parking brakes.

The result was screaming machine with smoking back wheels. The old fork lift would eat human gizzards tonight. The first six layers of rubber turned smoking hot and finally flew off the wheel. At the other end Papa Jake had already started for WB's machine when he realized that this was more than vengeance. It was a chance to become a "legend" and he felt he was Dwarf enough to show the gallery what true heroism could be. So instead of just slamming into the other fork lift he too joined into the violent dance. He was also handy with the fork lift. He professionally manipulated the control lever on his machine to cause it to go back and forth like a jumping mechanical monster. It leaped wildly. He made a clucking noise as the machine spat rubber out the back. The whole picture made him and his machine look a giant smoking chicken.

Then one of the dwarfs sitting in the audience went over to wall and grabbed two long grappling hooks. Quickly, he ran by each one throwing a pole at each contestant. Another dwarf in the audience screamed out: "Now we got us a "joust" goin!" The others clapped and yelled. A third Dwarf had run over to a candy machine and using his master keys, had opened up the contents to the crowd. They jumped for joy as they devoured the chocolate candy treats.

The two jousters backed up to each respective side of the building. Then almost as if no time had passed at all, there was a tremendous screeching. Smoke poured from each end of the building as the giant machines lurched forward. There was only one yell from the crowd before they hit. The pole held by Papa Jake found it's mark first. WB went flying off his steel mount. The forklift's dead man's switch stopped the machine from plowing into the wall.

But the electric motor didn't die. It sat there rumbling as if waiting for WB to remount. WB lay in a heap in the corner spread eagle on some old boxes. The Dwarf audience had risen to their feet and in unison and were tongue lashing WB. They yelled as loud as they could: "Hey WB, get up you piece a shit! . . ." Then they looked around to see if everyone agreed. They did. Then: "Get your ass back in that seat! It aint over yet." WB surprised everybody. He did get up. He staggered a little at first but then got a menacing look on his face as he stared at the old man on the far side of the building. Then he grabbed his pole and started to fiddle with the hook end. In another few seconds the hook end popped off and there was nothing on the tip but the socket end meant to allow replacement of the hook. Instead of replacing the hook with another new hook, he grabbed a small screw driver and crammed it into the socket opening. Now he had a lance. It wasn't pretty, like you see in the movies. The blade of the screwdriver didn't glisten in the light from above. It just lay there waiting to strike.

The screw driver was held firmly in the tip of the pole and anyone lucky enough to be on the receiving end of the lance would certainly feel it in the morning; maybe the rest of his life, which might be short. Papa Jake had been watching and wasn't sure just what WB had done. It was too far across the room to get a good enough look at what the young fool was doing. But the Dwarf audience had decided to keep the contest fair.

So a "thuggy" looking small man named "Pudden" came limping up to Papa Jakes forklift and because "Pudden" didn't like to talk, he made motions showing that WB had altered his pole. Papa Jake now was furious. He pulled out his big swatch blade knife and grabbed a roll of duct tape next to him, held by a rope on the wall. With a few skillful wraps of the duct tape, Papa Jake now had a very evil looking weapon. Maybe it wasn't the weapon of death, but it sure got your attention. It glistened as if it had a soul of its own and was anticipating some soft sinewy human chest that it could tear into. Papa Jake had just finished setting his knife in place when he heard the screeching of WB's machine. WB had jumped the gun.

The Dwarf audience started yelling about not letting Papa Jake get ready. But WB didn't see any judges, so in his mind he figured he'd make his own rules. By the time Papa Jake had revved up his machine, WB was already half way across the room. In a few seconds one of the two contestants would be the proud recipient of the seriously sharp end of a "home-made" lance. Well, in WB's case it would be the dull end of a lance. But coming at 30 miles per hour, if the screw driver took a bite first, there would be no quibbling. It would tear into its target just a wickedly as if it were an expensive saber, maybe even worse.

I once worked as a State worker assigned to administer State contracts. My area was the South East corner of the State but the big prison was in the North East end of the State. A girl was assigned to that area, but the supervisors didn't like her going out there, so they gave that project to me too. On the same grounds as the men's prison was the women's prison. I had to go out to review any work a State Contractor had done and to determine if it was in compliance with the Contract Documents. Well, they called me one day when I was scheduled to be looking at some work that had just been completed in the women's prison. They said: "Sir, I know you are scheduled to be out here today, but a guard was just killed by one of the women inmates." I said: "Oh?" Then thinking about how many times I had walked by the women prisoners. I asked: "How was he killed?" There was a silence and then the person on the other end of the phone said: "A spoon." Then silence. Then: "They killed him with a dull spoon into his ribs." I thought about this a minute and then said: "Ok, yes sir, no problem. I don't need to be out there today anyway." Missing that little drama was just fine with me. We hung up. But, the rest of the day I thought about how slow you might die when cut by a blunt instrument.

The screaming motors brought me back to reality. This time the two little sluggers would hit and one or both might not be working for GREMIS any more, or anyone else for that matter. Smoke filled the room. The two machines were about to smash together when a chiming sound came over the room speakers. "Bing Bing, Bing!"

All the Dwarfs sitting in the gallery, rose slowly with eyes as big a saucers. They seemed completely hypnotized. The jousters were also affected by the chiming, but they were set on a collision course. The driver's eyes also went bug eyed. One even started to climb off his motorized mount as it sped forward. But the forklifts were not affected by the chiming and were set to hit. "Kaboom!" Both machines smacked together. The drivers had dropped their "lances", but there was no stopping the crash. Both little men went flying into the air. One hit on some barrels and one hit against the wall. Both received tremendous blows. They lay there in their respective heaps for a few minutes, but then they slowly rose to a sitting position and stared at the members of the dwarf audience, who were now marching toward a door that had opened at the far end of the room. The jousters surprisingly got to their feet and followed. Both were bleeding in numerous parts of their bodies, but they didn't seem to notice. I lay in my green prison completely mesmerized.

Some signal was calling the group of watchers to an unknown place. They all were spirited out under some hypnotic control as they headed out in the hall. Their eyes were wide and completely blank. One of the Dwarfs rubbed his eyes and looked around for a second, but then went back into a trance as the group marched out. I lay there in shock for a few minutes. Nothing else happened. It got quiet in the room. The automatic lights went off. I lay there in my prison. I was just drifting off for a small nap when the door opened again and another fork lift appeared. It was the gorilla man from the Bug feeding room. I almost felt like we were friends.

I think he still had body parts on his shirt sleeves or maybe that was just my imagination. I found myself wanting to wave at him. It seemed like we were at least acquaintances, maybe more. He wiped his face with an oily rag and headed for me guiding his forklift as if he were cleaning up some accident. He picked me up deftly and proceeded to move me through an odd smaller door at the end of the room.

CHAPTER 47

The grinder

He dropped me with several other green box shaped blobs on the floor in the middle of the smaller room. I looked around as much as I could. I was completely a prisoner. I had just noticed a conveyor belt on the far side of the room when my gel prison was jolted roughly. Several other blobs had been dropped on me.

I was just getting use to the whole routine when I focused on the insides of the blobs that had just become part of my pile. I was shocked. It was the Dwarf gallery. I stared at them for a minute making sure I had identified the little revelers. Yep, it was them. Someone up stairs hadn't liked their "jousting" on Company time. They had cheered their last cheer.

Now, I looked back at the conveyor belt. The Gorilla man was over at the far end loading the green blocks on a humming belt. In the distance I could hear a giant machine grinding something up. It didn't take a "rocket scientist" to figure out that we were all going to be made into in a few minutes. That was: "bug salad". We were going down the belt whether we liked it or not. Then the complete thought hit me. We were going to be ground up into little "bite sized" pieces and fed to the bugs. I was in quite a pickle. The fork lift slowly loaded the conveyor belt and we all were being pushed closer to the "business end" of the machine in the slot at the end of the room. I would have about 3 minutes to figure out what to do.

I thought my deepest thoughts. It made my head hurt. I racked my brain. But, my three minutes were up and I had come up with exactly "zero" plans. My green jail was lifted into the air and dropped harshly on the conveyor. Strangely, my block didn't sit flat. The green blob in front of me was holding up one end of my green prison. My eyes were glazing over with the thoughts of being laid out in a feed bin in tiny pieces, wondering which bugs would eat me, when all of a sudden my eyes focused on the blob in front of me that was holding me at an angle on the belt. There was a person inside the blob held fast by the green block. The person looked at me as if it wanted to quickly tell me something, but alas, no luck. The person was bound in a mass of green brine.

My mind raced. I knew that person. It was . . . It was . . . Anna! I thought to myself: "Oh no . . . My Anna . . . She's going into the grinding machine with all the rest of us. What can I do?" It all was happening too fast. I strained against my bounds, but I was held fast. Then, almost without further notice Anna's block dropped on to a faster moving belt below my belt. I could see that she had about thirty seconds to live and I couldn't do anything. Sure enough, her green box dropped a few more feet and flew into a mouth full of giant blades. I screamed in dismay.

I pulled against my bonds. I ripped at my mussels but all to no avail. Pieces of green flew everywhere. I cried. I screamed again. And to make matters worse I was next. My block also fell on the faster moving belt and jerked forward following Anna's block. But then my block stopped. I looked up and saw a giant rope lassoed around me. Slowly I was lifted off the conveyor and set on a side shelf.

There was a long silence. Then a boot kicked the side of my green block. I couldn't quite see who it belonged to. Shortly after, a large chisel hit the top of my block and the block started to crack. After 15 minutes and the use of a pry bar, I was free, but just lying there is sorrow. I was ready to end my life. I looked up to my savior and was about to ask him to help me end my life. But then the site of his face made my eyes bug out. It was Max! The Scank! I didn't know whether to cry or rage at him. He quickly put his hand over my mouth and started to whisper. I was not in any mood to listen to this lunatic's excuses. I tried to lift my arm to smash him in the face, but to my surprise I found I could not do it. I just lay there like a sack of potatoes. Max looked at my strained expression and realized that I didn't have any idea what was happening. He whispered again: "You are ok. Just lie still until the drug inside the gel wears off.

I said something that didn't make any sense. Well, actually it made sense to me, but maybe to no one else. It went something like this: "It's time to change the rug racks in my jeans. Do you have the polisher?" It made complete sense to me. Why do you ask monkey brains? Actually, maybe it was a little weird. Anyway, time passed. Then the next words I heard that I understood were: "Renn, you've got to snap out of it! We've got to get out of here and we don't have much time."

Then I found myself saying "Anna . . . Anna . . . I saw her . . ." Max quieted me softly and I will remember this for all times. He said: "That wasn't Anna. It was her clone" I was now regaining some of my wits, which weren't that many on a good day. But, that's a different story and I am worried that we won't get through this one. Anyway, back to Max. I jerked a little as what he was saying fed into all orifices of my body. I was saying "What?" and he was saying: "It wasn't Anna!" I must have passed out. I don't remember. All I recall was waking up in a small closet under a back stair way. Max the "Skank" was gone, but he had left a loaf of bread. I tore into it ravenously. On the door was a note: "Stay put. I'll be back soon. Max".

I had just drifted off to sleep. Being the "fruit" inside a block of green Jell-O is more than I usually do. Sleep seemed the only way. I had some serious napping to catch up on. But just as I was between the clouds and the deep blue sea, some very pretty hands placed a pan of food in front of me. I looked up expecting to be carried off to become a dinner for large ridgeback beetles or something worse. But the hands that placed the pan in front of me belonged to . . . wait for it! . . . Anna! I tried to get up, but my back had been strained in the escape ordeal and I found myself sitting where I had been placed. My expression must have given my confusion away. She saw my dilemma and knelt down to hug me. I could not contain myself. "Oh . . . Anna . . ." She looked at me and placed her finger over my lips. She quieted me with: "SHHHHHH". I needed to tell her more.

I started again: "But I saw you drop on to the conveyor and . . . you got ground up!" She looked at me as if she wanted to tell me everything, but instead shook her head. "I know sweetie . . . I have a lot to tell you, but first eat some food. Then, we have to meet Max at the other end of building #6." I looked at her intensely, and then: "Max?" a long moment and then: "Max the Skank? . . . , the one who he ratted us out, the one who spilled the beans, the one who turned us in for "corn flakes?" She only shook her head.

Then she said: "Max can explain it . . . It is not what it appears to be" Then she paused as she looked into my eyes. "Max has been protecting us . . . I know it's hard to see." I grabbed my back and said: "With Max as my friend, who needs any enemies?" I chuckled a little. It was very confusing. One moment Max seemed to be snared in the trap with Anna and me and the next minute he is gone.

Then when everything looks the bleakest Max is dropping a rope to pull me out of the "grinder". No, it would take some convincing. I didn't just come in on a hay truck yesterday. You can fool me some of the time or whatever that famous politician said . . . just joking with myself.

We would meet with Max soon, and when he told his tale, I would be all ears. He had better be on target with his details. Otherwise, we might find out if the grinder will take objects without green blocks around them. Max might be the first to find out and I would be there to show him the way.

Our plans took another dive when the wall to the closet under the stairs smashed in. The huge tire of a forklift had crumpled the sheet rock and studs like butter. Both Anna and I were thrown to the opposite wall. Laying there we looked up to see Gorilla man reading a girly magazine as he drove through the area. He must have come to an extra "steamy" part. For sure, he was not concentrating on his driving. If we had been any closer to the wall, we might have been eating "tire sandwiches". As it happened he continued on down the hall to some other assigned job. But no one told him he couldn't have a little entertainment on the way.

CHAPTER **48**

The control room

We watched closely until he turned the corner in the hall. Then we pried the closet door open. After some coaxing from Anna I was on my feet and ready for the next debacle. Anna took the lead and we followed the hall that "gorilla man" had used. Instead of following him turning right as he did at the end of the hall, we turned left and immediately went down an industrial type metal stair. The light was faint as we got to the bottom of the stairs. There at the end of the hall was Max "the skank". He was sitting on several boxes he had piled up and looking intently through a glass window into a room with a low light level. I started to grab Max and throw him down but Anna stopped me. She said: "Wait . . . let him tell his story" I looked at her in mistrust, but finally acquiesced.

Max raised his hand asking for quiet. He motioned to me to pull up some more boxes. With both Anna and I seated, he began to explain what we were watching. Max started: "You see each one of the "Hoodsmen" on the computers is monitoring several events happening to "Outlanders". I looked on and watched. Most of the Hoodsmen were bent over computer screens actively watching "split screens". Max spoke: "The "Hoodsmen" who have been here the longest can monitor up to ten people on one screen. Then they handle even more of the poor bastards by "tabbing" though to second and third screens. They keep close tabs on their assigned poor souls. I watched and saw that the "thugs" were very focused. Well, actually most were, except for two slumped over Hoodsmen in the corner. Both had a bottle of something. I suppose they were on break. A funny thought ran through my mind. "They had been breaking someone and now they were on break". Ha ha, I couldn't get the thought out of my head. What a "corn ball" I am.

Sure enough, I could just barely see what was happening on the screen directly in front of us. A man in a brief case was walking along when what should happen? He slipped and fell. We watched him get up. Obviously hurt, but not bad enough to go to the Hospital, the man tried to fix his wounds. It would be just bad enough to keep him in misery for several weeks. The Hoodsman noted the event on some kind of tabulator to his side. Another part of the same screen showed a boy lying in bed with poison ivy. The boy was miserable. He lay with sheets completely off so as to not cause any additional itching.

Yet another part of the screen showed someone waiting at a railroad crossing for twenty five minutes as a long line of rail cars went by. Another part of the screen shows a man waiting in line at the Post Office. The line has gone down to just him. There's no one else there. He stands there politely waiting for the Post Man to ask how he can help the man. But the Post Man is busy filing letters and does not ask. The man stands there and waits and waits. Finally the post man looks up and realizes the man needs help. The post man blurts out: "Do you need help?"

Of course I couldn't help editing the whole scene in my head. I answered in my mind: "No, I am just standing here holding the floor down.The Contractor on the floor below believes that if someone does not do this, the floor will fly up and possibly go out the window". Or, I think further: "No, I am doing a report of "dumb asses". I thought I would drop by and get your name and ID number." Or: "No, I just had a back brace placed down my spine and the damn thing has jammed. Can you call maintenance?" The Post man of course says: "Oh . . . You looked like you had already been helped". I wandered off in my mind thinking about what a person looks like. I mean how do you look, when you look like a person who has already been helped? Do you stand there with an extra pleasant expression on your face?

A Hoodsman in a special black hooded outfit was located right in the middle of the group. He must have had more rank. Anyway his screens showed nothing but natural disasters. One screen showed rivers rushing through small towns as if the town had been built right next to the river bank. Huge storms had brought torrential rains. The rivers had come alive. They were devouring everything. People were seen in complete devastation. Everything they had owned was lost.

Another screen showed tornados cutting through populated areas like a chain saw cuts through soft wood trees. The damage was unbelievable. Cars were shown piled on top of each other. But the main focus was on the people. He was graphing how much they could take. A "Hoodsman" next to the one directly in front of me was feverishly noting something on his side "tabulator". I strained to see what was on his screen. His computer was tied to a camera in another part of the building. There were all sorts of moving things on his screen. I could not make out what they were. Then, the Hoodsman caused the camera to pull back a little and I was shocked. The view was of a flat filled with green food for raising bugs! Yes, they were hatching right before my eyes.

The Hoodsman was busy estimating the size of the "brood". He entered data as fast as his pudgy hands could move. The data was somehow tied to a big graph on the monitor placed on the wall in front of all the Hoodsman. As the bugs started to grow and flow over the hatching boxes, lights flashed on the monitor. Several Hoodsman stopped a few seconds and looked back at the "Bug Hatcher" Hoodsman. They were jubilant. They cheered at the Bug man. They Director would be pleased.

Suddenly several lighted monitors flashed on. A bell sounded. All the Hoodsman stopped working and looked up. It was an order from the Director. Large black letters came across the screen. They read: "Brethren! We need more accidents. Numbers 10, 14, 15 and 17. You are falling back. I will expect the numbers to increase by 11:00am. Don't forget your quotas. Otherwise . . ." The message repeated two more times and then both large screens went blank. I could tell there was a chill in the air inside the Hoodsmen's room. All the workers leaned forward in great concentration started working furiously with their computers.

Ok . . . I've got to take a minute here. You won't see this in many books. I've got to tell you that I just spent the last 2 hours trying to get back this manuscript. I was typing away when something went wrong. I tried a few keys and all of a sudden my whole book was reduced to two letters. "cc". I am not making this up. This book was started in jest. I never really thought I would hit a nerve. Maybe I did, maybe I didn't. But, only a few minutes ago the book was lost. You might say: "But Renn, haven't you been saving your work as you go?"

And, I would say: "Of course". But there are always factors aren't there. The factor here is that I just updated my "Word" program. I have been all over this new program trying to find a place where the 180 pages or so were saved. I save every time I quit, so you would think I would be current. No my friends. That is not the case. Some genius was hired to make things easier. But . . . Rather than get lost trying to explain what happened, let it suffice to say that the complete writing disappeared. Now that is something to think about. After much a due, I am back. I still have lost three pages. Not a big loss. I can remember most of what I said. I won't get caught again. Also notice that this incident only caused me to stay up and add more content to this document.

CHAPTER **49**

Back to the story.

Max leaned forward and motioned to us to quietly move off the boxes and follow him. We moved quietly down the hall and into a small room. Max whispered: "That's just one on many control rooms. They require each Hoodsman or at least the smarter ones to spend time in the tabulation rooms. Each Hoodsman has 8 cells on his screen with each cell showing a torment that the Hoodsman is inflicting. Then the same computer controls a number of "tabs" to different screens. In all, each Hoodsman might be working on 80 Outlanders at the same time. The poor sods don't even know what is being thrust upon them. They actually believe it's their fault." I was enraged. I blurted out: "But you were in the middle of the whole thing!" I paused and then: "You spoke to the people on the City Center stage." Max looked down and then: "I know how it looked, but I can explain." He paused and then: "While I was sleeping in your basement hideout the Hoodsmen surrounded the area and several broke into the basement room. They caught me completely off guard. They took me to the Directors Office and told me that they would give me power and money." I started in: "But you were so convincing!"

Max looked up and started to speak but instead rushed to the door and carefully opened it a small amount and looked down the hall. Quickly he shut the door and whispered: "We've got to get out of here. They're coming. They've get a thermal imaging device. They can see right through walls." With that we followed him through a door at the other end of the room and down a small corridor. Somehow, we got out of the building. It was dark and we had no trouble in finding my car. It had been a long day. Max still wanted to finish his explanation that he started when we were frightened off by the imaging device.

We jumped in the car and proceeded to vacate the parking lot and head for home. Max, grabbing the back door handle said: "You never asked me what I did before GREMIS took over."

I was looking back and a little worried, but I saw that he needed to tell me. I said: Ok . . . What?" Max jumped in right away: "I was an Actor!" I mulled it over as I fumbled with my keys. I said: "Oh . . . I see. I guess that would explain how you were so convincing." Anna spoke: "Renn, he's telling the truth. I saw them working with him. They knew what he could do. The Director's speech, coming from an Outlander would be very convincing." I shook my head and said: "Ok, I will think about it. But I still have some questions."

I was pulling out of the parking lot, except I had to wait for the one car that would come by, one in 3 hours. It would be exactly where I would hit it if I pulled out without looking. Then we proceeded to head out of the city. Our drive was uneventful except for the 13 yellow lights and the 4 trains crossing the street we were on exactly when we wanted to cross. Anna looked at me questioningly: "Does this happen often?" I just shook my head and said: "It's a long story". She looked at me as if to say: "You owe me a better explanation than that." But she let it drop for the moment.

We finally got to the dirt road leading to the Cave. It actually was my Uncles land. We crept down the road with the lights off carefully observing the Cave as we went. The whole area seemed empty. It had a small shack attached to the cave entrance. The whole shack was badly in need of a paint job. Well, that was 20 years ago. Now, it was in need of a "wood job". The ship lap siding that had stood pristine against the weather a number of years ago, now was held together by the vines that grew between the boards.

The siding, barely hanging on the roof, had given up the ghost for sure. It was covered with blue tarps. They were courtesy of our boys, the FEMA inspectors. Except in this case they should have gotten out of their car. The shack was falling down, but not because it had been hit by a big storm. Anyway I was happy to receive the help.

There was only one bed. All three of us piled in and we were fast asleep in a few minutes. Before sleep took over, I looked in Anna's eyes and told her that I loved her. She smiled and hugged me closely. Max started to snore, but we were both too tired to care. Later that night, I got up. I had some thinking to do. Things had gotten very complicated. Here I was facing a group that had man's torementation as their main purpose in life. Notice that "torementation" is not recognized as a word. I wonder why? Maybe it would cause too much attention. So the word was set to "never exist". Don't spend much time checking on this or you might draw more attention to yourself than you really want. Of course it's up to you.

This whole process, that of slowly breaking a man down with little events was grating at me. They thought that man would just take this in stride and always carry the greater burden until his back broke. Whoever was doing this I didn't know who, but I was determined to have one last kick in the kidneys if it was the last thing I did. And maybe it would be. But since I started my little manuscript I had been had balls of every kind of misery thrown at me. I had been beaten and thrown in jail. I had been berated and had my complete history thrown in a trash can. Finally I had been sprayed into a green block and sent to a grinder. I sat there and got angrier and angrier. I reached into my inner self to find the last bit of energy to fight them just as I had done with the "Dust" man. I would go after them one last time except this time I would have a plan.

I fell back asleep shortly before dawn and woke up an hour later to the smell of biscuits and coffee. Anna had gotten up and seeing me asleep, was completely unaware of my furry in the night. I got up and hugged her. She looked at me with surprise. It felt almost like a "going away" hug, but I told her nothing.

Later that morning, I put the red scarf on the bottom of my mail box out by the main street. Anyone seeing it might just think it was laying on the ground next to the wooden post that held up the metal mail box. However, it was a sign to the Bums that I wanted a meeting. They had all started to call me "Mirror Man" but I waved off the compliments. "Self pride" could only lead to failure. In 24 hours I would have the Bum leaders from the various sections of the City sitting in council. Before I left this shack to go to the City Center meeting and speeches a day ago, I had gotten some of the Bums to clear out an old barn behind the house. We built several benches. It would be a good place for the first full meeting of BAG. (Bums Against GREMIS.) It was sort of catchy, but not perfect. We had to make do. After all, we had no marketing team. Ha ha The Bums would be here soon. I had a lot to say. And . . . there were plans to be made.

I fixed some coffee and then crept down by a small stream behind the barn. I needed to get my head on straight. Up to now we were just reacting to whatever GREMIS threw at us. Many of the Townspeople were actually moving closer to "dream time." That was the wording I had heard used to describe someone getting to the end of their Torment cycle. Of course, what happened after that was well known. Death would be looked on with concern by GREMIS because they would be losing experimental subjects. Of course that might explain why I ran into a lot more trains crossing the streets that I drove down. Instead of just trying to hold me up, maybe they were bringing in more troops.

An hour had passed and I noticed that several Bums had arrived. They sat around a fire pit at the house and told tales. They knew where I was, but respected my privacy. I got up and threw the rest of my coffee in the stream. There was something I had to do.

I walked back to the shack and said hello to the "early Bums". Then, I told them to wait while I went into the house. Max was still in his bed. I sat on the edge of his bed and waited for him to feel my presence. Shortly, he awoke and looked up at me. He knew right away that I had something to tell him. I spoke: "Max . . . I think you were telling me the truth. I don't think you intended to harm us." Max rubbed his eyes and looked at me again. Then he said: "Ok . . . but what?" I sat there for a moment. Then: "Max, there will be a number of Bum leaders here in a half hour or so." I stopped and thought about how to tell him what I need to say. Then: "Max, I need for you to stay with Anna. I have not had enough time to completely figure out what happened over the last 48 hours." . . . I paused. Then: "But please don't take this personally. I don't want you in the meeting with the Bums." Max sat up a little more and looked at me as if I had accused him of trying to kill the Pope. But then, reason returned and he simply nodded and said: "Ok Renn. I understand. I'll keep the guard up at the shack." With that I walked off and he remained silent. I had a plan that might turn the tables on GREMIS and the Director. It might be very dangerous.

The meeting with the Bums lasted most of the day. Around noon Anna came down with cans of Chili; their favorite food. During the break we laughed and talked about all the experiments we had done. They were much different than GREMIS experiments. They of course, were part of a report I was doing that might someday change everything. The Bums didn't know how the different projects connected together. I am sure Max knew. And, I was just starting to understand the GREMIS process myself. The results were still a little past me, but I had sworn to figure everything out if it put hair on Dolly Parton's chest. Yes, that was a good way to put it.

The meeting resumed after a hearty lunch. After all the Chili cans were cleaned up and thanks given again to Anna, we again made some very intricate plans. I knew at some point that I would have to let Max in on the plans because he knew the GREMIS headquarters layout. But for now, I had resolved to wait until the last minute.

The next day several trucks arrived from the Chili Factory. The owner Bill Mathews was driving one of the trucks. He got out of the truck to help unload and I noticed that he was all bent over. He was of course oblivious. GREMIS had paid him a visit and he didn't even know it. He, like everyone else, just accepted his fate. He never even gave any thought to the possibility that he was on a master list of tormented souls and that there would be many more adversities to come. I started to tell him what had been happening to him, but then decided that it would just upset him and that the best thing I could do for him is to carry out our plan. I spoke to him: "Hello Bill, thanks for the materials." He looked up at me from his hunched over position and only smiled. He was checking a clipboard with all the supplies. He completely understood why I needed broomsticks, and batteries. The word had gotten out about "Mirror Man" and he knew it was me, even though we did not speak of it. I winked at him and it completely reassured him.

One final truck carried a number of 6 foot diameter "Sona Tubes" about 15 feet tall. The tubes were used in construction to pour concrete columns. We had a somewhat different use planned for them. The Bums spent most of the night spraying the cardboard tubes black. They were to be part of a stage we were planning on building if we got approval for a meeting with the Director.

A Bum courier came by to pick up a letter I had written to the Director. I was proposing the said meeting. It was brash of me to expect to meet with someone who thought they held everyman's fate in thier hands. But on the other hand, I thought it might just appeal to his sense of theatrics. I was asking to meet on a stage for a "public debate." To my surprise, the request was immediately accepted. Of course, if it came about, both sides would have some additional surprises planned. This time however, we would try to anticipate his moves. It might be the end; the end of something. Maybe it would be the end of me. But I was mad. It was time to pull all this out on the table.

CHAPTER **50**

The Crews

The next day I woke up early. We had several crews of Bums that had gone into the GREMIS headquarters with the Director's permission. They were all following a plan that we can carefully orchestrated over the past two nights. Max still was not a part of this plan. I had told him to not be offended and that I would ask him to help us navigate the giant facility. At the same time I had had a covert unit slip in at night to take care of a few additional items that we did not want to tip off. I sat there by the fire outside on the half overgrown patio and stared into the flames. It felt like "Game day." Everyone joked outwardly, but inside they were extremely tense. There was an "air" surrounding the Bums that was almost thick enough to cut with a knife. I tried to walk away from them so they could not read the concern in my face. It would all take place this evening. Maybe the other team would be better, but we would sure have some tricks up our sleeve. It was more than a game. It was the "Super Bowl". I had given the last speech early this morning to all the Bums. I had even pulled in the Bums still running experiments.

I was hesitant to bring them in since we were close to a break through on some of the projects. For example, I had one unit working the down town area. They had orders to work several of my "try this yourself" experiments. The first one was very straight forward. I had several public restrooms staked out. One set of bums went in and used the toilets. They closed the door and sat there on the toilets with their pants down. Another group hid around the corner and were there to record how many people came into the restroom while the bums were sitting on the toilet with the door closed. The answer: None.

After that data was recorded I had them try the same experiment with the bum sitting on the toilet with their pants down, but this time the door to the toilet stall door was left open for all who walked in to see. There they were with all of their manly glory exposed to anyone who might come in. New data was recorded on this second part of the experiment. The answer: Out of 25 tries where the door was left open, 23 had people walk in and were surprised to see the Bum on the toilet seat. Very interesting. #1120.

A second group was working with Clorox. I had them in a wash room doing daily chores. However, one group had dark pants on and one group had light pants on. After 25 separate washing attempts in the laundry rooms, it was noted that 20 washing attempts got Clorox on the dark pants. The lighter pants did not receive any stains. A second part of the experiment was an "add on" to the primary experiment. It was determined that 12 pairs of dark pants were expensive and 13 pairs of dark pants were not. The conclusion: All expensive pants were stained. Out of the 13 pairs of inexpensive pants still left, only 4 pairs had stains. #1121.

Still, a third group was riding around in old beat up vans. Each driver was given a newspaper with what I thought were very interesting articles in them. The stop lights in the area were very challenging. They were set to the maximum red time. If you had driven up and waited for the green light you might wait up to 4 minutes. During this time your whole life would be paraded in front of you. You would think that you would surely loose interest in anything that you had planned for the day. And in fact, you would forget where you were going and what you were going to do. I had them sit and wait through several red/ green cycles. Then I added the second part of the experiment. They were told to pick up the papers we had provided them and find an interesting article.

I had my "datatitions", (another one of my words), take close tabulations on how often the red light changed to green and in what interval. It was found that in 25 cases where the newspaper was raised to read, in 24 out of 25 cases the red changed to green in a time at least half of the time the regular light sequence was set for. It appeared that any "happiness" that might have been imparted to the reader by the newspaper, was immediately met by condensed light schedules. Many of the drivers were caught reading the paper while drivers in other cars behind them were honking at them. I called the lead Bum on his cell phone and had them clean up and record their project and head this way.

All the information would be copied just as it had happened into my black book. The book by now was getting pretty thick. I again made provisions that I can not tell you about to protect the information contained in the book. After all, how much would it take for you to tell someone about the black book? I could not be too careful. And just so you know, I made several copies. I went through an involved process that included the use of five Bums.

I gave a copy to be hidden to one Bum who in turn gave it to a second Bum who also was directed to hide the book copy. Then a third Bum placed 6 boxes down and a fourth Bum was blind folded. The blindfolded Bum was directed to go to where the book was to be hidden and then to place the book in one of the boxes. He did the job by feeling the boxes. He could not see. He was not aware in what order the boxes were in. He used duct tape to seal the boxes again by feeling the seams in the box. All boxes had the same weight in them. So when they were picked up it would be impossible to tell by weight which box contained the Black book. I called this my "Double Bum" test instead of the more official "double blind" test.

A fifth Bum was then asked to label each box and then to hide all 6 boxes. If GREMIS was using some sort of "Mind Reading Media", it would be impossible to read one of the Bums minds since they didn't know which box held the book anyway. I didn't think I would need to go to this trouble. But, I was getting more signals each day that the Director had made it his number one goal to learn what we had planned for the meeting, and where my book was. Several mornings I had gotten up feeling depressed. I guess I am a normally strong individual. Had the "suggestive" wave patterns been aimed at a weaker individual, we might have had a different outcome. I have heard of people committing suicide for unexplained reasons. I had actually done some research on this. So when these feelings of worthlessness came over me, I recognized it right away.

I slipped out that night. It was too dangerous to get close the GREMIS building. I already had several Bum crews working there. GREMIS knew about part of the team. But part of the team was our little secret. One of the Bum foremen a man named "Chad" met me at the top of a hill overlooking the GREMIS building. He looked somber as he approached. Then he looked up and said: "It ok chief, I think we will give'm a run for their money." With that I reviewed several drawings and sketches. They looked good. Tomorrow evening would tell for sure. With that we broke up and Chad disappeared. I headed back to the cabin for a fit full night. I held in my worry. It would do no one any good to know how concerned I was.

Morning came sooner that I thought it would. In fact I think "morning" made a deal with the "night". It might have said: "Look here, there's a guy down there who has had very little sleep. I think if you can slip a few hours out of the night and let me get in there earlier, I think we can break him." The night, being very willing to cause someone trouble, eagerly agreed. After all, points were earned in many ways. The Director would be very generous when he looked at the report of what the "night" had done.

So, several hours were just taken. No one could argue. No one could prove anything. There was no committee to complain to. And of course I needed to be awake by 9:00 to make final plans. I did notice the loss of several hours though, and before getting started on my final plans I made note in my book about the stolen hours.

CHAPTER **51**

The meeting.

I was early. We had set up a meeting with the committee who represented the Director. They probably thought it would be a chance for them to warn me to stay away from their business. "Business", I thought about that word. It had so many meanings. In this case did it mean holding a man's nose to an electric grinding wheel but yet, showing compassion when not grinding it completely off. It might even be called a "training" experience. I stopped to reflect and add special reverence to that particular idea.

On the other hand I had planned a "complete and total confrontation." You might say: "But the "Director' is so powerful. He could choose to not even pay any attention and then where would you be?" I had given that some thought, but I had a feeling that it would not turn out like that. I had the Bums working all night on items that we had gotten approval for, like a "Debate" stage, and tables for special exhibits and lighting, chairs in the big auditorium. I had another team, within a team, that had done some other small surprises. All I could say for sure was that it might be interesting.

GREMIS seemed to be completely in favor of the debate. They would bring their own contingent of ghouls. I was sure that it would be completely "stacked" in favor of the GREMIS view point. They were all aware of my book. The mere existence of the book copies represented the fact that the operation of GREMIS had been documented. I was pretty sure that whoever set GREMIS policy was under strict orders to keep the whole operation secret. I thought that just the idea of the books would set them on off. Maybe it could give me an edge in the debate. However, I expected much more than words. I was ready for that too.

The Dwarf sweeping the floor saw me first. He had an oversized Hoodsman's outfit on. The outfit dragged on the floor as he moved. It was almost like he was a Hoodsman "wanta be". The hood on him made him look like a character out of a fairy tale. Most of the outfit had been stepped on and ripped, but he still wore it with pride. He was working away with a push broom that he had obviously cut the handle down on. He stopped, wiped his head and then shook his head. I am sure he thought that I was far too brazen and that the committee would dispense of me quickly and send me out in complete embarrassment. I walked toward the stage giving him a completely wide berth. He saw me avoiding contact with him. As I walked by, he made little "barking" noises as a sinister jab at me. I acted like I didn't hear him.

I walked up the stairs to the stage. The auditorium was completely empty except for a man in a Long Black Coat standing high up in the bleachers. The man was talking into his coat sleeve. The stage itself was about 50'x50'. It had six large columns that were about five foot in diameter and rose to twenty five feet in the air. They served to define the stage space.

I had tables with exhibits on them placed all over the stage floor. There were tables with Radar Detectors that looked really good. They was everything you would wanted in a Radar Detector except for one thing, they didn't "detect". Next to that, I had gutters that didn't "gut". I had scissors that didn't "siz." Then, I had a pile of toilet paper much like the one they had kept as part of my personal belongings back in the warehouse. Of course the toilet paper didn't "wipe," at least without some surpriseing breaks at just the right moment. I had a pile of broken glasses. You know the pair you bought and they broke before you got them home. There were fast food cups that spilled in your lap. There were mechanical pencils that the leads broke as soon as you picked them up. There were reams of paper that you could not write on because of the slick surface.

You know like the back of a check. Ha ha, it happened to you too.

There were piles of socks without mates. There were shirts that shrunk six sizes upon contact with water. There was a whole pile of men's under wear that didn't "pouch". You know, last week when you were running up the stairs and your whole manhood was hanging out in your jeans. Yes, these people brought you that too. There were boxes of under arm deodorant that didn't "deoder." I was surprised to see a representative of a pants company here. The Bums had gotten him a chair and table. He had laid out his most recent designs. He had a company that designed men's slacks with extra wide legs to make the man look as foolish as possible when he had them on. They had a special "sought after brand" so that people would "overlook" the fact that they looked like a cartoon character with very short wide legs just to be able to show their friends that they had the "taste" to buy that brand.

Next to him was another man I was also surprised to see. The Bums ran out of chairs s so they found him a box to sit on. He was from a local sock manufacturer. He had laid out men's socks in front of him. You say: "we have already heard that one". But, I say no, these are special socks. The have an elastic band at the top. They tell you it is to hold the sock up so it does not slip down you ankle. But, what it really does is cut off the blood circulation to you ankle. After several hours of use the ankle has a huge indentation where no nourishment from the body has been able to flow. Continued use will cause loss of the ankle. Maybe you have some. He looked up and smiled at me with a full set of white teeth. I was revolted.

I looked at my inventory. I had jars of Mosquitos. I had poisonous snakes in wooden cages. I even had a skunk with Rabies. Rabies, that's a good one. Who would think of that? The list went on. There were so many torments to man on the stage that some had to be left on the arena floor.

I was checking my list when a guttural voice came at me from behind one of the large card board columns. "You think you can get them to listen to you?" I turned and looked. It was an old man in a Hoodman's outfit. I shrugged my shoulders and continued to read a copy of all the items I had set out. I spoke without looking back at him: "All we can do is try." There was a silence. Then the man spoke again: "This is not the first time someone has called their hand." I shrugged again. Then he continued: "Last time they "green blocked" up the whole mess, chopped 'em up and fed 'em to the bugs." I looked up when he finished that thought. Then: "That's pretty serious." He laughed: "Serious?" he chuckled. Then: "Listen Bob, you don't know serious."

He started to laugh. Then: "Serious is a man down in stance waiting to run a race. This was more like a Comedy except, the laughs were all with the GREMIS Group . . . ha ha . . . if you know what I mean." There was a long silence. Then he whispered: "I would watch your back in here if I were you." I shook my head in agreement and quickly looked around. Then he added one last thing: "Predictions are nothing but warnings . . . until they happen." I stood there and thought about that for a few minutes. It seemed pretty perceptive. Then, I turned to ask him what he meant, but he was gone. I stepped over to the cardboard column that he had been behind. There was no one there. I brought the clip board back from my side and continued to take inventory.

The stage was set up kind of like a boxing match well . . . maybe not like that at all. It all seemed very odd, except at opposite ends of the stage I had my podium and at the other end, the GREMIS podium. Maybe it would be more like a cage fight. But I was hoping to just use my wits.

I was just putting the last touches on the exhibit tables when the Arena doors opened and the GREMIS crowd started coming in. There were Men in long Black Coats. They marched in just like that did at the public meeting. They all sat in an area in the middle of the bleachers. The whole group sat completely at attention. Then in came a few Hoodsman carrying clubs. They were not so regimented. Most of them looked very serious. Finally the dwarfs came in. They had scooters and bicycles and even a few miniature horses. A small car drove up in front of the bleachers and out came 35 dwarfs. Right behind the car came a group of clown dwarfs came in marching in a parade. The leaders of the "show" were Dwarfs on stilts all with tall black hats. They came stepping over their shorter comrades yelling obscenities and throwing popcorn balls to the crowd. A Calliope played music in the background.

At one point a small car shot in front of one of the Dwarfs on stilts. The Dwarf didn't see the car. He hit one of the stilts and started to stumble. He threw his whole bag of treats into the audience as he slowly teetered to the side. The Hoodsmen in the audience fought over the treats hitting each other with their clubs. Finally, the dwarf on stilts, started to fall very slowly. He leaned over and grabbed part of a banner that someone had put up. The banner had a famous quote written on it. It said: "We are here on Earth to do good for others. What the other people are here for, I don't know." The banner was just made out of paper and would not take the weight. It ripped from one end to the other leaving the stilted dwarf holding a lot of air. Then there's a: "Shit Shit Shit!!" as he finally fell into some Men in Black coats. There was some yelling and cussing as they pushed him around. Then, to my surprise, one of the Men in Black Coats gets up and shoots a lightning bolt at the Dwarf. There's a loud crack and the Dwarf screams as he is trying to find his way out of the audience seats. "So" I thought, they have come up with another weapon; one we had not counted on.

CHAPTER **52**

The procession

At the other end of the arena my Bums started to come in. They had also dressed up. They had every color and every torn and tattered clothing piece known to mankind on. Some had layers upon layers of clothing articles on. They had hats from the dump. A lot of them wore white gloves and big shoes. Some of the Bums carried balloons. They didn't quite have the serious manner that the debate demanded. But, I sort of expected that. Behind them came a big truck hauling crates full of cans of Chili.

A cooker was on a chain behind the truck. It was not secured correctly so it jerked side to side as the truck pulled it in. One of the Bums had already fired it up. There would be all sorts of Chili treats in between events. Not to be out done, the Hoodsmen had rigged up two horses pulling a large block of green substance on a low slung wagon. They had flowers all over it to highlight the gayety of the event, but everyone could also see the "veiled" threat. I hoped the two groups could stay calm while we got our little discussion started.

At the same time we had rolled in three twenty five foot diameter balls of yarn. We had made a sign and put the yarn balls as a display next to the stage. The sign read. "These are all the broken shoelaces and all the runs in sweaters and all the pants that ripped when they were not supposed to."

I heard a wrap on the GREMIS podium. I turned to see the 5 men in white robes had filed in. Four of the robed men sat behind the podium to show strength. The fifth one was staring directly at me as he again tried to get the house to come to order. The wrapping continued even after several firecrackers went off in the Dwarf section. The man cleared his throat. "HMMMMMMMM!!!!!!!" Still the crowd continued. Frisbees were flying everywhere. The man again tried to call for silence: "HHMMMMMMM!!!!!!. Come to order!" But nothing happened. Finally, the man started clapping his hands on the mike making an irritating popping noise. "Pop! Pop! Pop! Pop! Pop!" The crowd started to get quieter.

But, it just left a hole in the noise for a few minutes giving a wise ass in the crowd the right cue to yell something: "Hey! Somebody stole my bag!" . . . There's a murmuring in the crowd. "Then across the crowd just far enough to make it really hard for the first wise ass to find him, someone yells out: "Hey butt head! I got it." The crowd murmurs some more. Then: "Hey "weasel breath", I sure do like your candy!" With that, there's a scrambling in the crowd where the first wise ass yells out. He yells back: "Listen Jack . . . You eat one bite of that candy and I'll ram the rest up your ass so high it'll come out your mouth!" The crowd laughs, but continues eating popcorn and peanuts. Someone from behind the first wise ass . . . actually a very big gorilla of a Hoodsman raises up and shoved the first wise ass back in his seat. He mumbles like he really can't talk very well.

"You shad up!" The first wise ass is shoved down so hard he falls off his seat and into the seats below. We lose interest as the wrapping and popping continues to get louder. The man in a white robe is now angry. He is about to order several of the crowd killed, but in the last minute the crowd quiets down. This time it seems like the silence will last.

The man in the white robe looks into the crowd and condescendingly yells: "Thank you!" I was looking back toward the excitement when the white robed man directed his irritation at me and said: "Mr. Higgins!" I turned around. That's not my name. I don't know where they got the name except it was the name of my College roommate.

Sure, now that I think about it, they must have tapped into some old college files and got the wrong guy. I was completely happy, because I hadn't used that name yet. Maybe I would. But, it also showed they weren't infallible. I looked up giving my most sorrowful look and said: "Me?" The man in the Robe just stared at me as if I was the biggest "halfwit" he had ever come across. Then he spoke: "Yes!" Syrup almost flowed out of his diction. "Yes, I mean you." I looked at him trying to play the person with no clue as to what was going on. I looked down to make sure my fly was not open. There was a quick "Slap!" as the man in the white robe quickly hit his podium top with the palm of his hand.

"Mr. Higgins!" I looked up quickly. He continued: "You may not believe this, but this is not a Circus!" He was silent a few seconds and then: "I don't know who authorized all this "fan fare." Now looking down at his papers he spoke again: "The Director expected a few witnesses . . . not this!" I looked back around as if I had not noticed the huge motley crew behind us.

Then: "Oh . . . I just thought we might have a few things to talk about and my Bums were in the area, and . . ." Of course I was trying to pack sand up the man in the White Robes butt. A lot of planning had gone into this meeting and now I needed it to appear that it was just thrown together. I was not sure the White Robed man was buying it. He stared out into the audience. Then, back at me. He started to speak, but I got the next word in: "But, what about your people? I didn't know GREMIS had so many "employees." He stopped formulating what he was going to say next and began studying his papers again as if I was nothing but a fly buzzing around him. This time he spoke softer as if it was not any affair of mine: "What GREMIS does or does not have is of no concern of yours." I decided to let it drop. After all, that was not what this meeting was about.

Then he spoke again: "Mr. Higgins, are you the same man that broke into the Bazaar twice, and started a fire in the hall. And are you the same man that broke out of jail and ran the guards on a wild goose. And are you the same man that Broke out of the Grinder room after you had received termination orders?" He continued to look at his list. He looked like he was finding more and more information. Then: "My, My, My . . . Here's more. Mr. Higgins, you've been a busy boy." I kicked the floor and looked down and then, as if I had gotten some courage, I stammered a moment. Then: "Yes . . . That would be me!" I stood my ground and stared back at him.

Then: "But . . . there was more . . ." The man in the White Robe quickly cut me off. He raged: "Mr Higgins! . . . Let me put you in the correct position here. You are a flea on a dog's ass, you are slime at the bottom of the sewer, you are spit on the street. You are nothing to us. You have pushed us to our limit!" He stopped and looked at me is if I might come up with some argument that would change his mind. But then he sniffed his nose in the air and said: "We have nothing further to talk about . . . You are terminated!" I stood there and raised my arms and looked them over carefully. I didn't feel terminated.

Then feeling a little playful, I continued: "It's nice to hear those words of commendation . . . I didn't know GREMIS thought so highly of me." There was a smirk from the audience as my voice was transmitted over a PA system.

The man in the White Robe's face turned bright red. It looked like he would pop a gasket at any moment. The man in the White Robe started packing up. He had a briefcase out and was loading papers into it. He had said his piece and now I had something to say as well. I was starting to get mad.

Up to now I had just tried to see what they would do. I stepped away from my podium and said: "Hey! Mr. White robes! What about all this?" I pointed to all my tables. Mr. White Robes just waved me off as if I were trying to sell a magazine subscription. I was getting a little heated now. I said again: "Hey! I didn't just make all this up!" I pointed to all the items on the tables representing thousands of torments to mankind. He continued to pack up. Then suddenly, there was a loud explosion and a drape dropped from behind Mr. White Robe's podium.

There stood a man in Black Robes maybe ten feet tall. The crowd grew completely silent. There was a low bellow as the huge being spoke: "I think I can answer your questions."

The crowd gasped. Mr White Robe backed away. He quickly said "Sir! . . . We can handle this!" There was a silence while the big man reached down and got some records. He moved like in slow motion. When he was standing again he spoke very slowly: "Mr. Stanks . . . You can go. I will handle this for here on." Mr. Stanks was upset. He spoke again: "Sir! But Sir! . . ." The giant Director turned and stared at Mr. Stanks. Mr. Satnks started to sweat and shake uncontrollably. The shaking man backed off hoping for no further punishment. Then the whole group of White Robed men shrank away as the giant Director moved forward standing behind the podium. His great height made the podium look like a toy.

There was a long silence as the Director gathered his thoughts. Then he spoke very deliberately. "Mr Higgins . . ." I could feel his deep voice in my chest. He continued: "I know you can't understand. So I will just try to give you some general information about the workings of GREMIS." I stood there with my mouth still open. "First of all . . . Please know that we LOVE you." I stood my ground and said: "What?"

The giant man again looked into my eyes and said very religiously: "Yes, Mr Higgins . . . We love you." I stammered and then said: "You call this love?" I looked at my displays on the tables.

Then to make a further point, I motioned to several Bums nearby. They had been waiting for the command. They pushed out about 15 gurneys with sick people on them. One man had the flu. One man was very old. One man had Rickets. One man had poison Ivy. One man had Pneumonia. One had a bad liver. All looked up at the Director with questioning eyes. I stuttered. I had to get this right. I started out: "You call this love?" I jumped down off the stage and walked among the sick. Then I continued: "If this is what you do to the people who love you, what do you do to people who don't love you?" There was a long silence.

CHAPTER **53**

The confession

Then, in a voice that was so deep it vibrated several glasses on a nearby table. He spoke very slowly: "You see . . . True love is taking people to the brink of their abilities in life. It's forcing them to face the trials and tribulations and responsibilities of living and because of this great "gift" I give them, they become better people from it." I shook, I was so mad. Then I spoke: "So let me get this straight. You torment people so that they will get better. Is that right?" The crowd gasped as if I had certainly offended the Director and just signed my own death warrant. But the big man kept his low voice intact and spoke again: "Yes. You have described what we have tried to teach for 20 years in a few sentences." He stopped and glared at me.

Then: "Yes. That is correct." I was red in the face. "You can't be serious!" I was shaking. "Who gave you the right to play with people's lives?" The quiet was deafening. You could have heard a clip of 55 MM rifle drop. In fact, I think that was what did happened.

The giant looked down at me and smiled. Then he spoke: "We test everyone. But, we do it out of love. We build up "Vectors" until you cannot stand anymore." He stopped to let me take in what he had said. Then: "Most die at some point, but in the march to the "after life" they overcome many challenges and . . ." He thought for a moment and then: "It makes them better individuals." He was almost crying he was so emotional at this point. I just shook my head. I answered almost as if I had to stand up to him: "Well, I'm here from the people." I stopped to let him understand that I was going to seriously stand up to him. Then: "I said, I am her from the people . . . and we're not buying it!" . . . I seethed a little. Then I continued: "You can take this whole operation, and shove it where the sun don't shine!"

The Director kept his composure, but raised one hand a little. I could not see what was behind me but I did hear some movement in the crowd. It must have been a signal. I turned my head a little but still watching the Director for any sudden movements. He continued: "You see Mr. Higgins, life is a journey not a destination." He thought for a moment. Then: "I have seen your kind; always hurrying to get somewhere." I was still seething: "You mean the ones who do the work?" He thought for a moment. Then: "Yes, if you want to put it that way. I have to worry about everyone, even the ones who don't add anything." He thought. Then he continued: "My burden is so great."

At this point I had just about had it. I needed to do something. But the Director beat me to it. There was a whooshing noise as giant straps dropped from the cat walk above the sick men in Gurneys. The straps had hooks on them. They tore into the men's flesh and then slowly the struggling men were pulled up with the hooks into the darkness above the stage. All the men screamed and writhed in pain. One man broke loose from the hooks and fell 30 feet to the floor. He lay there doubled over in pain. The Director spoke once again: "Yes, we have to see the big picture. These men you have brought me will serve as a "teaching guide" to everyone else . . ." I cut in: "And don't tell me." I paused.

"They will be better human beings from the experience." Now, the Director was getting angry. He spoke: "You can't see the good in this?" He thought again and reached for another "Pearl" of wisdom: "These men serve a higher goal. They show us where the path is. They "teach" us." I said: "Is that so?" But, all the time I was trying to figure out what to do next.

Bert one of my main Bums was waiting at the side of one of the big cardboard columns.

You see, we had a few lessons we want to teach as well. What could be better than two sides offering to teach each other? The whole area would be filled with "learned" individuals. This lesson would be very interesting. The question would be: "Can a ten foot man handle 2 tons of insects?" With that I said one last thing to say: "Sir, I am starting to see your side. Would it be possible for me to try teaching too?" He started to shake his head, to tell me that he was the only one with this ability, when I raised my hand and all six columns started to fall towards his podium. I yelled: "What about a lesson on how to handle two tons of insects?" and as an afterthought: "I also . . ." I thought a second. Was I going too far? But then I decided to kick the whole mule loose. I said: "I also do this out of Love!" The columns fell, and as they fell they ripped open.

We had wrapped wires around the tubes and tied then to weights on the floor. They appeared to be stabilizing wires, but in truth, the wires were going to cut the columns in quarters. The columns hit the big man with a "WHOSH!"

All parts separated and, Surprise! Insects swarmed all over the huge man. I stood there grinning. The big man stood very still. There was silence in the crowd. Suddenly the insects started to fall off the big man. It was almost as if he had commanded them to leave. They dropped all around his feet. A Bum nearby, started scooping the bugs up with a shovel and putting them in barrels. It was incredible how he had shed the insects. Maybe I had been wrong. Maybe he was a Deity. Maybe, everything he had said was true. We are on this world with one goal in mind, to live through as many torments as possible and then become wiser because of it.

I had thought about that argument. Many thought we born "bad nellies" and the only way to get better was to get "beat up" figuratively? If that were the case then did that mean that the Director was here to, in essence, clean up all the "spilled milk?" I thought about that a few seconds more and then I said loudly as I thought about it: "I . . . don't . . . think . . . so!"

The crowd had been under a spell as the drama unfolded on stage. But now it appeared that the Director had shown us his power. And the Men in Black Coats and the Dwarfs had taken this as a cue to "rub out" the Bums once and for all. The Men in Black Coats raised some sort of weapons. It was, of course, the same one that had almost fried the Dwarf earlier. While this was happening, the Dwarfs had pulled out several big arms from under the grand stands. They were the same ones used to feed the bugs. They quickly hooked the arms to several fork lifts.

Then, with a Dwarf in the top of the arm, green spray was pumped up to the hose that the Dwarf held. It was clear that the Dwarfs meant to spray the bums and turn the rest of the bugs loose on them. My mind raced.The Bums not so "on the ball", were busy eating Chili. They had chili sticks. They had cotton candy chili. They had Chili under glass. They were so excited about eating their favorite food, that they had allowed themselves to get into a sort of Carnival spirit. They were blind to what was really about to happen. How could I get their attention to emphasize the danger of the situation? Then, I remembered; the three giant balls of yarn. They weren't exactly what we had said they were. Actually they were all hollow inside. In the middle of each one was a Bum on a motorcycle. Each ball still weighed 1000 lbs so the Bum inside would have to "rev" up his cycle and slowly move forward. It was after the ball got rolling that they might get your attention . . . or not. But, it did remind me of a verse I had read somewhere about the "quick and the dead."

CHAPTER **54**

Buddies

Now, that the Director and I had become bosom buddies. (not really) Actually, I felt like there was iced oxygen in the air. I was startled. I didn't think anyone left a door open. The crowd seemed to read the tension. All the pent up frustrations of the Men in Black and the Dwarfs started to come to a boil. The cool calm of the "debate" was about to stop. Everything started to happen all at once. If the Director could really shed those bugs, he could probably do more. And I started to think my "goose" was cooked. At the same time, the Bum who was scooping up the bugs looked down at the Directors feet. He was closer than I was. Below the bottom edge of his cape was another material.

At first the Bum was so frightened of the massive man that he stayed as far away as possible. But, after working up a sweat shoveling bugs, the Bum started to let down his guard. He came closer to the Directors feet and noticed that the material hanging below his cape was plastic sheeting. The Bum stopped shoveling and secretly got my attention. He pointed at the plastic and I caught on. I spotted the plastic sheeting at once. Maybe the Director was not so perfect as he seemed.

I started to get brazen. "Oh? Don't like Bugs?" The big man stared at me and started to move slowly toward me. The Bum by his feet grabbed the edge of the plastic sheeting and pulled enough down so the next step of the giant would cause him to step on the sheeting.

At the same time there was a "schreech!" in the audience. A Bum eating several Chili dogs had been hit by a giant electric bolt. The Men in Black had turned on their electric sticks and were moving towards the Bums. The Bum was shaking from the shot, but would not give up his chili dogs. He rolled down the bleacher steps and hit the ground in front. His coat was smoking. Another Bum ran down and started to fan the smoking coat, but this just added air to the fire and the coat burst into flame. This got the other Bums attention and someone said: "Hey! They got Frank!" At that instant the Dwarfs in the spray rig started spraying the Bums with green bug food.

The bugs, sedated in the barrels, now, started to smell the food. They quickly began to pour out of the barrels and move towards the Bums. It looked like the Men in Black had caught the Bums in "Chili mode" and were going to teach them a few things until, . . . a large cracking sound was heard and the giant balls of yarn started to roll. At first they just rolled a few inches and then a few feet. It was really not enough to get your attention until . . . The crunching got louder and one of the dwarfs on the spray rig looked up as the giant balls started moving toward the crowd. One dwarf said: "Hey! Look out! The balls of yarn! It's a trick!"

There were Bums and Men in Black and Dwarfs running every direction. Before you knew it one ball hit the bleachers and crumpled one side as it bounced off and headed off in another direction. The Men in Black had stopped and under the direction of the lead Man in Black and had organized a fighting line. They stood bravely shoulder to shoulder with electric sticks drawn. The ball approached.

Meanwhile the Director had taken another slow step towards me. The plastic I spoke of was now under his foot and the next step would rip it from under his cape. The Director stopped and looked at me with gleaming red eyes. Then he spoke again: "Ok . . . I enjoy it." As if I understood his little joke. He paused. Then: "Does that make your insignificant heart feel any better?" He stopped, waiting for me to respond.

But he had more to say. "If I want to smash a man or break him in half or tear him down from the inside, I have just done it. There's no one to judge me. I make the rules" And he continued: "And yes . . . ok . . . I like it. But what difference does it make to you? You're just "Cannon fodder. There are a million of you. What's a few hundred thousand, beat up, maimed or mentally handicapped poor sods anyway?" Then refocusing on me he said: "I want that book!" I froze in my tracks. Now the shit was on the table. All good and bad, all in's and out's, all dreams and torments came down to this moment.

Of course, I was never good with a quick "come back" but I had to do something. It was the same moment where I stole the basketball from "Mr. Basketball". Well, maybe it was not exactly the same but whose checking me? I thought a minute and then said: "Two things." I hesitated a second and then: "My name's not Higgins! And your plastic is showing!" Right away I knew I had chosen the wrong comeback.

His arm reached out much farther than I thought it could. He grasped my neck and raised me off the stage. I was only a 12 inches from his face. The arm was too strong. Almost like a mechanical arm. But, I had no time to compare it with normal arms. I could see myself in front of a class. I might say: "Now Class" I might say. Then continuing: "The human hand can produce as much as 25 foot pounds of force."

I would point at the black board where I had done some calculations. Then continuing: "But a mechanical arm, with a mechanical hand attachment, can produce more than 100 foot pounds of force." The class ogled at my numbers as the scene faded out. I was back to the present and it didn't look good. Maybe I should have stayed with the class. He raised me even closer to his face and then said: "This is it Higgins or whatever your name is! Give me that book . . ." (in very slow speech) . . . he hesitated a few beats and then: "and I will take your torments away." He paused shaking his head and then: "Otherwise." a long pause. Then: "The bugs will have a nice treat today." Everything inside of me was screaming. My insides, if they could talk, (Maybe it was the liver or the intestine.) were yelling as loud as they could: "Give him what he wants! You idiot! . . . We want to live!" I was about to cave in. After all, I was swinging in the air held by some monster twice my size.

Then to my surprise he wanted to say more: "Your just one big "science experiment" to me anyway." He said, as he took another step. You know the step I told you about, the one where the plastic gets caught under his foot. Well, sure enough, the plastic did get caught under his foot and it started to pull out from under his black cape. At the same time something snapped inside of me. It was the same thing that snapped when I was in the trunk and ran after the Man in a Black Coat.

I couldn't put my finger on it at first. But I had to . . . I mean I had to reach inside and find out what drove me. What caused me to resist, under any . . . let me repeat that, under ANY circumstances. If I lost use of my limbs, I would pull myself down the hall on a skate board. If I couldn't see, I would fight you in the dark. If you cut my arms off, I would use my mouth to bite your nose off . . . Then I realized . . . after a few seconds . . . It was the "Human Sprit!" . . . Yes, that was it. Maybe not all human spirits, maybe not all people, but I knew of at least one. It was my soul! And my spirit was enraged. Not about the mechanical arm that was squeezing the life out of me. Not about the insults that this monster had hurled at me. No. It was much deeper than that. What was it? And then it came. It was about the "belittlement of man" Or maybe the "embarrassment" I had for man accepting such torments.

Yes! . . . That was it. I would show him that we were much stronger than he gave us credit for. We could fight back. I would not back down. Never! . . . Never! . . . Even if my life left me as I was making this statement. I grabbed his lapel as he was choking my last breaths and found the plastic sheeting. At the same time he took one more step and the whole situation began to change momentum.

CHAPTER **55**

Falling

He started to lose his balance and slowly very slowly his body was out of control. I pulled the plastic sheeting out but still kept my face close to his. His eyes flashed for a second as he started to realize what was happening. I got real close to his face and then said: "One more thing Jake! . . . I just wanted to tell you that . . ." I paused just like he did. Then slowly I said the words: "We're doing THIS out of love too." With that I kicked into his midsection and strained with all my might to break his hands hold on me. It worked! Just as we started to crash to the stage floor I tried to spring away, but that was not going to happen.

We hit the floor with a giant crash. The monster of a man lay there on top of me. The weight was crushing. His hood covered my head. All I could see were his glowing red eyes. Before, I thought I saw a weakness. The plastic had been a clue. Now I thought, he had to be just a man. But then, here I was lying under what must have been 500 pounds of dead weight. My insides came screaming back.

They said: "We told you so!" and I started to see that I had made a very bad mistake. I wanted to yell back at my insides: "You keep your little organ thoughts to yourself!" I thought for a moment and then spoke to them again . . . Then: "I'm working this out . . . you'll see." But I already knew that there was not any place those voices came from.

He was going to smother me to death. I started to question everything. Did he have powers that I didn't even understand? It seemed that the only answer was, yes. I had been wrong before. I misjudged the danger. I was completely powerless as his red eyes shot into mine. I started to think of death. An image came to me. It was not that bad. It would be like a vacation where they gave you candy sandwiches every day. There would be no more torments. No more losses of memory when I needed to remember. No more "super hot" days. No more sleepless nights. No more worrying about finances. I could break my bonds and sit with the bum in front of the closed down grocery store as he ate the free sandwich.

I could build a tent on shopping carts laid on their side with a piece of plywood on top, like Bob the bum (in real life) in the old mining camp. Bob lived there at night and during the day he dug for leftover metals that he could sell to the recycling company. It actually seemed peaceful. But there was just one problem. I was describing someone else, NOT ME!

I raised my head a few inches and looked straight into the Directors eyes. Then very slowly I started to let my true feelings come out. The ones that had festered in me all my life began to burn to the surface. Before I could put any sort of plan together, there was this flaming rage that tore through me. It blinded me from the Black Cape over me, from the Bums who loved their Chili, from the Men in Black who would almost for sure would wipe out the Bums and from the Dwarfs who kept helping this giant being. It boiled to the surface as I spoke: "You think we are all some sort of play toys? You think this world is yours to do with however you please? You think you can grab anyone you like and turn them into clay?" . . . I hissed . . .

Now, I was really getting mad. "You know you may have some of the people hypnotized, but not everyone! In fact, not nearly as many as you think! You think you can run experiments on us and we will just accept it as "fate"? Well, let me tell you Mister Black Hood, someone sold you a stinking bill of goods!"

I stopped a moment still shaking. Then: "We'll fight you at every turn. You think you have all the holes filled? Well, you don't!" I shook a little more. I hesitated a second. Then I blurted out something that had been inside of me for a long time. I said: "It's out!" It was more powerful than it sounded and I waited for him to realize what I had said. But there was no response.

I braced myself waiting for him to rise up and beat the life out of me. But, he just lay there. The plastic sheeting was all over the stage. Everyone in the audience stood in silence. They all stood with their mouths open. The quiet lasted for a very long time except, for the slight noise of a kettle being raised to the top of the bleachers at the far end of the arena.

Some of the Bums had rallied. At the top of the bleachers ten bums had hefted and large vat of hot chili. The Men in Black were getting more weapons from under the bleachers when there was a slurping sound and 200 pounds of very hot chili poured all over the Men in Black. It was not a pretty scene. The Men in Black tried to drop their weapons which were electrified. When the Chili shorted out the contact points on the weapons, the weapons discharged and sent charges into the Men in Black. About half of the Men in Black were depixeilized right on the spot.

I know that's not a word. But it IS now. I am taking charge! Move back! Whoever started making words anyway? They sure as hell didn't talk to me! We need it to describe what was happening. In laymen's terms, they electronically decomposed. The rest of the Men in Black in that group ran screaming from the area. One bum standing at the top of the bleachers turned to another and said: "Hey Fred, that was my best Chili. What a waste!"

In the meantime all three yarn balls had reached cruising speed. Ha! You forgot about those didn't you? There was a tremendous screeching as one of the balls ran right over the bleachers smashing everyone in the way. The Men in Black had had some weapons stored in the bleachers and under the crushing pressure of the yarn balls they started to explode. A second ball was heading for the miniature cars that the dwarfs had driven in. One of the dwarfs on the spraying device looked across the arena and yelled" Hey! Look out!" But it was too late. The yarn ball hit the cars and smashed them like match sticks. Several dwarfs were in the cars and we saw them hurdling out of the windows just as the yarn ball hit.

Meanwhile the bugs had gotten the scent of green bug food and were swarming toward the Bums. One large group of Bums had been so excited with all the different Chili concoctions that they had not even noticed that another group of the Men in Black were warming up their electric guns and had started to melt some of the large Chili cookers as they moved in on the Bum Chili eaters.

One Bum had a stack of Chili sandwiches on a plate. One sandwich fell on the ground. He reached down to pick it up just as tremendous electric charge shot right through where he would have been sitting. Instead it hit a big Chili boiler. The boiler quickly melted and spilled its contents on the ground. The Bum, oblivious to what just happened raised back up and placed the errant sandwich on his plate. He started sing an opera song as if nothing had happened. I think it was O Sol A Meo.

CHAPTER **56**

Not dead yet

Now, I lay there but I was not dead. So what could that mean? The Director had stopped talking. His eyes still glowed as he stared directly into my soul. But the longer I laid there the more I began to think I was laying under a big mass on cloth and machinery. I tried to move again but I was pinned like an insect on a wax board. I lay there trying to figure out what to do next when I felt some tugging from one side. Several moments went by and the weight on top of me started to lift. It was the Bums near the stage. They witnessed everything. They had grabbed all the cloth parts of the Directors outfit and had slowly moved him off my "beat up" body. My beloved Anna was standing there with the Bums.

The day had just brightened. I crawled out and they all lifted me into a standing position. I reached for Anna and held her in my arms. The hug lasted a very short time. Because, suddenly there was a rustling in the seat of the pants that the Director was wearing. We all moved back expecting the worst. Then to our surprise a hatch opened up. Some gas spewed out. Then, out the popped the bald head of Dwarf. He looked around at everyone before climbing out. He spit at us as he started to pull himself out through the hatch. He looked at one set of Bums standing close by and yelled: "Get out of the way!" He started mumbling to himself as he reached back in for a small tool box.

Then turning and seeing me, he seethed with anger. He pointed his finger at me and then raged" "You! . . . now look what you've done . . . !" He threw the tool box to the stage floor like a child having a temper tantrum. The impact caused the box to open and the contents spilled all over the floor. He looked at me as if I had caused that too. Then he continued his rant: "Now look . . . what you've done!" He jumped up and down in rage. Then: "You've ruined everything!" He reached down and "half-heartedly" grabbed a few tools and threw them in his box, but he was more intent on focusing his anger on me. He shook his finger as he adjusted his small white tunic. "You think you're so smart by getting in the middle of everything!" He looked around the stage at the Bums and Anna and me and then said: "We'll get that book of yours and then . . ." He stopped to reflect on what he was about to say. Then: "Then . . . you're all toast! And that's with a capital "T"!" . . . He made a break for one of the stage exit stairs, but stopped as he raced away to kick one Bum in the shin. Wham! The Bum yelled in pain and started jumping all over the stage holding his leg.

I was still aghast at what had just happened. I had to think fast. I knew the little man would vanish quickly if I didn't act. I blurted out: "Wait!" And to my surprise the little man stopped. I wanted to tell him one thing. It was the same thing I told him earlier, but I was sure he missed it in all the commotion. There was a long silence as the little Director turned and waited for me to tell him what I wanted to say. Then I just blurted it out: "You've already got it!"

He looked at me a little funny from across the stage and then he said: "Got what?" . . . I was ready. I knew he was still not on the same wave length as I was, but I continued.

"The Book! . . . You've already got the book." He looked at me as if I had completely lost my mind. Then: "What?" I continued. "The book . . . you've got it!" I stopped a second and then: " . . . and, so does everyone else" There was a long silence. Then I spoke again: "I sent it to you and everyone else including every newspaper and book publication companies." He stared at me. His mouth dropped open.

Then: "No!" He started shaking his head as he started to realize what I had just said. "Yes" I said: "It's true. We made the information public early this morning. It's on the Internet." The little man turned white in the face. He kept shaking his head. He looked at the floor and then looked back at us. Then: "You . . ." He hesitated. "You . . . You don't know what you've done."

He stood there not knowing what else to say. Everything was out. All the torments and tricks on mankind, all the sick people, and the broken appliances and yellow lights and the stolen socks and the false promises. He raised his hand toward me. He opened his mouth to say something, but then stopped and just glared at me. Then he snapped out of it! Quickly he said something into his white sleeve and jumped to the back exit. The bald Dwarf yelled his last words. "You haven't heard the last of this!" With that, the exit door slammed shut. We all stood there in complete disbelief.

The battle in the audience had started up again. Some had stopped to watch the drama on the stage and were caught off guard as all sorts of wrath flew at them. Some were shooting electric charges. Some were spraying green bug food and some were not paying any attention at all and busy eating Chili. The lights went off. There were more muffled shrieks. But then, sometime later, it got quiet. After that everyone on competing sides stopped and walked or limped out of the arena.

I had Anna by my side. We were hugging and kissing. My Bums had mostly gone. Several of the Bum Lieutenants were still standing guard around me. We also decided to leave. We walked behind two large Chili wagons that had been packed up and were slowly rumbling out of the arena.

All of a sudden it hit me. Where were the Hoodsmen? I knew a few had been in the audience, but where were the rest of them? I turned and asked the Bums, but no one seemed to know. The whole battle had taken place without the Hoosmen. It chilled me to think of what it might have been like had they been there. It was a lot to comprehend. We walked a little longer in silence. Then, we were just turning the corner to walk out of the arena when I saw a small dwarf with a push broom. He was doing his job no matter what the confrontation outcome had been. I stopped and spoke: "Hey Sparkie" No answer. I continued: "Hey Sparks, where are all the Hoodsmen?" He continued as if I didn't even exist. I shrugged my shoulders and decided to move on. I was tired anyway. I had taken a few steps when a little voice from behind me said: "They're all sick." I stopped in surprise.

CHAPTER **57**

Where are the Hoodsman

I said: "What?" The little man looked up and said: "You got Cheese in your ears Mister? . . . I said they all got sick." I was stupefied! They all got sick? I couldn't believe it! What had happened?

We again, started to move off when the little "Broom" man said one more thing. "They're all at the GREMIS infirmary." As soon as I heard that, I knew I had to do one more thing.

We all arrived back at the Cave. We dropped our packs and Anna and I hugged again. We fixed some left over Chili. The Bum lieutenants were ecstatic about eating this delicacy. We all sat down for one last meal. Then I took two Bums with me and excused ourselves. I had one plan left to set in motion.

I went down to my new lab in a lower level of the cave and worked all morning. I wanted to give all the Hoodsmen a last small parting gift. After looking around the lab, all I could find was little miniature cans of Chili. So, with great pleasure I wrapped 3 cans in each box and completed the package with a ribbon and brightly colored wrapping paper. In order to carry all the packages we had to enlist the use of a large wagon. Two of the Bums pulled it to my car and we tied its tongue to my back bumper. Later we arrived at a large building on the GREMIS campus labeled "Infirmary". We unhooked the wagon and proceeded to enter the building. A guard stopped us at the door, but quickly saw that we brought gifts. (he . . . he) We proceeded down a long hall until we were ushered into a large open room about the size of a basketball court. There were army cots strewn all over the floor. Most of the Hoodsmen were lying covered up with blankets.

Some Hoodsmen had kicked the blankets off and were sweating with a fever. There was an air of sullenness. I could barely hear the Bum behind me because of the nonstop coughing in the big room. Several Dwarf nurses were flitting between cots, helping as much as they could. I stopped one of the nurses. I spoke: "What's wrong with them?" The nurse looked up at me as if I were some sort of "Hayseed" who just came in on a farm wagon. Then she spoke: "Mister . . . They all got the flu!" I stepped back. "What?" She bent over and picked up some rags and then said: "Yeah . . . They were the Hoodsmen working the Bazaar and well somehow some of their merchandise backfired on them." She shook her head and then said: "I don't know how that could have happen." I looked at her with wide eyes. I was jubilant, but tried not to show it. I turned and winked at the Bums behind me. Then I thanked the nurse and moved forward.

I leaped up on two chests of medicine that stood about four feet off the floor. I started rapping my clip board against the wall. There was no stop in the coughing and murmuring. I hit it again against the wall. This time the large room started to quiet. I looked at my clipboard and tried to act as official as I could. "Could I have your attention?" Not much change in the sound level. Then I yelled:" Greetings from Central Headquarters."

The silence grew as they all turned to look at me. "We are sorry for your medical problems." The murmur completely stopped. "Yes . . ." I looked around hoping no one would recognize me. Then: "We know you Hoodsmen have been put through a marinade of issues." I look out over the crowd. Someone in the back yelled: "Hey! It's the "Outlander!" The room fell into complete silence.

Then : "Get him!" Several Hoodsmen grabbed the brooms nearby and tried to use them to push their cots toward the stage. One jumped up and limped my way holding a long stainless steel rod. Another one or two threw bananas. An orange smashed on the wall next to me. I held up my hand. "I come in peace!" . . . They stopped for a moment. But then someone else said: "That's the idiot with the mirror suit!" They all stopped for another moment as if someone had hit them in the face.

I tried to stop the "tide" from building. "Wait!" . . . They stopped for a moment. Then I spoke again: "I bring you gifts!" . . . They continued to stare. "I want to make amends!" The Bums behind me held up some of the pretty gift wrapped boxes. One Bum tossed a gift box to the nearest Hoodsman. The sick Hoodsman quickly opened it and saw the three miniature cans of Chili. He grinned and yelled out: "Hey! It's some Chili cans" Another Hoodsman limped over and looked at the gift. "Yeah, it looks good to me!" Quickly, my Bums started passing out the gifts and in 45 minutes we had over 500 gift boxes distributed all over the sick bay.

The Hoodsmen broke out some beer and were singing old war songs as we left. I didn't want to push it. Also, we didn't have much time. The bottom of each box had a compartment filled with . . . (he he) . . . bugs. We had stuck the bottom on with some wax laden with bug food.

I calculated that we had about 5 minutes left until the bugs had eaten through the wax. So, as we left the room we turned the corner in the hall and we all sat on the floor waiting for the Hoodsmen to receive the real "final gifts". It didn't take long. There was a scream from across the room. "Hey! . . . There's bugs in this box!" Then the whole 500 boxes seemed to break open almost as if I had given a signal.

We could hear the yelling in the big room behind us. "Hey! . . . What tha?" and someone else: "Hey! That "chowder head" slipped some bugs in on us!" and: "Ohhhhhhhhhh" Then: "Ahhhhhh" The bugs had started to fill in together and had formed a swarm that would need to be reckoned with. The swarm boiled over on a Hoodsman and ate all his clothes off. He shrieked and tried to cover himself up with a blanket. Another Hoodsman had been chased up a support column. He was clinging to the beams it supported. The bugs were slowly covering him.He started to shake as they got to his head. Another, not yet hit by the bugs, yelled out: "The Outlander did this!" . . . There was a roar from the field of beds. He continued: "Let's get the Son of a bitch!" The others filled in behind him. We took this as our clue for us to leave. As we ran out, I was thinking of changing my name to: "Bug Man". Ha ha.

We rushed out the door, found my car and headed for the Cave. It was a good thing. About the same time the double doors from the building burst open and a passel of sick Hoodsmen poured out. Some were limping. Some were pushing other beds. Some were being carried. But all they saw was the dust from my car as it hit the main road. We had to stop a minute as the one car that would come down that side street all day was just in our way. But, we waited. And then, we floated home on a cloud with a warm feeling inside. Kind of like the one you get right after Christmas.

CHAPTER 58

Oh I don't know . . . whatever

The drip hit me again. It woke me up. I wondered again why it had to hit me in the eye. After all it could have hit me anywhere. Why the eye? I lay there in darkness. It was time to sleep. But somehow the emptiness in the trunk didn't seem the same. I felt a hand next to mine. It was my partner's hand. Yes, we had found a car with a larger trunk. Now, we had a larger felt lined sanctuary for two. You guessed it. My beloved Anna was with me. I looked over at her childlike face as she slept. She was my true joy.

Well you say: "Renn, I thought you were going to change everything. Here you are back in your car trunk. You had the "goods" on the Director. You exposed all of his plans to use the earth as a testing ground for all sorts of experimental torments." I would shake my head as I listened to you. You actually had some very good points.

The day we exposed the Director with the entire contents of my black book, was a red letter day. The book contained what I thought was indisputable evidence of the Directors intentions. We . . . had made it public. There were of course investigations. At first there were many debates between one group who claimed that we had endured a heinous injustice. We had been used as lab rats to expand the science of torment.

But then there was the other side. The group that claimed that man was meant to endure and that the Director was actually "teaching" us. He was our "Guide" in a world of turmoil.

I was interviewed a number of times. But at every interview, there were Protestants claiming that I was just being a big "baby". They claimed that I should knuckle down and carry the large stones of life like everyone else.

I argued that you did not have to smash your hand with a hammer in order to build a wood shed. Most people did not understand what I had said. I thought it was very insightful. In the end, more than you might think agreed with the concept, though they still wanted to know where the wood shead was. Time marched on. They were, "the silent majority." But alas, they were also the "complacent" majority".

Six months after the great "Exposure", the Government reworked their services. GREMIS was out and a new and friendlier "GRANIE" was in. GRANIE stood for Government Recovery and Naturalization Institute. I never could figure out what the "E" stood for. The group claimed to want to work with the people to find a better way. No more social profiling. No more digital spying. No more convincing people that they were "extra special" if they spilled their private "guts" on the internet.

At least, that was what the Government line. The pixelating Men in Black were real. It turned out that the Men in Black had a big problem with electrical charges. The whole program went underground. I am sure there is a lab somewhere hidden away right now working on fixing the electrical charge problem. I can promise you we haven't heard the last from them. As for the clones, well, I thought I saw Anna the other day, but I had just left her in our trunk, so I knew it wasn't her. As of this writing they seem harmless enough. Check with me later.

And, for the soulless ghouls that roamed the night, they were still there. We heard them screaming every night. We still shook in our trunk whenever they were close. Later on, I heard them referred to as "Politicians". But that's another story.

As to the world, Anna and I watched on from the privacy of our trunk. Nothing had really changed. Civilization moved forward. More people than ever before were becoming "Lemmings". You know, the little animal that would follow its own species right off a cliff. Such was the way of the world. But, we had not given up. We just needed some rest. The trunk would serve as our island in the stream. Maybe I would get another campaign started someday . . . maybe I wouldn't.

The Bums still checked in occasionally. I would find a note taped to the top of the front tire of our car. They just rambled about nothing except to ask where to order more Chili.

A small surprise came to me from Anna. She said we would have to get an even bigger car with an even bigger trunk. I asked why, like the dunce that I sometimes am. Of course, the answer caught me of guard. We would be expecting a third occupant to our trunk and it wasn't a rat. Little "Haddley", named after me, would be joining us soon. Oh I forgot to tell you, I changed my name again.

Remember always . . . Fight the fight . . . Never give in!

This isn't the End.